discard

I AM NOT A PSYCHIC!

RICHARD BELZER

WITH MICHAEL BLACK

SIMON & SCHUSTER

New York London Toronto Sydney

SIMON & SCHUSTER
1230 Avenue of the Americas
New York, NY 10020

First Simon & Schuster hardcover edition October 2009

SIMON & SCHUSTER and colophon are registered
trademarks of Simon & Schuster, Inc.

For information about special discounts for bulk purchases,
please contact Simon & Schuster Special Sales at
1-866-506-1949 or business@simonandschuster.com.

The Simon & Schuster Speakers Bureau can bring authors
to your live event. For more information or to book an event,
contact the Simon & Schuster Speakers Bureau at
1-866-248-3049 or visit our website at www.simonspeakers.com.

Designed by Suet Y. Chong

Manufactured in the United States of America

10 9 8 7 6 5 4 3 2 1

Library of Congress Cataloging-in-Publication Data

Belzer, Richard.
    I am not a psychic! / Richard Belzer with Michael Black.
        p. cm.
1. Comedians—Fiction. 2. Motion picture actors and actresses—Crimes
against—Fiction. 3. Las Vegas (Nev.)—Fiction. I. Black, Michael A.,
1949–. II. Title.
    PS3602.E6545I36 2009
    813'.6—dc22

                                                        2009012249

ISBN 978-1-4165-7089-9
ISBN 978-1-4165-7338-8 (ebook)

I would like to thank my loving family:
Harlee, Jessica, Bree, Timbo, Franklin, Django, Bebe,
Papa Bear, Mama Bear, Tulip, Lacey, Sonny, Star, Cupid, and Patch.

I AM NOT A PSYCHIC!

CHAPTER 1

I watched my part-Lab, part-mutt, Django, and my part-poodle, part-mutt, Bebe, run through the park, circling some bushes and zigzagging between a couple of benches, startling the young couple who had been sitting there immersed in each other. Owing to the season, early February, it could almost be considered a rite of the false-spring we'd been experiencing in the Big Apple. As I kept an eye on the frisky dogs, I was feeling a bit of the old false-spring fever myself, and longed to wrap up this year's filming and head back to my home in France. But first, I had another commitment.

I whistled and their ears shot up. Like they were attuned to catch their master's voice, even in the middle of Manhattan. They changed direction, moving as synchronously as the Blue Angels in flight, and trotted back toward me. Ah, the simple joys of life when you're a dog. Or a stand-up comic/television star with a couple days off.

A pair of NYPD's finest rolled by in a blue-and-white, the officer in the passenger's seat giving the thumbs-up sign.

"Great episode last night, Belz," he yelled.

I waved as both dogs came to a stop at my feet and obediently sat down. As I refastened their leashes, my cell phone rang. The number was unfamiliar, but it had an LA area code. I wondered who the hell this could be, and against my better judgment, answered it anyway.

"Richard Belzer, is that you?" the voice asked.

"Yeah."

After a few seconds the voice said, "It's Paul."

Paul? I knew quite a few Pauls, and this one sounded like he'd imbibed his lunch. Actually, it would be closer to his breakfast time if he was calling from La La Land. "Paul who?"

"Paul Venchus." His tone sounded both hurt and surprised. "Don't tell me you don't remember me."

It was close, but I actually did. "Damn, what's it been? Thirty-some years?"

He laughed. "Yeah, thirty-something. Man, you sound the same. Exactly the same." His words ran together, slurring with a drunk's sloppiness.

"Yeah, right," I said. "How you been?"

His voice brought back a period of my life full of bittersweet memories. Paul Venchus and I had been reporters at the *Bridgeport Connecticut Post* back in my college days, when we'd meet at McDonald's and write jokes on the back of the paper napkins, dreaming of a career in stand-up comedy. Mine had finally taken me to some of the smaller clubs on the Atlantic City circuit, and eventually I moved up from there. I left the newspaper on good terms. The same couldn't be said for Paul. I'd come back from a gig in New York and found out through the grapevine that he'd been fired for showing up drunk one too many times.

Some things never change, I guess, or if they do, they don't change much.

"I been doing all right, Belz," he said. "And . . ." His voice took on a conspiratorial whisper. "I'm working on something big. Real big. And I think you'll be interested."

Now, any of you who've read my previous books, like *UFOs, JFK, and Elvis: Conspiracies You Don't Have to Be Crazy to Believe,* know I'm no stranger to the art of conspiracy theories. But mine have to be grounded in fact, more or less. It sounded like Paul's might be anchored in a bottle of

Jim Beam. This was one Pandora's box I wasn't sure I wanted to open. He didn't let my silence deter him.

"Belz, listen. I know who really killed Brigid Burgeon. And there's more. Way more."

I gave it a few more beats, then tried to sound as noncommittal as I could. "That's almost ancient history now."

He snorted. "I know you're thinking I'm full of shit, but I've got the goods on some big people. Real big."

Every conspiracy theorist's dream. "Like who?"

"Shhh, not on the phone," he said. "This is your cell, right?"

"Yeah, and how'd you get it, by the way?"

"Belz, I—" He stopped and I could hear him in a brief conversation with someone else. "Look, I can't go into that right now. I need to meet with you. You're still filming in New York, right?"

I could've said no to the whole thing, and avoided a lot of trouble, but I tried for a gentler brush-off. "Actually, no. I've got a week or so off from the show, but I have another commitment." Mistake Number One.

I could hear his sonorous breathing—the sure sign of deep concentration. "You gonna be in L.A. anytime soon?"

"Not really. I'll be in Vegas cohosting a telethon with Johnny Leland."

His tone picked up. "Vegas is perfect. I just got back from there myself. It's where my source is. And it's only a quick road trip away from L.A."

I certainly didn't want him showing up at the show, especially in his usual condition. Dino's old "drunk routine" might have worked with the Rat Pack, but it would be a disaster on a prime-time telethon. Time to nip it in the bud, as the late, great Don Knotts used to say. "Paul, I told you, I'm involved in a telethon. It's to benefit charity, and it's nonstop, around the clock."

"Belz, you gotta listen to me." His voice picked up animation as he talked, almost obscuring the faint trace of the boozy slur. "Like I told you, I got the scoop on who really killed Brigid Burgeon. Mark Kaye Jr., too."

"You and half the rag writers in L.A., I'll bet." Although a little voice was telling me to extricate myself from this conversation and then see about getting a new cell number, another voice was urging me to hear what he had to say. I've always been a soft touch for an old friend. Especially one with a conspiracy theory. "So what kind of an angle you got?"

"I told you, not on the phone. Lots of people involved in a huge cover-up. Puts Iran-Contra to shame. And I know who did it and why."

Iran-Contra? Now I suspected he might have been on some kind of heavy psych-op drugs in addition to the booze. "Iran-Contra's not exactly cutting-edge news anymore, either."

"Yeah, yeah, I was just being metaphorical, but you got the connections in law enforcement we need to do something with this."

"Listen, I am not a cop."

"Yeah, yeah, I gotcha. When you leaving for Vegas?"

"Tomorow," I said, realizing I'd just made Mistake Number Two.

"Great, call me when you touch down." He rattled off his number but it was already on my LCD screen. "Got it?"

"Yeah, Paul, but—"

"Belz, please." His voice suddenly took on a drunk's plaintive lilt. "Call me, okay?" Before I could answer, he added, "I gotta go. I'll be in touch," and hung up.

The dogs looked up at me, their chocolate eyes almost echoing what my good judgment was telling me. Django cocked her big, dark head and Bebe's tongue lashed out to slick back some errant gray fur. I sighed and met their reproachful stares.

"Look, he used to be a really good friend, and I could tell by his tone that he really thinks he's onto something." Django's head tilted slightly. "I know, I know, I can't be sure unless I could read his mind, and I'm no psychic. But I don't think it was all due to the booze. Plus, he's coming to me because he thinks I have connections in law enforcement . . . and I do, sort of, but . . ."

I was suddenly cognizant that the pair of young lovers had been listening to my phone conversation, and were now watching me explain myself to two dogs.

Oh well, I thought with a shrug. I am not a cop *or* a psychic.

●　●　●

I pondered all this the next day as I leaned back in my first-class seat and studied the occasional clump of cottony clouds down below us. They looked like a frozen sea, so firm and substantial that you could almost imagine getting out and walking on them. The stuff illusions were made of.

Illusions . . . Leave it to good old Paul to resurrect a story from a moldy grave. It was more than twenty-six years since Brigid Burgeon had been in the movies. A generation ago now. Sure, she was beautiful, and some argued that she even had some real acting talent. She had made just a handful of pictures when she died unexpectedly—"found in the nude," the papers had said. Her last picture, a screwball comedy with movie star/singer Sal Fabell, was never completed. All this probably wouldn't have separated her from all the other young, talented rising stars who have heard the Grim Reaper's beckoning call, except that Brigid's not-so-secret boyfriend at the time was an equally charismatic young California congressman named Mark Kaye Jr. Kaye had the looks of a movie star himself, but the intellect of a flying squirrel, and the sexual fidelity of a rabbit. Although he was married to a gorgeous trophy wife, he was rumored to have trouble keeping his pants on in the presence of attractive women. His brother, Lawrence, who was state senator in neighboring Nevada, was rumored to suffer from the same affliction. Perhaps it was hereditary. Except that Good Old Lar was rumored to be "on the down-low," as they say in the ghetto. The other side of a very old coin.

Regardless of the roots, the story had surfaced that Mark Kaye Jr. and Brigid were an item, seen skiing together on his daddy's mountain resort near Reno. And this sighting came at a very inopportune time for the young California congressman, who was being groomed for a possible vice presidential spot on the next ticket. Personally, I think he would have fit right in with the era. At the very least, he could have made Dan Quayle sound like a Rhodes Scholar. Then Brigid suddenly turned up dead, and the tabloids had a field day. "Did She Just Die, or Was She Murdered?" the tawdry headlines screamed. I figured the answers to those questions were yes, and maybe.

But headlines change as new news replaces the old, and about a year later Mark Kaye Jr. was killed in an automobile accident. For a while the

Brigid ball got rolling once again, then brother Lawrence, affectionately called "Little Larry" by the press, had a rather nasty late-night scrape outside a Reno bar in which his male "companion" and he were involved in a fight with a "gang of men." Larry somehow came out miraculously unscathed, but his campaign aide was beaten to death. The perpetrators were never caught, sparking rumors of Larry's cowardice and fueling an unsubstantiated rumor that he was a closet homosexual. As they say, God protects small children and drunks, but not often enough with the former and way too often with the latter.

So Brigid's demise sort of faded into the ether, like all those young starlets who had met untimely demises or possibly emulated her with a pill-laden early death . . . from Marilyn Monroe to Natalie Wood to the more recent Anna Nicole Smith, their memories kept alive by an occasional anniversary article or a rerun of an old movie on the late, late show.

And now my own blast from the past, Paul Venchus, had dredged up Brigid's corpse for another round of inking. Now, don't get me wrong . . . I love a good conspiracy as much as the next guy. Well, maybe a bit more than the next guy. But I had too much going on in my life to get involved with this one. In addition to the usual end-of-season scripts to be reviewed for the show, I'd promised Johnny Leland months ago that I'd cohost and do a stand-up routine on his telethon. Johnny and I go way back. He'd helped me break into the business. It was like Luke Skywalker getting lessons from Yoda. Johnny had been a legend in comedy for as long as I could remember. And not only was he my idol and mentor, he was my friend. There was no way I could let any of Paul's crackpot schemes interfere with my commitment to the telethon.

"All the proceeds are going to help autistic kids," Johnny had told me. "I've got some big names already on board, and was hoping you'd help me out, Belz."

"Just tell me when and where," I said.

"Vegas," he said, with a slyness in his voice that suggested something more.

"What is it you're not telling me?" I asked.

His laugh sounded just as strong and rich as it had thirty years ago when we'd first met. "It's the same weekend as one of those big Mixed Martial Arts fights you're always talking about. Reeves versus somebody, I think."

"Scott?" I could barely contain my excitement. I knew both men, and figured their collision course would result in one hell of a fight. "You're kidding me, right?"

"Nope. It's legit. They'll be at the same hotel where we'll be shooting, and natch, I already talked to someone about getting you a ringside seat for the festivities."

I've been a big boxing fan forever, and I had to admit that the MMA fights were starting to appeal to a lot of us devotees of the "sweet science," including me. These Mixed Martial Arts guys were some real rough dudes, and you were practically guaranteed to see good fights on every card. We even had a couple of students at my martial arts school in Manhattan training for them.

"Johnny, that would be great."

He laughed again. "Just help me cohost and do a routine on the telethon, okay?" The best thing about Johnny was that he genuinely enjoyed doing nice things for people. I couldn't have asked for a better mentor.

"Like I said, just tell me where and when and I'll be there."

"Come hell or high water?"

"If the creek don't rise."

The lines had come from a stand-up routine that we'd done once, parodying folksy aphorisms. I couldn't even remember where we'd first done it, but the exchange had become something of a catchphrase for us.

And so, here I was, cruising westward at five hundred miles per hour and thirty thousand feet, headed for a rendezvous with Johnny, the telethon, and a chance to see Reeves and Scott pound the hell out of each other for the MMA World Heavyweight Championship of the World. What more could a stand-up-comic-turned-actor hope for?

Then my thoughts drifted to Paul Venchus again. How the hell had he gotten my damn cell phone number? Before this was over, I'd have to find out. But then again, given his history with the booze, he might not even remember he'd called me, much less call me back.

The flight attendant came by and asked if I wanted a drink. I opted for cranberry juice instead of red wine, and wondered how much longer we'd be suspended between the upper atmosphere and the low-lying topography below. At least I was in first class. I took advantage of the room and stretched, thinking how good it would be to see Johnny again. I leaned back in the comfortable seat and must have dozed off, because the next thing I remember was the pilot telling us the temperature in Las Vegas was a balmy seventy-eight, and that we'd be landing in about ten minutes.

CHAPTER 2

As limo drivers go, this guy was cleverer than most. Instead of standing there with a sign advertising he was waiting for Richard Belzer, he'd written "Detective" on the card instead. Of course, he had a pretty good idea what I looked like, too, but I admired his ingenuity. The kid's name was Hector and he spoke with a Spanish accent. After loading my suitcases in the trunk of his white limo, we were off to the races.

"Hey, Mr. Belzer, man, how you doing, sir?" He'd left the screen separating the front section from the back open, and tipped back his black chauffeur's cap. He had enough hair slicked back on the sides to start a Korean wig shop.

"Call me 'Belz,' " I said. "And knock off the 'sir' crap."

"Belz," he repeated, "okay, cool. You got it. You need to make any stops before we go to the hotel?"

The hotel was the Monticello, one of the oldest on the strip. The last time I'd been here, they'd been demolishing some of the older hotels to make room for the newer versions. My guess was the Monticello was probably on borrowed time. That's all Las Vegas seemed to be doing now: trying to reinvent itself by tearing down the old image to replace it with something new. Sort of like an enormous snake shedding its skin in sections.

Now, don't get me wrong—I love Sin City, but I harbor no illusions about the tawdriness lurking just below the glitzy veneer. Built by the mob, for the mob, and paid for with the unfortunate contributions of millions of suckers hoping to leave here richer. Whatever happens in Vegas, stays in Vegas. Too bad their heartaches didn't stay here, too.

"No stops necessary," I said. "Just get me there."

I caught his grinning expression in the rearview mirror as he nodded.

We passed the big, white, diamond-shaped sign bidding us WELCOME TO FABULOUS LAS VEGAS, NEVADA, and beyond it the swelling expanse of the Strip. Lush vegetation and palm trees lined the streets in the desert. Even though it was daytime, the sea of neon seemed ready, somehow, to spring into artificial ultrabrightness. In a few more hours the real city that never sleeps, except maybe from about six to eight in the morning, would be lit up like the Ginza on steroids, drawing the unsuspecting moths closer to its flame. But we do live in a society of consenting adults, and no one was twisting anybody's arms to pull the levers on those slot machines.

I'd gained three hours flying west from New York so it was only a little after noon. I turned on my cell phone and figured I'd give Johnny a call, but three messages popped up on the screen. The first was from my wife, Harlee, hoping that I had a good trip and reminding me that I was supposed to call her as soon as I landed. It was like she knew in advance I'd forget. The second was from Johnny saying that we'd have to grab lunch at the Monticello instead of Binion's, our original choice, because he had a couple of appointments. And the third one was from Paul Venchus asking me to call him as soon as I touched down. Yeah, right.

I called Harlee immediately.

"Your husband is back on terra firma," I said. "All safe and sound."

"Glad to hear that. You meet up with Johnny yet?"

"On the way now." We shot past the MGM and New York–New York. It made me miss her all the more. "I wish you would have come with me."

She must have detected the wistfulness in my voice. "Next time, honey. You know I couldn't miss the time with the girls."

I sighed. "I know. See you in a couple days."

"I'll be looking forward to that," she said, then added, "Richard . . ."

"Yeah," I said, drawing out the word.

"Just do one thing for me, okay?"

"Name it."

"Stay out of trouble."

I almost replied, "What trouble can I get into in Las Vegas?" but thought better of it. Instead, I said, "For you, my sweet, anything."

Famous last words.

"We're almost there, Mr. Belzer," Hector said.

"Hey, it's Belz, remember?" We were making good time on the Strip.

He swung off Las Vegas Boulevard and onto the long drive in front of the Monticello. One of its benefits was the central location on the block. Supposedly it was one of the few hotel-casinos that was actually paid for, but the latest rumor was that it was up for sale, and like I said, the wrecking ball was probably waiting in the wings. Hector turned to me as we pulled up in front.

"Mr. Leland said for you to go check in at the VIP lounge. I'll give your stuff to the bell captain." He grinned. "Sound okay?"

"*Está bien,*" I said, slipping him a hefty tip.

The grin widened when he saw the cash. I started to open the door, but as quick as a welterweight, Hector was already out of the car and opening the rear door for me. I passed a crowd of people meandering along the red-carpeted route to the front desk. In the old days, hotels used to have their front desks near the entrance, but never in Vegas. You have to walk through the casinos to get anywhere, and that means running the gauntlet of pinging slots, mumbling drunks, and scantily clad cocktail waitresses trying to keep them drunk and feeling lucky. Today, I was feeling pretty lucky myself, but that was because I'd be seeing Johnny. He'd walked into a small club in Jersey where I'd been doing my stand-up. Afterward he came over and bought me a drink. I couldn't believe it. Here was one of the true comedy legends offering to buy a drink for a struggling, no-name comic.

"I caught your act, kid," he'd said. "You write your own material?"

In total awe, I told him I did.

"It shows," he said with a grin. "Keep at it and maybe someday you'll think of a funny line that works."

His grin had taken the edge off the harsh words. We sat in a booth and I bombarded him with question after question: How did he get started? How did he perfect his delivery? How many writers did he have? What was it like working with his partner, singer Sal Fabell? And, most importantly, could he give me any advice on how to be a better comedian?

He took his time answering each one, and ended by giving me his card.

"Keep in touch," he said. "Toss me some of your jokes sometime and we'll see how they work."

It was, as Bogie said at the end of *Casablanca,* "the beginning of a beautiful friendship."

I pushed through the glass doors and saw the lighted neon sign directing me to the lobby. The red carpet had sprouted a gold brocade pattern that wound through the rows of machines. I passed an older lady feeding bills into one of them, then pulling down the lever and watching her credits spin away. She pulled the lever down again, after muttering a few choice words.

They found when they redesigned all the slots, back a few decades ago, that a lot of people still preferred to pull down the side lever instead of pushing the button on the front. More gestalt in it, I guess. So they kept that method as an alternate way to lose your money. One of the few traditions that Vegas tipped its hat to. Otherwise, the place tended to reinvent itself every few years.

I continued to follow the golden brick road through the cacophony of bells and whistles, finding the lingering cigarette smoke a bit unsettling. It reminded me of the old days, in the clubs where the smoke hung in such a thick cloud while you were onstage that half the time you thought you were lost in a fog. Or was that the audience?

Finally things opened up as I got beyond the fringes of the casino and the front lobby materialized. This one was a beaut, looking about the size of a football field. The entire back wall was a collage of high-def video screens, each flashing an individual image before coalescing into one huge picture. It was currently depicting scenes of two beefy men beating down a variety of opponents before superimposing big red and black letters spelling out:

TWO TRAINS COLLIDING . . .

MMA—MIXED MARTIAL ARTS MATCHUP

REEVES VS. SCOTT FOR THE HEAVYWEIGHT

CHAMPIONSHIP

It looked like it was going to be one hell of a fight.

And Johnny had tickets for me. I smiled at the thought as I walked into the vacant VIP lounge, getting glares of anger from the people twisting through the lengthy feeder line. While I sympathized, sometimes rank does have its privileges.

The pretty young thing behind the desk asked if she could help me, squinted slightly, then said, "Oh, Mr. Belzer. We've been expecting you, sir."

More "sir" stuff? Who says this younger generation has lost its politeness?

She picked up her phone, saying that Mr. Leland told her to call him as soon as I arrived, and handed me the envelope with my keys. I stood there soaking up the ambience. If there's one thing Vegas has a lot of, it's ambience—some of it good, some of it bad.

Speaking of bad, I heard another voice, this one distinctly male and eminently more forgettable, call my name.

"Well, Richard Belzer. What's a broken-down ex-comic-turned-TV-actor doing here in Vegas?"

I turned and saw a pudgy guy wearing a dirty T-shirt under a shopworn sport jacket and beltless blue jeans hunched under a sagging gut. His greasy, black hair was drawn back into a ponytail. Some guys can pull the ponytail look off. This guy couldn't, even with the blond highlights. His face pinched into a squinting grin under the circular, wire-rimmed sunglasses that went out with John Lennon.

"Harvey Smithe," I said, not offering to shake hands. This dude was on my walk-to-the-other-side-of-the-street-to-avoid-him list.

"Smithe with an E, don't forget," he said, obviously thinking that was something akin to a punch line. But maybe for him it was as close as he was going to get. "Don't tell me you're here for Johnny's telethon, too?"

"Okay, I won't tell you."

It took him a couple of seconds to get it, then he pushed himself into an exaggerated but phony guffaw. Like the old Chinese saying goes, Never trust the man whose stomach does not shake when he laughs. Smithe frowned, licked his lips, and looked around. A cocktail waitress in a low-cut, black bodysuit and translucent stockings strolled by with a drink on a tray. Good old Harv plucked it up and drained the martini glass with the deftness of an experienced drinker.

"Hey," the waitress said. "If you want a drink, all you have to do is ask."

"And if I want something else?" Smithe said, leaning close and lifting his sunglasses while leering at her cleavage. Not that I hadn't noticed it myself. It was hard not to. She turned and left.

I heard someone call my name. Johnny was coming through the opaque glass doors into the lounge. There was a slender young man next to him carrying a laptop. Johnny had put on some weight since I'd last seen him in person, but still had the vitality in his step that spoke of an eternal youth. But as he stepped over and we embraced, I thought his face looked way more drawn than usual.

"Great to see you, Belz," he said. "I really appreciate you coming."

"I wouldn't miss it."

Johnny turned and extended a hand toward the young guy. "Richard, this is Barry Goines. He's the guy who's helping me keep track of all the scheduling."

Barry smiled. "I call it keeping order in the face of chaos."

We shook hands and I told him I was glad to meet him.

"Hey, Johnny," Smithe said, setting the empty cocktail glass on the counter and stepping forward with an extended hand. "Good to see you again."

Johnny shook it, but from the look on his face it was clear he didn't have the faintest idea who this joker was. He turned back to me. "Come on, I was up in the Tahiti Room nursing an iced tea. We got a lot of catching up to do."

"Sounds cool," Smithe said, insinuating himself into the conversation again. "I could go for a tea myself, as long as it has 'Long Island' in front of it."

Johnny shot him a correcting glance. "Sorry, pal, but do we know you?"

"Well . . . ," Smithe said. If he was trying to impress us with his Jack Benny imitation, it wasn't working. This joker probably didn't even know who Jack was. "That's why I'm here."

Johnny looked to Barry, then at me. I shrugged.

Smithe's jowls trembled a bit in panic. "Hey, it's me. Harvey Smithe."

With an E, I thought.

"Smitty, for short." He reached into the desk area of the VIP check-in desk and grabbed something. "Here, watch this," he mumbled, bending over and faking a sneeze. When he popped up again the end of a long rubber band hung suspended from one nostril. "Hey, I got a booger, I got a booger."

I caught Johnny's grimace. Smithe must have, too. He grinned, still leaving the oscillating rubber band suspended from his aquiline nose. "In my drunken frat boy routine I unzip my fly and claim that I got the clap instead, but this gives you the idea, right?"

"Yeah, it sure does," Johnny said.

"Don't worry," I said. "He's going to charm school, but he hasn't graduated yet."

"Harvey Smithe." Johnny's brow furrowed. "Why does that name sound familiar?"

"My agent," Smithe said. "Elliott Collins. He must have told you about me being in the telethon. You know, besides the drunken frat boy routine, I can also do the one about the guy who steps in dog shit in his bare feet."

Johnny canted his head and nodded, placing a palm gently on Smithe's shoulder. "Oh, yeah, I do remember Elliott saying something about that. Tell you what, why don't you get yourself a drink, or something in the bar. I'll have my assistant, Barry, see you in a bit and get your contact information, where you're staying . . . Richard and I have some important matters to discuss right now."

"The bar's right this way, sir," Barry said.

Smithe's face turned a shade darker. "Barry, huh? Rhymes with fairy. I'll bet your parents were hoping for a boy, right?" Smithe grabbed a hotel flier and began fanning himself.

Barry's cheeks flushed.

"Shit," Smithe said, "I haven't even fucking checked in yet."

"You staying here?" Johnny grabbed my arm and began steering us toward the elevators. "Good. It's a great hotel. I'm sure you'll love it. Make sure you check out the fitness room for a steam. Ahh, Barry, would you mind helping Harvey here get checked in?"

"Not at all," Barry said, but I could tell he was gritting his teeth.

Johnny deftly pressed the button. The elevator opened immediately and we stepped inside. As the doors slid closed, I saw Smithe's petulant scowl framed between them.

"I feel guilty leaving Barry to deal with that asshole," Johnny said. "You know him?"

"Only through a set of unfortunate events. We played at the same club once in New York."

"He any good?"

I shrugged. "If this was vaudeville, they'd have a stagehand standing by with the hook."

Johnny pursed his lips and nodded. "That's what I figured. Elliott has a habit of picking losers."

"So I take it he's not your agent anymore?"

Johnny shook his head. "No, but I owe him a couple of favors from way back. Plus he's helping me set the telethon up here. He's friends with the owners." He sighed. "I guess he's gonna call in one of his markers."

"Johnny, say the word and I'll go put Smithe on a one-way trip back where he came from."

He smiled. It was a wistful-looking smile. "I heard you've become quite the ass-kicker lately. That why you want to go to this big fight? To check out the competition?"

Now it was my turn to grin. "The tales of my exploits have been greatly exaggerated."

The elevator doors opened, treating us to a view into an exotic jungle. Palm trees and drooping fronds, all completely artificial, of course, pointed the way toward a bar made of something polished to look like teak, and bound with thick coils of rope. I knew most of the scene was artificial, but in Vegas, perception is reality. The whole place survives on illusion.

I followed Johnny over to a table that was fashioned to look like a hut. Phony straw fastened around phony logs, bound together with phony ropes. Like I said, here illusion is everything.

"What are you drinking?" Johnny asked.

It was still early in the day for me, even on New York time. "Coffee will be fine."

He nodded and gave the waitress my request and ordered a seven and seven for himself. I guess he'd already acclimated to Vegas time. When he saw my expression he brushed it off with a grin and a shrug.

"Don't go thinking I have a *problem* now," he said. "Because I don't."

"Furthest thing from my mind."

"Yeah, right. But Christ, can you blame me? Look at this fucking place." He snorted as he tossed his hand in an encompassing gesture. "Not a clock anywhere in sight. Except in my room, and I don't like to drink alone."

"Point well taken." I smiled, covering the uncomfortable feeling that was starting to eat at my stomach.

The waitress came back and set the seven and seven in front of him. By the time she'd set my cup down and filled it from the carafe, he'd already downed almost half of it. His face sagged a bit and I thought again how stressed-out he looked. He must have read my mind because he pushed the drink away and leaned forward, both forearms on the table.

"So how's everything, Belz? How's Harlee? The kids?"

"They're great."

He grunted an approval, and sat there, his jaw gaping slightly like he was searching for the right words. "I really appreciate you doing the telethon for me, buddy. This is a cause close to my heart."

I've found the best way to get people to open up to you is to nod and say nothing when they give you an open-ended statement. Some of my police-interview technique training coming into play.

"All the proceeds are going to help fight autism."

I nodded.

He pursed his lips. "My boy Joshua . . . his son, my grandson, he's autistic."

I nodded in commiseration and let him go on.

He sighed and shook his head. "Like he's in his own world, you know? And nobody can break through. It tears me up. Like I said, this one's close to my heart."

Family tragedy had been no stranger in my life. I was about to offer whatever sympathy I could when my cell phone rang. My eyes automatically drifted downward to the clip holder on my belt and I hit the ignore button. About forty seconds later the persistent ringtone, sounding like a slice of classical music, started again. I shook my head and swore.

"Maybe you better answer that," Johnny said, his grin returning. "They sound desperate." He swirled his drink and brought the glass to his lips.

I grabbed the phone off my belt holder and said a gruff, "Hello."

Silence, then, "Belz? Is that you? It's me. Paul."

The slurred S sounds were just sloppy enough to let me know that he was soused.

"Yeah, it's me."

"Where you at? Vegas?"

Another sloppy S. "Yeah, I am, but I'm right in the middle of something. I'll call you back."

"Whoa, whoa, whoa, wait. Don't hang up. Please."

I sighed and waited.

"Belz? You still there?"

"I'm here, Paul. But I told you, I'm in an important meeting."

"I know, I know, but just do one thing for me, buddy. Okay?"

"I'm listening."

"Meet me in L.A. tomorrow."

"Paul, look, I'm right in the middle—"

"You gotta come, Belz. Please. I'm begging ya."

I didn't reply.

"It's about who killed—" His voice cut off.

"Brigid Burgeon?"

Johnny perked up.

"Right, right. And things are getting ugly real fast. It's like a matter of life and death that I see you, okay?"

I blew out a slow breath. "Okay, Paul. When and where?"

"You know where the old Farmers Market is?"

"Farmers Market. The one on Fairfax?"

"Yeah. I'll meet you at Philly's at two. Sharp. Got it?"

"Two sharp. Got it."

"And Belz, make sure you're not being tailed."

"Tailed? By whom?"

"The Indian." He said it with the assurance of someone reciting a known fact.

"Who the hell's the Indian?" I asked.

Across from me Johnny's eyes narrowed and he canted his head.

"Never mind," Paul said. "I'll explain everything to you tomorrow. Don't forget. Two sharp. I'll call you if anything changes."

"How the hell did you get my cell number anyway?"

He hung up. Johnny's eyebrows rose as I reclipped my phone to my belt. His grin was wry. "Who was that?"

"A guy named Paul Venchus. I knew him back in Bridgeport."

"Bridgeport?"

"Connecticut. Where I grew up."

"What's he been smoking?"

"Drinking," I said. "He and I used to be reporters together. He's convinced he knows the scoop on who killed Brigid Burgeon. Says he's got somebody who can blow the lid off things."

Johnny's face crinkled. "Man, that sounds like it's right up your alley. Mr. Conspiracy Theory himself here."

"Some mysteries are best left unsolved. Or at least undisturbed."

He laughed. "Brigid Burgeon . . . She was making her last movie with Sal. That was right before we split up, though."

Johnny and Sal Fabell had been unlikely comedic partners in an act that catapulted them both to stardom. Johnny more so than Sal, who had fallen in with Marco Sastra, another dark crooner, after his not-so-friendly split with Johnny. But by clinging to Marco's coattails, Sal had embarked on a successful career of his own, singing, acting in some pretty bad B movies, and finally finding his niche as the host of a TV variety show in the late eighties. I always wished I could have guest-starred on his show before it went off the air. But no such luck.

Somebody called Johnny's name. We both looked over.

I'd met Elliott Collins about fifteen years ago and the man hadn't aged well. His hair had gone totally white, and his jaw seemed more prognathic than I remembered. But his dark eyes hadn't changed. They still looked like dark, cat's-eye marbles trapped in the folds of his eyelids.

Johnny's mouth twitched slightly. "Elliott, sit down. Join us."

Collins shot me a quick nod and pushed onto the bench next to me so he could look across at Johnny, but his head turned toward me.

"So how you been, Belz?"

"Great," I said.

"That's what I been hearing. So you're out here to take part in our little telethon, eh?"

I was about to question his use of the plural possessive regarding the telethon, but out of the corner of my eye I caught Johnny's slight wince. So I just nodded.

"But he has to meet a friend and find out who killed Brigid Burgeon first," Johnny said in his clowning voice.

Elliott looked perplexed for a moment, then looked at Johnny. "I heard you met Smitty downstairs. What did you think of him?" His mouth reset itself into a tight-lipped line.

"Not a lot," Johnny said.

Collins grimaced.

"He stuck a rubber band up his nose, then launched into a gay-bashing routine," I said. "Mentioned something about unzipping his fly for his drunken frat boy act for the telethon."

This time Collins tried to pass things off with an old Ronald Reagan–style grin-and-shrug.

Johnny frowned. "Look, Elliott, this is going to be on network TV. It's for the kids. I can't afford to have some knucklehead fucking things up."

Collins raised his palm. "Harv won't. He's going to be okay."

"Famous last words," I said.

Collins turned to me. "Aww, come on, Richard. You've been known to use the F word time and again."

"Only on cable, and when I did it, it was funny."

He worked his lips together. "The kid really has potential. You'll see once you catch his act."

"I caught it a couple of years ago in New York. I felt like scrubbing up and gargling after touching the same microphone."

His face contorted into a frown. "Johnny, look, he may have been a little bit raw, but we need the exposure."

"We?"

"The kid. I'm his agent, after all. I'm supposed to look out for him, just like I did for you, once upon a time. This could be the break he needs."

I felt like telling Collins I'd give his boy a break. Right across his collarbone. But I was working on being less confrontational, more pacifistic. Johnny seemed to sense that I was itching to tell Collins to take Harvey and put him on a plane home, wherever that was. But it wasn't my call to make.

Collins shot a glance my way, then turned back to Johnny. "And after all, I am helping you set this whole thing up, right?" His tongue moved over his lips. "We need to talk about some stuff. Privately. You don't mind, do you, Rich?"

I've always hated it when people called me "Rich."

Johnny was quick to move in. "Belz, you want me to have Barry set my pilot up to fly you to L.A. tomorrow so you can meet your friend?"

I shook my head. "I think I'll drive."

"Hell, I'll have Hector drive you."

"No, thanks." I patted Collins on the arm and motioned for him to let me out of the booth. The longer I stayed here, the more likely it was that I would say something I'd regret later. And since Collins was obviously a bigger wheel in this whole thing than I was, I didn't want to jeopardize

Johnny's telethon. It was too important to him. "I'm going up to my room and unpack. Let's do dinner later."

"You got it, Belz. I'll call you. You still got the same cell number, right?"

I said I did and wondered again how Paul Venchus had gotten it so easily.

CHAPTER 3

Early the next morning I left Las Vegas and headed southwest toward the mountains in my rental car. I'd chosen a Ford Taurus for the trek. Not that I couldn't have afforded an upgrade, but there was something about going out to L.A. to meet my old buddy Paul, who had a new conspiracy theory to run by me, in a car named after a bull that seemed totally apropos.

I took I-15 and started to fly. By the time I'd hit the winding section through the mountains, a fine layer of mist had settled over the top of them. It was like riding through a dreamscape. I was glad I'd decided to drive instead of taking Johnny up on his offer of the plane. On the other side of the mountains things flattened out as I came through the long stretch of desert separating the lower end of the Sierras from the rest of the Golden State. I still had about three hours to go to L.A., and I became less enthralled by the scenery and more introspective.

Last night Johnny and I had finally made it to the Fremont East District and our old favorite, Binion's, for dinner. We'd originally planned to go there for lunch, but time had run out on that plan and it was early evening by the time he'd gotten some free time to eat. Fremont was actually Las Vegas city, proper. The Strip, where all the big casinos and hotels are, is actually unincorporated Clark County and not within the official Las

Vegas city limits. Fremont, or "downtown," as the locals call it, reminds me more of the old Vegas: a bunch of smaller casinos, a couple of low-scale hotels, and some strip joints. Just the basics. Certainly this is what Bugsy Siegel had in mind when he'd envisioned the place. Now Fremont Street is covered with a panoramic canopy, and the street itself is off-limits to cars. A far cry from the days when Elvis and Ann-Margret were filming the racing scenes for *Viva Las Vegas*. Of course, most of that one was probably filmed in Hollywood anyway.

I'd hoped eating at Binion's would make Johnny feel more relaxed, but he still seemed troubled and ordered another seven and seven as soon as we sat down. I guess the pressure of setting up something as immense as the telethon was getting to him. I asked if he needed me to give him a hand.

"I appreciate your offer, Belz." He smiled and took a pull on his drink. "But it's lots of pressure you don't need."

"What's that old saying about friends? They take half the burden and they double the joy?"

He smiled again. "You do that just by being here."

Our conversation meandered to the old days when he was just starting out. He told me how he and Sal Fabell had played one of the clubs down the block from here.

"Sallie's doing some shows at the Mirage through next week," he said. "Man, I'd love to see him again. Catch up on how he's doing, but hell, we haven't talked to each other since . . . shit."

It was rumored that he and Sal had split under less than the best of terms. I'd never asked him much about their partnership, and he hadn't offered, but I figured that now, since he'd opened the door . . .

"Why did you guys break up anyway?"

He looked down, shrugged, and took another long sip of his drink. "Things change. People, too. I guess we just sort of outgrew our relationship."

"That happens sometimes." I still wondered about what had caused the bitterness that had lasted all this time. Word was that they hadn't spoken in about twenty-five years. But he didn't offer anything in the way of an explanation.

His voice turned wistful. "I remember the first time we met. We were playing on the same bill in Jersey. He was the coolest guy I'd ever seen. But, like you said, things and people change."

I didn't press him and the conversation segued to a new subject. We talked about happier things. Movies and television, and the telethon. All the standard stuff that two stand-up guys who'd caught their respective brass rings like to talk about. When Hector dropped us back at the Monticello, Johnny looked exhausted. I told him I was going to take a short walk up the Strip, and he said he was going up to his room and have room service bring him a cocktail.

"I thought you didn't like to drink alone?" I said, hoping my smile would offset the concern I felt.

"I lied," he said, and wandered inside.

I silently hoped he'd forego the drink and just hit the sack.

I strolled down to New York–New York and called Harlee from the bridge over to the MGM. After talking for about fifteen minutes, and exchanging our standard "I love you"s, I caught the monorail back to the hotel.

I came in the back way, thinking about picking up the rental car in the morning, and saw the elevator doors closing about twenty-five feet in front of me.

"Damn," I said.

Just then a black hand shot out from inside the car and hit the retractors. The elevator doors jolted to a stop and opened wide. As I stepped inside I nodded a thanks to the guy who'd stopped them for me, a well-built African-American gentleman with a hint of gray in his fade. He also had the hotel crest on the pocket of his blazer.

"What floor, sir?" he asked.

"Lobby," I said. This guy looked familiar, but just why I wasn't sure. I stole a glance at his name tag, which said GRADY A. SANTA FE, NM.

Then I did a double take. The thick ridges of scar tissue above each eye told me I was right.

"Excuse me," I said, "but aren't you Grady Armitage? The boxer?"

His face twitched into a smile. "Yeah, well, I used to be."

"I saw you fight for the cruiserweight championship. Alfonso Ratliff, wasn't it?"

He nodded his head slightly. "Yeah, I went the distance, but lost the decision. Came close one more time against Holyfield. Thought I won it, but the judges, they saw it different."

"That time against Ratliff. It was in the Garden, right? I was there. You got robbed."

"'Preciate you saying that."

"I mean every word of it. Didn't you win another title, though?"

His chuckle sounded genuine and deep. "I won the IFBO belt after they split them all up, but it never was worth much."

"Well, you're still the champ in my book. Can I buy you a drink?"

He shook his head and pointed to the emblem on his jacket pocket. "I appreciate the offer, sir, but I'm on duty. Can't go socializing with the guests in the bar."

"The next time you're off, then. I'd like to hear about some of your fights."

The elevator slowed to a stop and the doors opened at the lobby level.

"See you next time, Mr. Belzer," he said as he stepped out. The doors closed behind him.

Grady Armitage had been one of those pros you could count on to come to fight. He always gave his all, and was as tough as a bag full of nails. During the fight with Holyfield his left eyebrow was ripped wide open and he left more blood on his opponent and the canvas than the Red Cross collects in a week. But he never quit. Rumor was that he finished a fight with a broken right hand once, going nine full rounds just jabbing and hooking with his left. I was looking forward to buying him that drink and hearing all about his experiences in the fight game. Funny how many ex-pugs ended up doing doorman jobs in Vegas hotels. Like the place they all migrated to once the square jungle kicked them out.

I saw a sign for the I-40 turnoff to Palm Springs and knew I was getting close. More mountains loomed to the south, and more cars had started to show up. Pretty soon I'd pass the Barstow exit and then hit the heavy traffic. It was 10:30, so I was making pretty good time. I hoped that

Paul would be there and this meeting of the minds, or maybe one mind, could be handled with expediency. In and out. That was my goal. Listen politely, for old time's sake, offer him any encouragement I could while I disentangled myself from his rantings. With a little bit of luck, I'd be back on the road to Vegas by late afternoon. Hopefully the rush hour wouldn't be too bad coming back, but then again, when is traffic ever good in L.A.?

I kept asking myself that question as the bumper-to-bumper crawl started when I got past Hesperia. How far out did people live to commute to L.A.? The Ten, as the locals called it, was proving true to its namesake, in that the top speed felt like about ten miles per hour for the last forty miles into the city. Once I got to Melrose, I managed to escape the freeway and cut through side streets until I got to Fairfax.

The old Farmers Market was a throwback to the 1930s, when the farmers would drive in from the nearby farms and sell their wares from the backs of their pickup trucks to the citified folk. They did it on such a regular basis, they built a group of ramshackle sheds and stands that could be closed and locked up until the next produce arrived. Pretty soon more enterprising vendors were constructing places to shop for other trinkets and incidentals. Hats and belts for the gents, blouses and scarves for the ladies, toys for the kiddies, and a couple of small greasy spoons where you could grab some ham and eggs (as long as you weren't kosher), along with a cup of coffee while you waited for the fresh fruit to be unloaded.

As the area surrounding L.A. began its inevitable encroachment on the contiguous farmland, it took longer and longer for the farmers to drive in, and the old Farmers Market grew into a state of semipermanence. The gridlike collection of stands and small stores got rebuilt and roofed over, so they could stay open during the week, and they began to thrive. The area continued to grow, but allowed the Farmers Market to remain, in all its quaintness, and labeled it an historic landmark, making it untouchable. And why not? It held a lot of Hollywood history. Walt Disney sat on one of the vinyl stools to design Disneyland, and James Dean purportedly ate his last meal there before roaring into the desert and an early grave.

Inevitably, a huge shopping mall called the Grove was erected right next to the Market. You can take the trolley that runs between them and literally go from the thirties ambience to the new millennium with only a short ride. Or you can be really old-fashioned and walk. It's not very far.

For my money, though, I'll take the Farmers Market any day over the glitzy chain stores of the adjacent mall. As you walk through the old, labyrinthine passageways, you can almost imagine Walt or Jimmy Dean sitting there dreaming. Or even Jake Gittes standing in one of the Market's open-air aisles, smoking a cigarette and pretending to look at the fruit while shadowing an errant husband.

Forget it, Jake. It's a long way from Chinatown.

Luckily for me, they'd long ago disregarded Joni Mitchell's lament and also paved paradise and put up a parking lot right next to it. At any rate, I was able to put the rental in a convenient place and take the short walk to Phil's Deli in the bright California sunshine. It was an easy seventy-five . . . a little cooler than Vegas had been, but a hell of a lot warmer than New York in February. I was wearing a short-sleeve polo shirt and slacks and I felt pretty close to perfect comfort until, that is, I remembered why I'd come here and whom I was meeting. I caught a whiff of something frying at Phil's, one of the surviving open-air diners. There were certain advantages to being here, and having an excuse to partake in some goodies from the greasiest of the greasy spoons was one of the major ones.

I glanced up at the obelisklike clocktower. It was 1:45. Paul had told me he'd be there at 2:00, but in the language of a drunk that more than likely meant I shouldn't hold my breath. I grabbed a stool at the counter, positioning myself so I could keep an eye on the two main aisles, and ordered a Philly cheesesteak with fries. With all the disingenuous politicians passing clean air and food laws these days, you almost have to carry a pack of cigarettes and a small bottle of transfats to greasy spoon restaurants and darkly lit bars just on general principles. But one look at the large, flat griddle full of frying meats, onions, and sliced peppers, and I knew I was in the right place. What the hell was Thomas Wolfe thinking when he said you can't go home again? I was there. The Philly cheesesteak would have even made W. C. Fields believe he was in Philadelphia.

Despite taking my time and savoring every mouthful, I finished my meal and was nursing my second cup of coffee as people sauntered by with a brusqueness that marked them as locals. Luckily, no one recognized me, or if they did, they kept their distance. Of course, the place is well known for celebrity sightings. Plus, it was a weekday and the ice cream–licking tourists, the kind who might have pestered me for an autograph when I least wanted to sign one, were probably in the Grove hunting souvenir T-shirts. It was obvious that Paul had gotten sidetracked. I wondered if it was by a bottle. It was closing in on 2:45, and my patience was feeling as thin as a sheet of the onionskin paper my sandwich had been wrapped in. Plus, the coffee was running right through me. I hated to think about what the drive back was going to be like. Of course, one of the bennies of driving through the California desert alone was no one would say a word if I had to stop and take a whiz along the side of the road.

I hit the facilities, thinking the whole time if Paul wasn't sitting at the counter at Phil's when I finished, I'd get in my car and drive back to Vegas, putting the whole thing off to an extended lunch trip.

If I leave L.A. now, I thought, I can get back to Vegas by 9:30 or 10:00. I didn't relish the thought of driving through the mountains in the dark, but once I got past them, Vegas would be lit up like a beacon in the East. The refrain of "this road trip was a mistake" kept ringing in my ears, over and over again.

Still, I'd come all this way . . .

I pulled out my cell and found the number Paul had called me from on my screen list. Time to shit or get off the pot, buddy, I thought as I pressed the button to call him. It rang three times before someone answered it with a barely audible, "Yeah?"

"Paul?" I asked. "It's Belz."

"Who?"

"Richard."

"Richard who?"

"Belzer." This was ceasing to be amusing, and the voice sounded a bit off. "Is this Paul Venchus?"

"Huh? No." He disconnected.

So much for manners on the cell phone crowd.

I rechecked the number. It was Paul's, no doubt about it. He'd called me from it twice. But not a third time . . . and I had to think he would have once he realized he was going to be late for our meeting today. Which meant that he couldn't call because . . . his phone was lost. . . . Or stolen, and the schmuck who'd just answered it had probably found it. Hopefully, Paul would report it before the asshole could call South Africa or the Netherlands and run up the bill. But that was Paul's problem, not mine.

My next move was a no-brainer. It was time to hit the road, Jack, as Ray Charles used to sing. As I was walking to my car my cell phone jangled. Maybe this was my tardy friend.

The number was unfamiliar, but it had an L.A. area code. I answered it.

"Is this Mr. Richard Belzer?" a male voice asked.

Anytime I get a call on my cell from someone I don't know asking for "Mr. Belzer," the hair on the back of my neck stands up. It usually means what will follow is either about business or bad news. This guy's voice didn't have the light ring of a business discussion. In fact, he sounded official . . . too official.

"It is," I said. "What can I do for you?"

Hesitation. Another bad sign. Then, "Do you know a Paul Venchus?"

"Yeah." I was starting to get that little sick feeling in the pit of my stomach more from what I anticipated this guy was going to say than the greasy meal I'd just consumed. "Why?"

"When was the last time you saw him?"

Great. Twenty questions. "Maybe thirty years ago. Who is this, by the way?"

"This is Officer Pearsol, sir. LAPD."

Shit, that meant that either Paul had been cracked for DUI or something, or . . .

"Is he all right?" I asked. "We were supposed to meet over on Fairfax for lunch. I've been waiting for him."

Another brief pause. "I'm afraid I have some bad news."

The sick feeling was beginning to spread upward now. "And what might that be?"

"It's Mr. Venchus, sir. I'm sorry to have to tell you that he's expired."

"Expired? You mean dead?"

"Yes, sir."

"How did it happen?"

"Um, we're not quite sure at this time, sir."

A feminine voice in the background screamed, "Not quite sure! What do you mean, not quite sure? I told you he was—" The voice faded out.

Pearsol came back on the phone a few seconds later. "Sorry, Mr. Belzer. His girlfriend here is kind of hysterical."

"I am *not* his girlfriend!" the feminine voice in the background screamed again. "And I am *not* hysterical!"

I heard Pearsol instruct someone to "take her and put her in the back of my squad."

Sounded like the party was just getting under way.

"She sounds like a handful," I said.

"You got that right," he said. "Called nine-one-one screaming bloody murder and we get over here and it looks like the guy drank himself to death."

I considered this but didn't know if I should be surprised or saddened. "He did have a drinking problem."

"His place is a mess. Blood and fecal matter all over the place."

Blood and fecal matter? It was gratifying to experience firsthand the benefit of LAPD requiring a more extensive education for its officers. This guy's must have been in English. Or scatology.

"We're waiting on the ETs now, to process," he continued, "but if I had to make a guess, I'd say his stomach exploded. Happens sometimes with drunks."

"Yeah. Is there anything I can do?" I gave myself a quick, imaginary kick in the ass for asking.

"Well, sir, like I said, we're treating this as a death investigation at the moment. Would you know how to reach his next of kin?"

"Not really," I said. "We grew up together in Bridgeport, Connecticut, but that was a long time ago. Like I said, I haven't seen him in years."

"Okay. I can reach you at this number if I need to get back to you?"

"Sure, it's my cell. How did you get it, by the way?"

"Ah, the decedent's girlfriend gave it to us."

This was getting ridiculous. "Did she say how she got it?"

"No, sir. Maybe—" His voice dropped off abruptly and I heard him yell, "Shit! She's kicking my fucking window."

I heard some muffled sounds, then more yelling. Mostly Pearsol reading the riot act to the girlfriend. When he came back on the phone he was breathing hard. "Sorry, Mr. Belzer. A little problem here."

Sounded like a big problem to me. One that I wanted to avoid.

"Look, Officer, I don't suppose there's anything I can do over there, is there?"

"No, sir. Were you en route over here?"

"Actually, I was just getting ready to head back to Vegas."

"Vegas, huh? Man, I wish I was you."

Girlfriend must have been listening to his side of the conversation because I heard her yell again. "He's not coming over? Oh, my God! Tell him he has to get over here."

Pearsol told her to shut up and that she'd better not kick his car's window again, or she'd be going to jail. He cleared his throat and came back to our conversation. "You know, I really enjoy your show, by the way."

"Thanks," I said. "Just out of curiosity, what's going to happen to his body?"

"The ME will most likely do an autopsy. If it's ruled natural, which it appears to be, then they'll close the case out and release the body to the next of kin, if we can locate them. You said Bridgeport, right?"

"Yeah. Not sure if his parents still live there."

"We'll look into it."

"If no one claims his body, what then?"

I heard him sigh. "Maybe his girl will do something and bury him. If not, the county will."

That meant a mass grave with a lot-marker number in a field somewhere.

"Look, Pearsol, do me a favor."

"What's that, Mr. Belzer?"

"First, call me Belz. If no one claims his body and it's going to be dumped in an unmarked grave, give me a call and I'll make some arrange-ments."

"Okay, I'll make a note in the report."

"And second, I'd appreciate it, if girlfriend there doesn't know my number by heart, you'd not give it to her. And maybe if you could check her cell and if it's on there, hit the delete button for me?"

"Consider it done, Belz."

I almost said, "I am not a cop," but this time I thought it better to let it slide and beat feet out of L.A., thankful that, for once, I'd been able to dodge the bullet.

CHAPTER 4

"So you drove all the way out there for nothing?" Johnny asked the next morning over a late breakfast. The drive back to Vegas had been dark and monotonous as I traversed the expansive desert and wound through the mountains, thinking about Paul's untimely demise. A sad way to go, but one that didn't surprise me too much.

"Yeah," I said, "more or less. But at least I got to eat a cheesesteak at Phil's."

He smirked. "Ain't that what Jimmy Dean supposedly said?"

"Yeah, right. To Elvis, Marilyn, and Bogey in one of those Edward Hopper paintings." The long drive had left me exhausted and I'd slept a good ten hours. Johnny had awakened me with a brisk knock and a waiter pushing in a three-course breakfast. My room had a nice view of the distant mountains off the seventeenth-floor balcony.

"Jeez," Johnny said, "I leave you alone for one day and look at the trouble you get into."

"Actually, I spent the day avoiding trouble."

"I thought trouble was your business."

"Unh-uh, that's what Marlowe used to say. Avoiding trouble is my business."

"Right. But being Mr. Funnyman is what's important now. Anyway," he pointed at the tray, "your eggs are getting cold."

I was just about to make a snappy comeback when my cell phone rang. Thinking it might be Harlee, I answered it before checking the screen.

"Mr. Belzer?" Not Harlee, but definitely female.

"Yeah, who's this?"

"Veronica Holmes."

The name rang no bells. "Do we know each other?"

"In a manner of speaking," she said. "I was at Paul Venchus's yesterday when the police called you."

Ah, the screaming girlfriend. And good old Officer Pearsol had promised me he wouldn't let her have my number. "I thought your voice sounded familiar. What can I do for you?"

"It's not what you can do for me," she said, "but what I can do for you."

She made it sound like an offer I couldn't refuse. Except I did. "Look, Ms. Holmes, I'm sorry for your loss, but—"

"Paul and I weren't seeing each other. We were working together."

"That's nice to hear, but unfortunately I'm in the middle of something very important—"

"Paul was murdered," she blurted out.

"That's something I'm sure the LAPD will look into."

"You of all people should know that won't be the case."

Me of all people? I needed to get out of this phone call, but she continued. "We both know they'll want to sweep it under the rug. Keep things quiet."

"Maybe," I said. "Look, Ms. Holmes, I'm in the middle of something. And for the record, I am not a cop."

"Fine," she said, "I'll see you this afternoon, then."

"Excuse me?"

"I'm on my way to Las Vegas, Mr. Belzer. I have my Greyhound ticket now, and we're set to leave in one hour. I should be there this afternoon."

"That's nice. I wish you a lot of luck at the tables. They say Vegas is very pretty this time of year."

"I happen to know you're there."

I sighed. Paul must have told her. "And you know this how?"

"The same way I know your cell phone number," she said. "I happen to be blessed with extrasensory perception."

"ESP?" Visions of Carson's old Carnac the Magnificent shot through my mind.

"Otherwise called psychic abilities."

"Look, miss, I'm really very busy and I don't have time to commiserate with you on Paul's passing. In fact, I hadn't seen him in about thirty years."

"Time doesn't matter to kindred spirits."

"Well, it matters to me, and right now I don't have a lot of it. Please don't call me again." I hit the disconnect button and tossed the cell phone against the pillow. "If this keeps up, I'm going to put my fucking cell phone number on a billboard with the caption 'Please call me.' "

Johnny grinned. "Why not just put 'Please fucking call me'?"

"Or maybe, 'Fucking call me, or else,' " I added.

He laughed. "We do work well together, don't we? Too bad this telethon is on network. We'd tear them up if we had the freedom of cable. Remember Buddy's routine about the guy who farted in New York and his ex in L.A. fainted?"

"He was a great one."

His face had a nostalgic look as he nodded, then after a few seconds said, "Go ahead and eat 'cause I have a special treat for you. It's why I woke you up."

"Really? I thought it was your sadistic streak."

"I'm saving that for later. As soon as you're ready, we're going to be going over to the MMA gym to tape some of their training prep. They're going to let us use it on the telethon."

"Great filler," I said. "Plus good advertising for them, right?"

"You betcha, even though the big fight will be over by then. Who you picking, by the way?"

I shrugged. "Hard to tell. The smart money's on Reeves, but Scott can be tough." I picked up a piece of toast, slathered on some butter, and made a scrambled egg sandwich. The orange juice and coffee made it go down easier, but it still felt like a lump in my stomach. I needed some fruit or yogurt. And some answers.

I waved my finger up as I finished chewing and said to Johnny, "Excuse me a moment, brother. I have to make this call."

He held his palms open in a supplicating gesture and gave me his most obsequious grin.

I reached over and picked up my cell phone, scrolling down until I found the number I needed and hit the speed dial. He answered on the third ring.

"Officer Pearsol," I said.

"Hey, Mr. Belzer. Or should I say 'Belz'?"

"Belz is fine. I was wondering how things turned out yesterday with the death investigation."

"Paul Venchus, right?"

"Good memory. What did you find out?"

"We had the ETs process things. Man, were they pissed off. Lots of fecal matter and blood all over the place. One guy said he'd had to double-bag everything because of the smell."

"Anything on the cause of death?"

"They took the body to the morgue. They're probably doing the autopsy as we speak, depending on how many shooting victims came in last night." He paused. "I thought you said you and he weren't close."

"We weren't, actually. Went to school together, worked on the same paper for a while. Just one of those accidental friendships. Think you could do me a favor and ask the pathologist what the cause of death was and let me know?"

"Sure, I can do that. I mean, we coppers have to stick together, right?"

"I appreciate it."

"Say, I got something to ask you. I got a screenplay I've been working on. Police story. You know anybody in Hollywood I could hand it off to when I get it done?"

Three-quarters of the cops in L.A. were aspiring writers, all hoping to be the next Joseph Wambaugh. But for every Wambaugh or Paul Bishop who succeeded, there were a couple thousand broken hearts with piles of rejections slips. Still, I'd been there, too.

"I might be able to ask around," I said. "Let me know when you've got it done."

"Great. I'll call the morgue and get back to you later, okay?"

I told him it sounded great, but had one more thing to ask.

"Say, remember how you mentioned that Paul's girlfriend gave you my cell phone number yesterday?"

"Yeah, the psycho chick said you were as close to a relative as the dead guy had." He quickly added, "But I deleted it off her cell like you asked."

"Well, she knew it by heart. She just called me a few minutes ago."

"Aww, shit, I'm sorry to hear that. Want me to look her up and tell her to quit bothering you?"

"I'll let you know on that, too. Right now everything's cool. Besides, I'm in Vegas."

"Say the word and I'll work up a telephone harassment case for you. Of course, it would necessitate you signing a complaint and coming to court."

"Like I said, let's just let it ride for now. If she can find me in this city, she probably really is a psychic."

He laughed. "She lay that shit on you, too? The psychic crap?"

"Oh yeah."

"She just about went nuts at the scene yesterday, screaming first at you on the phone, and then demanding to be let in to the crime scene. I told her, 'Lady, believe me, you don't want to go in there now.' But did that stop her? No way. She kept babbling about it being murder and a big conspiracy. We finally had to threaten her with obstructing to get her to shut up."

His account was making her sound like a tenacious bulldog. Just what I needed hopping on a Greyhound bus and heading to Vegas to track me down. I asked Pearsol what Veronica Holmes looked like and he gave me a quick rundown.

"White, about twenty-five or -six. Brown hair and eyes. About five five, maybe a buck and a quarter. Brown hair pulled back with some kind of rag on her head. Not really a bad-looking girl, if she'd fix herself up. She wore kind of a long dress and carried this huge canvas bag instead of a purse. Sort of like a cleaned-up bag lady."

At least I knew who to be on the lookout for now. I thanked Pearsol and told him I'd be expecting his follow-up call at his convenience. When I ended the call I saw Johnny staring at me.

"Sounds like you're getting ready to launch one of your full-scale investigations, Detective," he said.

"Yeah, right. That'll have to wait till I get my next script. Right now, all I'm interested in is helping you out with the telethon."

"And if I believe that one," Johnny said with a grin, "you got a part of Hoover Dam you want to sell me?"

About an hour later we were taking the elevator down to the lobby. Hopefully, Hector would be waiting in the front driveway in his limo, and I wouldn't see any cleaned-up bag ladies. Of course, if she was just leaving L.A. now, on Greyhound, she wouldn't be here for several hours. Plus, Vegas is a big place and how could she know where I was staying? Unless good old Paul had remembered my talking about the telethon. At one time he'd been pretty sharp. How much of that had been dulled by the booze, I didn't know. My gut told me that even if the girlfriend did make it to Sin City, she'd have to ask around plenty before she could track me down. Hopefully that would prove discouraging enough and our paths would never cross.

It started me wondering again about Paul, though, and if his death was really from those natural causes. Pearsol made it sound that way. An exploded stomach. *"Happens sometimes with drunks,"* he'd said. Not a good way to go, but then again, there aren't many of those anyway.

"Hey, hey, hey," a voice behind me said. I didn't have to turn to know who it was.

"Come down to try your luck at the crap tables?" Harvey Smithe said, sidling up in front of us, blocking our way. Johnny's face took on a real sour look.

"It's craps," I said. "Now say good night, Harvey."

"But, it's morning, isn't it?" he said.

"I'm sure it's dark in Australia or someplace on the other side of the planet." The same place where I wished he was at the moment. "Why don't you go check it out for us and report back. Like next year sometime."

He pursed his lips and turned to Johnny. "Did Elliott get things straightened out with you yesterday? He said he did."

Johnny nodded. "Everything's cool. Look, kid, we're on the way somewhere."

"Oh yeah? Where we going?"

"Not to the same place you are," I said. "You bilingual by any chance?"

"My grandmother spoke Polish." He puffed up his chest. "I'm half Italian, too."

"Good," I said. "Go give Grandma a call and ask her which half is which. And also how they say 'scram' in the old country. That way you'll know it in two languages."

He fudged his lips again, obviously trying to capture that smart comeback line that kept eluding him. "Maybe you could call Johnny's fag boy Barry and ask him how to say it in Homo-eze."

"Real good," I said, letting the sarcasm exude. "It's hard when you have to think this early in the morning, isn't it?" He stiffened and I suddenly got that feeling he was considering taking a swing at me. His mouth gaped and I realized he must have had a couple of shots of vodka in his morning orange juice.

The gape twisted to a scowl. "Why don't you shut the fuck up for a change?"

Someone had soaked this worm in too much tequila.

"If you're feeling froggy, I wouldn't leap. Not unless you want your head handed to you."

"Why, you think you can take me?" His pudgy hands balled into fists as his face darkened. "You'd just better quit fucking with me, Belzer." His voice was a growl.

"Or what? You'll go steal a clever line somewhere and hit me over the head with it?"

"Listen, Mr. Big Shot. Or should I say Big Shit? I got just as much right to be here as you. Plus I got connections you can't even dream about."

This was taking on all the earmarks of a grade-school playground confrontation. I dropped my right foot back, ready to put him on the floor if he came at me.

"Sure you do, kid," Johnny said, stepping between us, giving Smithe an avuncular pat on the shoulder. "Look, we'll talk later. Right now me and Belz got to be somewhere."

The drunken prick didn't move and I made up my mind if he did anything to Johnny he was going to be eating some carpet. But I didn't have to move. A dark hand clasped Smithe's shoulder and Grady Armitage stepped between us.

"Everything cool, gentlemen?" he asked. He towered over Smithe and had an aura of quiet power.

Smithe blinked twice and nodded, giving me the cold stare that looked out of place over his simpering lips. "Cool. I was just leaving."

As he turned and walked down an aisle between machines, he bumped into a waitress, knocking her cocktail tray over. Whirling, he swore at her and kept walking. I moved forward and started to help her pick up the fallen glassware, but she told me thanks, but no thanks. She'd get it. Grady was right beside me.

"You all right, Belz?"

I straightened up. "Yeah, I was just trying out a new routine." Grady grinned as I went back to Johnny. "I still can't believe you're letting that asshole on the show."

His eyes flashed with an uncomfortable glint. "I know, Belz, but like I told you, it's a favor to Elliott."

I leaned close so he'd be sure to hear me over the constant dinging. "Elliott can kiss my ass, too."

"I'll tell him you're interested," he said. "Who's the black dude? He acted like you knew each other."

"Let me tell you about Grady Armitage," I said as we steered through the crowd.

Hector was out front waiting and jumped out of the car to open the door for us. He was back in the driver's seat before we'd completely settled in. The screen lowered and he smiled back at us. "Where to, boss?"

Johnny gave him the address and he nodded, leaving the screen down.

"Look, Belz," Johnny said, a look of concern spreading over his face, "I know that guy Smithe kind of bugs you."

"Bugs me? Are you trying for understatement? He's like that pesky smear of dog shit that you can't quite scrape from your crepe-soled shoes."

He scrunched up his lips before he answered. "Admittedly, the guy is kind of an asshole."

"Very admittedly."

He grinned slightly. "I just don't want to worry about you grabbing him and breaking his arm, that's all."

"My powers are only used for the greater good," I said. "Of course, throwing good old Smitty in the fountain in front of the Bellagio could be considered a public service."

"Belz, please."

It was my turn to laugh. "Have Barry put the prick on at three in the morning and our paths will probably never cross again."

"Sounds like a plan," he said.

"A good plan," I added.

We didn't speak of the asshole again until we pulled up in front of a one-story brick building with a big sign labeling it as WORLD COMBAT TRAIN-ING CENTER—THE PLACE WHERE CHAMPIONS ARE MADE.

"Hey," I said, "maybe we can drop Smitty off over here to learn some manners."

"Nah, he kind of reminds me of the kid who kept getting beaten up in fifth grade."

"No, that was me," I said. "Smithe would have been standing off to the side cheering the bully on because he was afraid he'd be next."

He chuckled.

Inside the place was extremely hot. If they had air-conditioning, they weren't using it. It looked like a larger version of the *dojang* where I study martial arts in New York City. My place has a more comfortable feel, though. This place was hard-edged. As if I needed another reminder of this, I saw an enormous guy in a black T-shirt and blue jeans stroll over to meet us. When he saw Johnny he shot us a wide smile.

"Mr. Leland," he said. "And is that *the* Richard Belzer with you?"

"The one and only," Johnny said, shaking the guy's hand. I followed suit. It was like putting my hand into a catcher's mitt.

"I'm Trace Gordon," the big guy said. "No relation to Flash. It's a real honor to meet you, Mr. Belzer. I watch your show all the time."

I felt like saying, "Call me Ishmael," since I was in the presence of somebody the size of Moby Dick, but instead told him just to call me Belz.

"I own this place," Trace said over his shoulder as he led us into the adjacent room. As we approached I kept hearing this guttural grunt followed by an incredible thud. Stepping through the door, I saw another big guy. This one had on a shiny vinyl sweatshirt and pants to match. He was standing in front of a huge tractor tire. The guy beside him, obviously his training coach, urged him onward and the vinyl-clad giant stooped and grabbed the underside of the tire, raised it straight up, and pushed it down. The grunt and the thud followed almost simultaneously.

"Man," Johnny said. "How much does that thing weigh?"

"A hundred and sixty kilograms," Trace said.

"Meaning what?" I asked. "About three-hundred-plus pounds?"

"Three hundred fifty-two, point seventy-four," Johnny said.

I shot him a sideways glance and he shrugged.

"All the time I spent in Europe, I had to pick up a thing or two."

"Hey, Stevie," Trace called out. "I want you to meet somebody."

The trainer scowled. "Come on, man. We got less than an hour before Reeves gets here."

"It's best not to disturb him," I was saying when Stevie skipped over the fallen tire and came trotting over. He shook hands with Johnny, then turned to me.

"Hey, I know you. TV, right? Cop show."

As I shook hands with my second baseball-mitt-size hand of the day, I told him I was glad to meet him, adding, "But, I am not a cop."

"Too bad. I'll bet you'd make a good one."

"Stevie," the trainer yelled. "You gonna do some work, or what?"

Steve grinned at us and rushed back, reaching down and picking up the tire again.

"He have something against tractors?" Johnny asked.

Trace laughed. "This is perhaps the only way these guys can train for

MMA. They have to be able to do a variety of boxing, wrestling, jujitsu, Muay Thai . . . it's like the ultimate fighting contest."

With that, Steve's trainer announced they were moving to the cage. He eyed us suspiciously.

"Don't mind Stevie's trainer, Riker," Trace said. "Since I own the best gym around these parts, I have to let both guys train here."

"That must be interesting," Johnny said.

Trace shook his head. "Nah, they respect each other. Just between you and me, though, I don't think poor Stevie's got much of a chance. Reeves is too good."

Johnny elbowed me. "Now we know who to put our money on."

I wasn't so sure. I'd seen Gordon Reeves fight and he was pretty awesome, but the determination I'd just seen in Steve Scott had been inspiring. "I wouldn't want to pick a winner in this one. I'm just glad to be able to see it."

"Ringside seats," Johnny said, patting his jacket pocket. "The only way I could get him out here."

He knew he could get me out here with a voicemail, but I let him have his moment of exaggeration. Trace took us upstairs to a room that had a long, glass window overlooking the gym area and, God bless him, air-conditioning.

"Whew," I said, fanning myself. "I thought I was going to have to change my shirt after this one."

"This is my VIP section," Trace said. "Go ahead, watch him go through his stuff."

We did. Steve went six five-minute rounds, alternating kickboxing with wrestling and ground techniques. He had six different sparring partners, and never showed any signs of fatigue until the sixth round. I was impressed as hell.

We stayed in the air-conditioned comfort as Steve's workout wound down and Reeves arrived. After a quick introduction to him, we watched from above. Reeves looked slightly bigger and perhaps stronger. Steve had a little more quickness, though. One thing was for sure, both guys packed a lot of power. Johnny asked me who I was going to pick as we went back to the waiting limo.

"It's too close to call," I said.

"An expert like you not being able to make a simple prediction?"

"Yeah, like I told Stevie, I am not a cop."

Immediately after I said it I looked at my watch. We'd burned up a good portion of the day, and it was stretching into early afternoon. Enough time for the Greyhound to traverse the distance between L.A. and Las Vegas? But still, I reminded myself, Vegas is a big place.

But not big enough, as I found out as soon as we pulled up in front of the Monticello. Hector parked and was out opening the door for us in world record time. I got out first and was waiting on Johnny when I felt someone tugging my sleeve.

"Mr. Belzer? Mr. Belzer?"

Slowly, I turned and got my first glimpse of the young woman grasping the material. I recognized her immediately from Officer Pearsol's accurate description: rag on her head, searching brown eyes, a comely face. The cleaned-up bag lady who might not be bad if she fixed herself up. In an instant I knew this could only be Veronica Holmes.

CHAPTER 5

"Mr. Belzer, pleeeeze."

Even the sound of her voice drove me nuts. It elevated to a whine that sounded like a dull razor blade dragging over glass. Apologies to Bogey, of course, but I couldn't help wondering of all the casinos in all of Vegas, how did she happen to end up in front of mine? What the hell. I asked her.

"I told you I'm gifted that way," she said. "I'm a psychic."

"Good. Then you can read my mind and leave without an incident."

"Wait," she continued, "you just absolutely *have* to look at Paul's notes. I've got them in here." She held up her large, brightly colored canvas bag. Her other hand held a beat-up suitcase.

"I don't absolutely have to do anything except pay my taxes on time," I shot back. The retort made her blink, as if she'd been clipped in the face. Her eyes welled up and began to glisten.

Aww, shit, I thought. Not that.

Just as I was starting to feel that twinge of regret, Johnny imposed himself into the conversation. "When's the last time you had something to eat, sweetie?"

"Yesterday," she said. The tears were starting now, rolling down her cheeks like twin gussets.

Johnny moved between us and put his arm around her shoulders, handing her his handkerchief and ushering her toward the elevators. "Come on. I'm starving and the place upstairs has a great corned beef on rye."

"I take it you're buying her lunch?" I asked.

He glanced over his shoulder and grinned back at me. "Actually, I'm putting this one on your room service account."

"Since you're paying all my expenses anyway, right?"

"Exactamundo." His finger shot out and hit the elevator button. "Come on."

I followed, feeling the regret starting to creep up my spine. All I needed now was Harvey Smithe to make one of his pain-in-the-ass appearances.

But we lucked out, sort of, because Harvey didn't show. I said "sort of" because just as we tucked ourselves into the booth, Johnny and Veronica on one side, me on the other, his cell phone rang. Johnny frowned as he looked at the screen, but answered it.

"What's up?" he said. I watched his face crease slightly. He licked his lips, listening, then said, "I'm in the Marebello Room. We just sat down to eat." Another few seconds, and he added, "Yeah, Richard and his friend . . . No, I don't think so . . . Can't you get with Barry?" He sighed and finished with an "Okay," after which he flipped the phone closed. He flashed me a grin that looked as genuinely mirthful as an emergency room doctor expecting a flood of victims from a train wreck.

"Look," he said, "I have to tag up with someone."

I didn't like the feel of this one. "I thought you were hungry?"

"Yeah, well, I was." His eyes avoided mine, scanned the room, and blinked. It was almost like a reflexive gesture. Like he'd seen something repulsive. I turned around and saw Elliott Collins separating himself from the buffet crowd and sauntering over to us.

"Ah, here comes Mr. Sunshine and Roses," I said. "That explains your sudden loss of appetite. Mine's starting to wane, as well."

Veronica eyed Elliott suspiciously as he approached.

"Don't mind him," I said. "He's trying to perfect his human zombie imitation in case they decided to do another body-snatcher movie."

I wasn't sure if I spoke loud enough for Elliott to hear me, but the ends of his mouth twisted downward as he stopped at our table.

"What was that last line, Belz?" he asked. "I didn't quite get it."

I shrugged. "Just a bit of witty humor. Nothing you'd appreciate."

"Isn't humor by definition supposed to be funny?" he said. It was more of a statement than a question, but the anger in his tone shored up the last inflection just enough to make it sound like a half-assed interrogative.

"Ask your boy Harvey," I said. "He's been sticking rubber bands in his nose and making bad jokes about gays and fecal matter and thinking he was being funny. Since you represent the little creep, I figured your sense of humor might be a bit skewed."

"Fecal matter?" Johnny guffawed. "What are you trying to do? Appeal to the Mensa fan base?"

"Mentioning Richard and Mensa in the same breath is like comparing a Ford to a Rolls-Royce," Elliott said. His tone dripped causticity like acid from a ruptured battery.

"So that must make your buddy Harv a full-fledged moped, right?" I stared right at him. "You remember those mopeds, don't you? More than a bicycle, but not quite a motorcycle."

Elliott's lips pursed, but he kept them tightly closed. After a three-second slow burn, his head swiveled toward Johnny. "As I told you, we have to talk."

Oh, please, I thought. Johnny, don't invite him to join us. But a second later, he did.

Elliott shook his head. "There's been a . . . development. We'll need some privacy."

Johnny frowned and traced his index finger and thumb over the wrinkle bracketing his mouth. He exhaled slowly, then said, "Okay, give me a minute, will you?"

Elliott nodded, and said he'd meet him downstairs in the bar.

I stared at Johnny. "Don't tell me you, the man who was saying how famished he was a few minutes ago, are now going to forsake nourishment and go off with the walking cadaver?"

"Okay, I won't tell you." His accompanying smile didn't cover the worried look in his eyes. I wanted to ask him what the hell made a jerk like Elliott think he could yell "Jump" and have Johnny ask, "How high?" But I didn't. For one thing, we still had Ms. Veronica Holmes in our presence. Something I hoped to rectify very shortly. Give her a hot meal and put her on a bus back to L.A. And if there were no buses running, I'd have Hector drive her there, so long as he promised to not bring her back. Black-and-white, clear and simple: she'd be gone as soon as she'd eaten her fill of the dessert.

The other thing was more complicated and painted in shades of gray instead of stark black-and-white. This telethon was very important to Johnny, my mentor and friend, and for whatever reason, he felt he owed Elliott some unspoken courtesy. Like Elliott held some sort of key to things. Elliott and the telethon . . . those two things were disparate in my mind, but I was looking at a jigsaw puzzle without all the pieces on the table.

Johnny offered his apologies as he slid out of the booth and winked at me. "You two kids enjoy a nice, friendly get-acquainted meal, on me."

And then he was gone, leaving Veronica Holmes and me staring at each other across the table with precious little to say. At least from my end. There was even less that I wanted to hear.

"Mr. Belzer—," she began.

I cut her off. "Look, kid. Put a lid on it, okay? I hadn't seen Paul Venchus in a long, long time. Since the real old days when we were both reporters back in Bridgeport, Connecticut, and I really don't have the time to listen to any cock-and-bull conspiracy theory about what really happened to the second half of Khrushchev's memoirs."

"Who?"

I sighed. These kids today had no concept of history, modern or otherwise. I pointed to her menu. "Never mind. Pick out what you want to eat before your trip back to L.A."

"Won't you even listen to me?"

"No."

"But I have Paul's notes with me," she said. "They're very comprehensive."

"I'll bet." I buried my nose in the menu. Nothing looked good to me, though.

"Mr. Belzer . . ."

I ignored her. Or tried to, as I set the menu down as a signal to the waitress after deciding on the onion soup. It was liberating not to have to worry about the social amenities. The soup wouldn't be real conducive to stimulating conversation.

Veronica sat across from me in total silence, not moving a muscle, like she was trying to impose some kind of trancelike state upon herself. Either that, or she was trying to act out a half-assed version of a Chuck Norris stare-down. Nevertheless, it was just this side of disconcerting, but I wasn't about to let her know that. I reached over and tapped a finger on her menu. "If you don't decide what you want to eat, I'll order for you, and you probably won't like it."

Veronica shook her head. The eyes were starting to glisten again. "I . . . I . . . I just can't . . . help believing . . ." Her voice trailed off.

"Look, kid, B. J. Thomas already did that song back in the seventies. Elvis, too. Both way before your time," I said.

"Aren't you even the least bit interested in what Paul and I were working on?"

I raised an eyebrow. "Look, kid—"

"I am not a kid. Quit calling me that."

"Okay. And I am not an investigative reporter."

"Can't you just listen? For Paul?"

It was like trying to reason with a shoot of bamboo. Telling it to stop growing. Maybe it would be better to let her talk and then walk her to the bus station. Besides, she had the pathetic look of a frightened baby bird that fell from the nest too early. Underdeveloped wings that wouldn't quite provide a liftoff.

"Okay," I said. "Order something, and I'll listen while we eat." And then you can go back to L.A., I silently added.

Her lips curled into a Mona Lisa smile. "Thank you."

"Don't mention it."

The waitress came and we ordered. Veronica seemed to be collecting her thoughts. Finally, she asked, "How much do you know about the death of Brigid Burgeon?"

Here we go again. "Probably not as much as you're going to tell me. She was found dead in her house in L.A. about twenty-six years ago. It was ruled accidental overdose. Case closed."

The lips-only smile didn't budge.

I waited. For someone who wanted to talk, she wasn't doing much of it. After tiring of trying to wait her out, I exhaled loudly. "All right. There's speculation that her death wasn't totally accidental. There were rumors ranging from suicide to murder, but it doesn't change the fact that the coroner's jury ruled it an accident."

She waited a few beats, then said, "Do you know who she was involved with at the time of her death?"

"None other than Congressman Mark Kaye Jr., proud son of the Golden State, and reoccurring nightmare of anybody with an appreciation of halfway intelligent politicians."

"And Kaye . . . you know how he died?"

"Car crash, about a year or so later, wasn't it? Sort of like James Dean, racing toward destiny in the desert." I took a sip of my water. "You know, they say he ate breakfast at the Farmers Market in L.A. right before he crashed."

If the last comment threw her off stride, it didn't show. She waited a few more seconds, then fixed me with a stare that was six parts quiet determination and one part condescension. "You've heard the theories about both of their deaths, I take it?"

"That Brigid was murdered by Kaye's family, the mob, or was it the CIA? Sure, I've heard 'em all. Which one did you and Paul believe?"

"All of the above."

Now it was my turn to shoot back the seven-part stare. After an appropriate pause, I used my most serious tone to say, "So, I take it you subscribe to the eclectic theory of everything being relative and relative being everything."

The double-talk didn't faze her. "It's why Paul was murdered."

Our eyes locked for a few seconds. "And who killed him?"

"The same people who killed Brigid Burgeon."

"Oh, of course. Why didn't I think of that?"

"Mr. Belzer, please, this is serious." Twin creases appeared between her eyebrows. "You can't possibly think Paul just conveniently died right before he was meeting you."

I took a deep breath. Did I really want to get into this discussion with her? I tried for the softer, gentler approach. "Veronica, that's something the police will look into, if they feel it's justified."

"Is that what you really believe? You of all people? Paul believed in you. Said you wouldn't be hoodwinked by bureaucratic bullshit."

I liked the alliteration, but the message was leaving me flat. My martial arts training has taught me that in conversation, just like in physical confrontation, sometimes it's better to use your adversary's momentum against him. Or her, as the case presents itself. "And why do you think he was murdered?"

"Because he was getting too close."

"Close to what?"

"The truth."

Ah, the old conspiracy theorist's standby, I thought. The truth shall set you free, if it doesn't get you killed first. I opted for silence and just arched my eyebrows, waiting for her to continue, hoping maybe she'd burned herself out.

She hadn't. "Brigid's death was part of a cover-up. Mark Kaye Jr.'s, too. And now Paul's."

"It just took them about twenty-six years between murders?"

She frowned and reached in the magic carpetbag again. After pulling something out, she looked at it, rotated it, and extended her hand across the table. "Please, look at this."

Her slim fingers held an old color photograph. Paul and me, resplendent in garish fashions of the seventies. God, why hadn't someone told us what we'd look like thirty-plus years later? We were both smiling with the optimism of young men when they're on their way to conquer the world.

"Well?" she asked.

"Well, what?"

"Doesn't this do anything for you?"

I shrugged. "You mean other than remind me how bad the clothing styles were back then?"

"Paul kept this on his desk. Told me how proud he was of you. Of being your friend."

"Listen, before he called me the other day, I hadn't spoken to him in about thirty years. It's not like we were bosom buddies or anything."

The frightened bird look came back, along with the tears, just as the waitress was bringing our food. Veronica dropped the photograph on the table and grabbed a cloth napkin. Holding it to her face, she slid out of the booth and bolted for what I assumed was the ladies' room. The waitress gave me a skeptical look. I shrugged and got out of the booth myself, mumbling that I'd be back in a minute.

Dammit. There's nothing worse than cold onion soup.

After pacing in the vicinity of the women's washroom for a good five minutes, I was approached by the maitre d'. "Is everything all right, sir?" If he recognized me, he had the manners not to mention it.

I cocked a thumb toward the door. "I was having lunch with a young lady and she's a little bit upset. You got anybody who could go in and check on her?"

He gave me a knowing wink and left. A few moments later a demure woman in a dark dress with a name tag that listed her as Emily came up and asked, "What's your friend's name, Mr. Belzer?"

"Veronica," I said, not adding that she wasn't really my friend.

Emily went inside and was gone about three minutes. She came out alone and said, "She'll be right out."

I lifted my glasses and massaged the bridge of my nose. The door opened and out she came, eyes as red as an old-fashioned road map staring up at me.

"Look, why don't we go back and eat," I said. "We can discuss your theories."

"You'll listen with an open mind?"

"I will," I said. It sure beat hanging around outside the ladies' room.

●   ●   ●

Two hours later we were in the back of Hector's limo heading west on Interstate 515 in the late afternoon sunshine toward a small trailer park outside Henderson. At least they used to be called trailer parks. Now the preferred designation, in our ever-changing, politically correct society with extreme efforts not to offend anyone with insensitive appellations, was "modular" or "manufactured homes." The only thing I knew was when I was growing up back in Bridgeport they were called trailer parks and they were full of, well, trailers. And hence the term "trailer trash." Now, the really big trailers had subsequently morphed into something called "mobile homes." But back in the day, the old joke was, How can you tell the deluxe mobile home from the not-so-luxurious one? The deluxe one has the chrome hubcaps stacked next to the cement blocks.

I was still trying to figure out how I'd gotten talked into this. I guess it was the old photograph that tipped the cart for me. Seeing Paul smiling alongside a much younger, and more naive, version of myself, something just clicked inside me, like a shutter speed-delayed by almost four decades. I'd agreed to go with her to talk to the woman Paul had interviewed on the phone, Mrs. Henrietta Perkins, after which Veronica agreed to go back to L.A. if the interview didn't provide anything earthshaking. Mrs. Perkins claimed to be the mother of April Mae Turner, who won an all-expenses-paid trip to Hollywood in a local beauty contest in Ohio that set her on the road to semisuperstardom as Brigid Burgeon. After hearing Veronica talk about how Paul had held it together, fighting the booze to work on the story, I did feel a twinge of nostalgia. He'd been a decent reporter at one time. Knew the ins and outs of the business. But that was long ago and far away. Still, despite my initial reticence, my old conspiracy theorist juices were starting to flow a little. As I studied the reddish patterns of the McCullough Mountain range through the limo window, I couldn't stop myself from thinking about an occasional "what if . . ."

We exited the expressway and got onto a highway that stretched past a lot of nothing except sage, mesquite, and tumbleweeds. I tapped on the screen and it lowered electronically.

"What's up, Belz?" Hector asked.

"You sure we're going the right way?"

I saw his grin flash in the rearview mirror. *"No tenga cuidado,* I've got GPS."

"How much farther, then?"

His dark eyes in the mirror flashed toward the GPS screen, then back. "Two and a half miles."

I gave him the thumbs-up. We were cruising past an old, decrepit billboard now, urging us to visit WESTERN WORLD—COWBOY ENTERTAINMENT AT ITS BEST.

"Hey, Hec, what's that place all about?"

He glanced to his left, then said, "Some kind of old amusement park. Closed about ten years ago, at least. Had a bunch of rides and a cowboy town where you could play dress-up. What's that real old movie from the seventies with that bald guy?"

"I hope you aren't talking about my childhood idol Yul Brynner like that," I said.

"Yeah, whatever. Anyway, the place closed and has been tied up in land deals ever since. Word is that somebody bought it for peanuts and is waiting to sell it so they can build a bunch of condos. You may have noticed things are growing pretty fast out here now."

"That I believe," I said. It set me thinking of the times I'd first played Vegas thirty years ago. Before the Strip took off and before the area became a sea of ever-expanding housing developments.

"Pretty soon they'll pave over the whole desert," Veronica said. She didn't try to mask the derision in her voice.

"That's progress," I said. "The population bomb is still ticking after all these years." My cell phone rang and I checked the screen. *Unknown.* Perplexed, I answered it, but got no one in reply. After a couple more "hello"s, I disconnected. With all the people getting a hold of my damn cell phone number lately, I figured I shouldn't have been surprised. Next it would probably be someone trying to sell me a subscription to *The National Review.*

Another few minutes and I felt the car leave the highway as the tires popped over loose gravel. A cloud of dust stirred up as we proceeded on a dilapidated-looking, two-lane blacktop road with no center divider. A sign loomed ahead, advertising J & M MOBILE HOME PARK in big block letters, under which was one of those marquees with the removable plastic letters. It read, No Vacancs at Prsnt. And under that, in smaller letters, was Clubhous Closd. Obviously, spelling wasn't on the list of high values around here. Or maybe they were just short of Is and Es.

The park, if you could call it that, had a gate shack at the entrance with heavy metal guardrails surrounding it, seeming out of place with the dilapidated speed limit sign posted at 15 mph. But you can't be too careful sometimes, I thought, as I saw the heavy, jowled face of the security guard perk up at the sight of the limo and what was left of the broken beam of a moveable gate barrier, patched with several strategically placed winds of duct tape. The guard made some furtive movement and the beam raised to let us pass. Not that it would have made much difference either way. The first trailers were about fifty feet beyond the entrance and circled around a series of ringed streets like the jutting spokes of a bicycle tire against a rim of more unlined blacktop. Of course, it was stretching things to call these slim strips of asphalt "streets." Still, they had signs designating them with names like "Willow Avenue" and "Peachnut Drive."

"What address are we looking for again?" Hector asked. His voice sounded a bit agitated as the wipers and solvent spray worked to clear the windshield. He was probably wondering how many times he'd have to run his limo through the car wash tonight.

"808 Windom Lane," Veronica said.

"Guess we should've asked the security guy at the gate where it was," I said.

Hector shook his head. "Most of these parks have one main drag where all the rest of the streets connect." He snapped his fingers. "See? Here it is."

We turned on Windom and started following the numbers. Why they needed a three-digit designation was lost on me, but at least they were easy to follow. In what must have been a last-ditch attempt at maintaining individuality, none of the trailers looked like its neighbor. Instead they were a mishmash of various colors, ranging from tan and brown to gray and peeling. Many had dandy little aluminum prefab sheds next to their modular units, as well as a sprinkling of old car tires cut in a scallop and flipped up to form makeshift flowerpots. A couple even had wiry strands of almost living plants sprouting in them. One enterprising mobile-home owner had invested in a large concrete slab over which he'd started to erect a minigarage roof. The effort was half finished, leaving not only the sides wide open, but most of the roof section as well. A set of wooden steps, with a railing in a state of semicompletion, led to the door.

808 Windom had even fewer luxuries. Instead of half-completed railings and wooden stairs, this one had that tried-and-true trailer park standby, cement blocks, leading up to its doorway. Three window air conditioners, cut almost neatly into the side of the structure, duct tape sealing the ruptures in the aluminum, jutted out from the rippled wall. Hector pulled as far over to the side as he could and said he'd have to leave it on the street.

"No way I'm getting this baby into that space," he said, cocking his head toward the narrow strip of cement next to the trailer.

"That's okay," I said. "We don't want to get a ticket for blocking the sidewalk."

"But, there isn't any sidewalk," Veronica said.

"Hey, you are a psychic after all, aren't you?"

She frowned as I got out and held the door for her.

"Does Mrs. Perkins know we're coming?" I asked.

Veronica shook her head. "I tried calling, but her phone is out of order."

As is my brain, I thought, for agreeing to come on this trailer park treasure hunt. But for once I kept my mouth shut and just smiled. Get this interview done, and when she sees it's going nowhere, she'll be more amenable to getting back on the bus for L.A.

The trailer was closed up tighter than a shrink-wrapped CD. I rapped my knuckles against the screen door. Inside I heard some rustling, followed by an older lady's voice asking, "Who is it?"

"Mrs. Perkins, it's Veronica Holmes. I talked to you last week on the phone."

A swath of cloth moved aside at the side window, showing a glimpse of a suspicious eye behind it. More noises of movement followed, then the interior door popped open.

An old lady with cottony white hair and the plastic connection of an oxygen hose fastened under her nostrils opened the door. Her eyes were framed in a brocade of wrinkles but looked bright, alert, and wary.

"Are you Mr. Venchus?" she asked me. Her voice sounded as reedy as she looked.

"Actually, I'm not." I smiled as disarmingly as I could. "I'm a friend of his."

Her lips compressed. "Why didn't he come himself?"

I was trying to figure out a way to break it to her gently when Veronica, with all the tact of a New York City bus driver, blurted out, "They killed him yesterday."

The old lady's head reeled back like she'd been struck and I saw her retreat from the door on unsteady legs. I glanced toward Veronica, who had an equally pallid expression on her face.

"Nice move, Nancy Drew," I said as I tore open the screen door and moved up the cement block steps. I placed a steadying hand on Mrs. Perkins's forearm, stabilizing her as I walked her across the small living room to a chair. She brought her hands up to and wiped her eyes. Veronica had followed me inside and kneeled beside her, offering profuse apologies and rubbing the old lady's blue-veined hands.

"Are you all right?" I asked. "Could I get you some water or something?"

She nodded and pointed to a refrigerator within an arm's length. I pulled the door and saw a plastic gallon jug full of clear liquid. There wasn't much else inside. A bunch of opened cat and dog food, two TV dinners, half a loaf of white bread encased in plastic, and an open can of heavy syrup peaches. As I looked for a glass in the tray of the adjacent sink I noticed something else that disturbed me greatly. There were no pet dishes on the floor. This made me wonder if the Purina and Fancy Feast were the old doll's dessert. I took a glass and poured it half full, replaced the jug in the fridge, and handed the water to Mrs. Perkins. She thanked me after taking a small sip.

"How are you feeling?" I asked, sitting in the chair across from her. Veronica was still on the floor by the old lady's knees. "Can we call anyone for you?"

She shook her head. "No one to call. I live alone."

I nodded, wondering how much I had in my billfold and where best to leave it in an unobtrusive sort of way.

"I do have Mr. Henry who lives across the way," she said. "He keeps an eye on me and fixes things."

I smiled. "It's good to have a friend close by when you need him."

She took another sip of the water, staring at me over the rim of the glass. It was one of those old-fashioned glasses like my mother used to have, with a pattern of little red hearts in rows around the outside.

"Young man, you look so familiar," she said.

I smiled again, especially at the "young man" part. I was just about to say I had a common face when Veronica chimed in.

"He's Richard Belzer, the television star."

The old lady's eyes widened. "You know, I was thinking he was looking mighty familiar." She extended her hand. I shook it. "You really are a friend of Mr. Venchus?"

"Yes." I didn't want to remind her that she should have been using the past tense. But I didn't need to.

She sighed. "And now they've killed him, too. Just like my poor April Mae. Goodness, mercy. When will it end?"

"We're going to find out," Veronica said. "Mr. Belzer's going to help us."

If I made a practice of slugging dames, like some uncouth individual, I would have come pretty close in this instance. But my gentlemanly nature won out. I did, however, shoot her a rueful stare while taking control again.

"Mrs. Perkins, we owe it to you to be honest. Completely honest. I'm not at all sure that we'll be able to do anything to set things right for you. And I'm not even sure that Paul Venchus's death wasn't anything but a tragic accident."

"But—," Veronica started to say.

I raised my palm like a stop sign. "The matter is being investigated by some very competent people in the LAPD, and I'm sure if there's anything suspicious they'll give it a thorough going-over."

Veronica looked ready to toss in her two cents but I kept the stop sign up.

"So," I continued, "what I'd like now is to hear what you were going to tell Paul about Brigid Burgeon."

The old lady's eyes acquired a sudden sadness and her gaze fell to the floor. Afraid that Veronica would insinuate herself into the conversation again, I pressed onward, trying to open the information floodgates.

"She was your daughter, April Mae Turner, before she changed her name?"

"She never really wanted to formally change her name, you know," Mrs. Perkins said. "They made her do it."

"That happens a lot in Hollywood," I said. Just keep her talking, Belz, my little inside voice told me. "Did she keep in contact with you after she became successful?"

"She moved me out here from Ohio. She was always a good girl. Never forgot her mother. Sent me flowers every Mother's Day." The old lady looked around. "I had a real nice house at one time. April Mae bought it for me, free and clear. I didn't always live here. Had to sell it once I got sick. We'd lived in a trailer park before, back when she was a little one, so I thought it would be nice. A lot hotter here than back in Massillon."

Almost full circle, I thought. But waxing about irony wasn't going to get this interview over with and me out of here. "I know this is difficult, but you must have had some information that you wanted to talk to Paul about, right?"

"I do." Her face took on a look of new determination. "Sweetie, will you get me that brown folder, please?"

We followed her crooked finger pointing toward one of those cheap paper accordion files with a long rubber band securing it. For a brief moment I thought about taking it and reenacting Harvey Smithe's "dangling booger" routine the next time I saw him, sneaking up and using him as an unknowing participant. Of course, I had a different orifice in mind. But I pushed the thought out of my head, not wanting to smile on what was evolving into a solemn occasion. And after all, good old Harv wasn't such a bad guy. He was just a crude idiot who, for some strange reason, was taking up way too much of my time. And my thoughts.

Mrs. Perkins undid the rubber band and sorted through the contents.

Most of them looked like notebook paper, wilted and starting to yellow. She pulled out a faded sheet of plain, letter-size paper with the dark swirls of a handwritten note on it. She handed it to me.

It was an old, handwritten letter. A love letter. The penmanship looked rushed, the punctuation sporadic. Like whoever had written it was in a hurry. I read it.

Dearest Brigid,

I know things are difficult for us right now but please know that I love you and am overjoyed about the new development. I have certain things I must do on my end to make things right. My father has worked hard all his life to give Larry and me the best opportunities. He's been difficult to deal with, but I am making progress.

Bear with me a little longer my love, and we'll be together with the baby.

All my love,

Mark

Then-senator Mark Kaye Jr., darling of the Nevada social set and upcoming potential VP candidate, to his paramour, Brigid Burgeon? I turned it over and looked at the other side. Blank.

"This the original?" I asked as I handed it back to Mrs. Perkins.

"Mr. Venchus made two copies." The old lady's lips puckered and her eyes shot toward Veronica. "He said he was going to show one to those awful Kayes to see their reaction."

"I only have one copy here," Veronica said, pulling a plastic slip-sleeve out of her bag, with a faded copy of the letter I'd just read inside. "I didn't show them to you before because I knew you'd probably want to see the original."

"And you'd be right." While I knew it was entirely possible to get fingerprints from paper, after more than a quarter century of handling, the results might be dubious rather than conclusive. Plus, identifying prints was based on whose were on file. Brigid's probably weren't, unless she'd been in the military or had a police record somewhere.

"I was so relieved when Mr. Venchus took it to make the copy," Mrs. Perkins said. "I thought he'd lose it for sure. You have the ultrasound copy, too, right?"

Veronica smiled and pulled out a plastic-encased item. This one was the size of a snapshot, with a bunch of black and white lines and shading.

Mrs. Perkins got a blissful look on her face. "That would have been my grandbaby. She would have been about your age now, honey."

I didn't want to break it to her that you couldn't tell the sex of the fetus at that stage from an ultrasound. The old lady had enough problems without me bursting whatever bubbles she'd managed to cling to.

She handed the item back to Veronica, who started to slip it back into her bag. "You're still all right with us keeping it, right?"

Mrs. Perkins gave an emphatic nod. "As long as I know you're going to be doing something with it, like that lady reporter promised all them years ago. That's why I gave her everything. She seemed so nice. So forthright. She would have done something, if she'd lived."

"Lady reporter?" I asked.

"Constance Penroy," the old lady said. "She contacted me about a year after April Mae died. Came to see me when I was still living in California. Told me she was investigating my little girl's death." She paused to sniffle and wipe her cheeks. "Sorry. Even after all these years I still get so sad. She was so special, my little girl. And like I said, she never forgot her mother."

Veronica reached over and gave her hand a commiserating squeeze.

"I showed her the letter. April Mae brought it to me when she told me she was pregnant. And the ultrasound. Gave it to me to hold, like it was going to make everything all right." She shook her head, her mouth twisting into an ugly scowl. "I knew that damn Mark Kaye Jr. never had any intentions of marrying her. His father wouldn't have let him. They're old money and they don't look at people the same way we do."

"What else did April Mae tell you?" I asked.

"Just that she was in love with him. He was going to get a divorce and marry her. All the foolish dreams of a young girl in love with the wrong man." The tears started to fall again. Veronica's eyes were misting over as well. She must have been something every time Turner Classic Movies reran *Love Story* or *Gone with the Wind*. "She called me the week before she died. Told me that—" Her voice cracked. "Told me that Old Man Kaye Sr. had contacted her, offering her money for an . . . an abortion. And his family always making such a big show of being good Catholics. They were trash. Just trash."

Rich trash, I added mentally. Striving to steer out of the maudlin fog bank, I asked, "You said Constance Penroy contacted you? How did she come to do that?"

Mrs. Perkins shook her head. "Out of the blue, it was. Of course, after they printed some of those terrible lies about April Mae, saying that she might have intentionally killed herself, I threatened to sue them. I'd gone to some of the papers telling them that my little girl would have never done that, especially being pregnant. She was raised Catholic. But Miss Penroy, she said she was going to write a series of articles that was going to blow the lid off all of them. Expose Mark Kaye Jr.'s father for what he was. She knew that they'd killed my little girl."

I hesitated for a moment, then said, "I wasn't aware that your daughter was expecting. This is the first time I heard of it."

"Those all-powerful Kayes hushed somebody up at the coroner's office." She held up her hand, rubbing her thumb and index finger together. "Bought them off to say she wasn't pregnant and rule it an accidental overdose. I mean, April Mae did have trouble getting to sleep, working all the odd hours she did in the movies, but she would have never taken too many pills. It wouldn't have been good for the baby."

I nodded, thinking, Why ruin an old lady's memories of someone long gone? But this was going nowhere fast.

"Constance Penroy," I said. "She passed away as well, didn't she?"

"A year and a half after Brigid," Veronica chimed in. "I mean, April Mae."

A smile crept over Mrs. Perkins's lips and she glanced toward us. "That's okay, honey. Most people think of her as Brigid, but to me, she'll always be my little April Mae."

"Wasn't Constance Penroy known mostly as a gossip columnist?" I asked. "I mean, she didn't seem the type to be working on a story with a lot of substance."

"She was actually a very good reporter," Veronica said. Her voice had taken on a tone of dominant umbrage. "She really was."

I nodded. Being between two zealous women, even if they were conspiracy buffs, had its drawbacks. I said my next line with slow deliberation, hoping to avoid another outburst of indignation. "Do we have any more proof of April's pregnancy? Any way we can prove that's her ultrasound?"

The old lady shook her head. "Her doctor's long gone now. The Kayes bought him off, too. Made a statement to the press about her not being pregnant, just like that crooked medical examiner."

"Constance was working on that angle," Veronica said. "She was getting to the bottom of it. That doctor was retired soon after that. Then he disappeared. She was tracking down the whole story."

"But," I said, "she's not around anymore, either."

"That's because she was murdered, too," Veronica snapped back.

I suddenly felt caught between two sets of staring eyes, like feathered raptors waiting for the field mouse to make his move toward the hole in the tree trunk.

After another half hour of going over their theories about Brigid's, née April Mae's, demise, we extricated ourselves from the claustrophobic trailer and sped off in the limo, heading back toward I-515. Now it was my turn to give Veronica the raptor's stare.

"Why did you tell that old lady that I'd agreed to help solve the mystery of her daughter's death?" I kept my voice low and even, making it sound like I was doing an interrogation of a suspect.

"Because," she said.

I lifted an eyebrow and waited.

"I knew that once you heard the facts of the case, you'd agree." Her voice cracked slightly as she muttered the last words.

"The only thing I agreed to was to come out here with you and listen to what the old girl had to say. Now that I've done that, I've fulfilled my part of the bargain. Now you fulfill yours and get on that bus back to L.A. tonight."

She shook her head defiantly. "I don't even have a return-trip ticket."

Marvelous, I thought. I reached back and tapped a knuckle on the screen. It lowered and Hector grinned. "What's up now, Belz?"

"Can I hire you to drive this young lady back to L.A. as soon as we get back to Vegas?"

"Aww, sorry, but I got another gig booked for tonight."

I frowned and pointed my index finger toward the ceiling. The screen went back up.

"See?" she said, pressing a finger to her temple. "As I mentioned, I do have psychic abilities."

"Okay, Wonder Woman, have you at least got a hotel room? Please don't tell me you came all the way to Las Vegas and didn't book a room in advance."

"Well, I sort of figured I could sleep on the floor in your room. I wouldn't be any bother at all."

"Yeah, right. My wife would love that idea."

I glanced out the window and watched a black Hummer with opaque windows zoom past us. I wondered if he was going west, toward L.A. I took out my cell phone and dialed Barry's number. He answered with a crisp, efficient "Hello."

"Richard, how fortuitous. I was just going to call you."

"Yeah, I'm in the presence of a psychic and was getting the vibes."

He laughed. "Johnny has something special planned tonight for you and him. Shall we say seven o'clock in the lobby?"

I glanced at my watch. It was closing in on 5:40. "Shouldn't be a problem, but I need a small favor."

"Name it, of course."

"Can you dip into your hotel contacts and get a room for Veronica

Holmes for tonight? Just for tonight." I watched her lips compress, but she said nothing. Barry told me he was on it and we disconnected. As I put my cell phone back in my pocket, I pointed toward her. "Let this be a lesson to your psychic abilities. You can think about them all the way back to L.A. tomorrow."

CHAPTER 6

Johnny's surprise turned out to be two tickets to a dinner show featuring his old partner, Sal Fabell, at the Mirage, which was practically right across the street. So we walked. Big mistake. First, we had to go down to the end of the block to use the elevated crosswalk bridge. Don't try crossing Las Vegas Boulevard that time of night any other way. Then, after doubling back, we began our long trek from the sidewalk to the dining room. Nothing like a mile-long hike from the front entrance and through the endless casino to work up an appetite. We stopped in the hallway to look at the white tigers in their glass prison. One of them slept on the pristine marble shelf as the water cascaded next to him from the fake waterfall. The big cat was oblivious to the unending series of flashbulbs and camcorders.

"Sometimes that's how I feel," Johnny said. His voice sounded wistful.

"Reminds me of the pictures of Elvis in his Zen garden."

"Wow, the King," Johnny said. "He's been gone as long as Brigid Burgeon, hasn't he?"

"Longer," I said. "And why'd you bring her up?"

He chuckled. "Just wondered how your quest for justice with your girlfriend went today."

"Oh, puh-leeze. She is *not* my girlfriend."

He laughed. "I meant to say your buddy's girlfriend. What was his name? The guy that just died?"

"Paul Venchus. And to hear her tell it, he was killed by the same evildoers who bumped off Brigid twenty-six years ago. Plus, you remember Constance Penroy?"

Johnny whistled. "Man, you are talking ancient history here. She always took delight in blasting my movies in her column. Can't say I was too upset when she passed, although she did give me good reviews when I was in the movies with Sal. I think she had a thing for him."

"Her and the rest of the female population in the seventies," I said. "Well, Veronica is certain that good old Constance was bumped off as well."

Johnny grinned. "All part of the same big conspiracy, huh?"

"Those guys were busy, weren't they?"

We started walking again. "You know," Johnny said, "Brigid's last movie . . . the one she never finished. It was with Sal."

"I remember. *Two to Tango,* wasn't it?"

Johnny nodded. "Good recall. Anyway, as far as tonight, we're gonna be sitting way in back. He doesn't know we're gonna be there."

"We going to surprise him?"

Johnny shook his head. "Just the opposite. We got to be ghosts on this one tonight. I just wanted to see him perform since I was out here."

"Why not drop in to his dressing room? We're early enough."

He shook his head again, more vigorously this time. "Belz, no. As a favor to me, he can't know we're here. Okay?"

"Whatever you want," I said. And I meant it.

He seemed to sense this and half of his mouth tugged upward into that crooked smile of his. "I got another favor to ask, too."

"Name it."

He inhaled, blew it out, gave a quick look around, and licked his lips. "I got to ask you to lay off Harvey Smithe."

"What? Lay off?"

"Yeah. I guess you kind of hurt the guy's feelings earlier." His face had taken on a serious look.

I felt my own face twist into an angry frown. "The guy doesn't have the couth to be offended."

"Just the same, I have to put him on the show, as a favor to Elliott, and he asked me to ask you to lay off insulting the kid when you see him."

"Me insult *him*?" Johnny made a quieting gesture with his hands, trying to shush me. "He's got all the sensitivity and tact of Idi Amin's grandson. And who the fuck is Elliott to go running to you?"

"Belz, please. For me?" He looked down. "Elliott got us the tickets tonight."

I sighed. "You know this is like asking a dog not to scratch at a pesky flea."

He grinned.

I shot him another one. "It's like asking an elephant not to swing his tail at an obnoxious horsefly."

He bounced one back. "It's like asking a jeweler to use tweezers to pick up a mouse turd."

I looked at him. "That one doesn't even make sense."

"I know." The crooked half smile was back. "But if I didn't put a stop to this banter, we'd never get there in time to see Sal's opening number."

Sal Fabell was terrific. Even though he was long past his heyday, he could still croon with the best of them. As specified, our table was in the back. We had a clear view of the stage area, where the band sat against a white background curtain, and Sal hammed it up with the microphone. The subdued lighting on the floor made distinguishing anybody's face from up there next to impossible. Still, I wondered what his reaction would be if he caught sight of Johnny sitting there. They'd been friends once, the tall, handsome singer and the crazy comedian. Together they'd parlayed a frenetic and offbeat nightclub routine into one of the best acts in showbiz. A TV show and a string of movies had followed until their parting of the ways.

Johnny leaned across the table and whispered, "Man, would you listen to him? His voice hasn't lost a note. And he looks great, too. Doesn't he?"

He did. He was doing a jazzed-up version of "L.A. Is My Lady," and sounded exactly like he had thirty years ago when he'd first recorded it. Then he ended abruptly, sacrificing the finish by ad-libbing, "Hey, I forgot. I'm in Las Vegas, not L.A. What was I thinking?" He smiled that fabulous Sal Fabell smile, adding, "That one was for all you guys out there who've ever called your lover by the wrong name at the worst possible moment." Laughter from the audience . . . another smile . . . "So why do you think they invented the word 'baby,' baby?"

Johnny snorted a laugh. "That was one of mine from the old days," he whispered. "I gave it to him to use and he loved it. If I close my eyes, I can almost think I'm back there, in the day."

Sal had a broad-shouldered look and big, rugged build that had stood the test of time well. His dark hair was streaked with gray now, but it suited him. The elder statesman of the essence of coolness. His black tux still made him look like a model for working out and clean living, which I'm sure he did plenty of, despite his carefully constructed image as a wild party man. But then again, we were in Vegas, where nothing is as it seems, and illusion regularly trumps reality until you've got all your chips on the losing number.

Sal had opened with some of his old standards. Soft-rocking ballads during which he purposely flubbed or jazzed up the lyrics, poking fun at himself without being irritating, conversing with the people sitting up front, smiling, and obviously enjoying himself. He had, as the French say, savoir faire. When he finished his version of the old Sinatra tune "One for My Baby (and One More for the Road)," Johnny nudged me and jerked his head toward the exit.

"Come on, let's get outta here."

We got up as unobtrusively as we could, making our way to the exit as Sal did an a cappella version of "Brahms' Lullaby." His trademark swan song. I could hear the fading lyrics as we stepped out into the long hallway that took us toward the casino lights and noise and cigarette smoke. Johnny kept a brisk pace through the place, past the bar and the omnipresent pinging machines, to the hallway with the slumbering tigers, and finally to the doors leading outside. The night air felt cool and fresh as the glass doors slid open, allowing us to exit. He kept moving and we got on the metal grate of the moving sidewalk escalator that propelled us toward the street as scores of other people passed us, going in the opposite direction. The night was still young and we headed south with the flow past the massive front of Caesars, the foregrounds looking like a sumptuous estate hosting a party.

Johnny seemed lost in thought, occasionally glancing behind him like he was worried he'd lost me in the crowd. We crossed the Flamingo and finally stopped to watch the singing fountains in front of the Bellagio. Ironically, they were dancing to a remix version of one of Sal's old songs, "Baby-O."

"See?" Johnny smirked. "I can't get away from him, no matter what."

Sensing that he wanted to talk, and for me to listen, I just smiled and nodded.

He leaned forward and placed his elbows on the cement railing. I did the same. "I remember the first time I ever saw him. I was as green as they come. Just got this gig at a club in Jersey, and was all excited. I was walking in, shooting the shit with the doorman, when all of a sudden this guy walks by in a suit and tie wearing this neat Borsalino hat." He shook his head. "He was the coolest guy I'd ever seen. I figured him for some big shot, the way he carried himself, and asked the doorman who he was. The guy turned to me and said, 'He's nobody, just like you. You two are playing in the same shit card here tonight.' " Johnny laughed. "I was so overanxious, I pissed off these two big goombahs with two nice-looking chicks in the audience during my number. Asking the girls if they worked for the city zoo, mild little stuff like that, figuring everybody could take a joke, you know? They couldn't. I go out afterward to catch the bus home and they're waiting for me. Grab me and start working me over. All of a sudden somebody growls for them to stop, and when they don't, this dude lays both of them out, one, two, three, just like that." He clapped his hands together. "It was Sal. He used to be a boxer, you know, before he decided to try and make it as a singer. He picks me up, dusts me off, and we catch the bus together. He didn't have a car, either. We were both broker than the guy in the shithouse without a dime."

"And that was the beginning of a beautiful friendship, right?" I said.

He nodded. The fountains were in their final flurry now, lights flashing, skyrockets arcing.

"How long's it been since you two talked?" I asked.

Johnny's lower lip jutted out. "Shit, I don't know. Since we broke up the partnership. Twenty-five years, maybe."

"Long time."

He nodded fractionally. "Yeah, sure is."

The fountain show ended and Johnny asked if I wanted to get a drink back at the hotel. I glanced at my watch. It was twenty after 10:00 p.m. and I hadn't called Harlee as I'd promised. I reached in my pocket and took out my cell phone, turning it on again. As it lit up, it made that little lilting jingle that told me I had a message. Maybe she'd tried to call me already. I selected voicemail and listened to the computer litany telling me I had three messages, the first one sent at 10:05 p.m.

"Mr. Belzer, where are you?" The irritating, razor-squeaking-over-glass quality was back in her voice. Why hadn't I bought Hector off and persuaded him to drive her back to L.A. tonight? "Have you seen the news?" She sounded on the edge of panic. "You've got to call me. Please. Call me right away. This is terrible. Mrs. Perkins. I think she's been murdered, too."

The other two messages were more of the same: both from Veronica telling me to get in front of a television ASAP and watch the news. She sounded practically hysterical. I dialed the hotel and asked for her room as we crossed the street. After being connected, it rang until it went to voicemail.

Shit, I thought. She's probably out looking for me. Not that I wanted her to be successful in that endeavor, but I couldn't help feeling sort of an avuncular responsibility toward her. Something had cultivated it in me. That frightened bird look in her eyes, maybe.

I persuaded Johnny to step inside Bill's Gamblin' Hall, which used to be the Barbary Coast, where they had a bar with a TV close to the entrance. I bought him a seven and seven and a slug of tequila for myself as I asked the bartender to turn up the volume. Not that it did any good. Trying to listen to the news in a bar, much less a Vegas bar, was like trying to carry on a conversation at a NASCAR track. We watched a couple of newscasters in pantomime through the weather report, the sports review, and finally we saw them get solemn looks on their faces as the screen shifted to an aerial view of a trailer park with one of the rectangular boxes totally engulfed in bright flames as a fire truck showered it with an ineffective spray of water. The black border along the bottom of the screen scrolled, *Breaking news . . . firefighters battle blaze at manufactured home park near Henderson . . . one believed dead.*

Johnny glanced up at the screen and clucked sympathetically. "Man, when those things go up, they really go up, don't they?"

"They sure as hell do," I said.

Johnny made a funny expression and reached inside his jacket pocket, coming up with his cell phone. After glancing at the screen he flipped it open, and said, "Yeah, Barry." A furrow appeared between his eyebrows and he added, "Hold on a minute, he's right here." He handed me his phone. "It's Barry."

"What's up?" I asked.

Barry's voice sounded mildly nervous. "Richard, I'm so glad I found you. That young lady, Veronica Holmes, that you had me find a room for . . .'"

Oh no, I thought. This can't be good. "Yeah?"

"She's down at the front desk, demanding that they do something to contact you immediately. Says it's an emergency." He paused. "The clerk knew you were associated with the telethon and contacted my room."

Aww, hell, I thought. What's next? "Can you tell them to tell her to sit tight there in the lobby and that I'll be there inside of five?"

"Be glad to." Barry laughed. "But probably not as glad as the hotel people will be." He paused again. "Is she . . . someone special?"

Yeah, a special pain in the ass, I thought.

"She's a friend of a friend," I said and disconnected, figuring the faster I got off the phone, the faster he could call down to the front desk and have them tell Veronica to put a lid on it. I turned to Johnny and pointed to his drink. The glass was still half full. "How about if I buy you a fresh one at the Monticello?"

He shrugged. "You haven't even touched yours."

"That's because I'll probably be needing a double shortly. Come on."

It took us closer to ten to make the half-block walk. The Strip was wall-to-wall pedestrians, and everybody seemed intent on strolling along at half speed. Not to mention the tons of Hispanics handing out cards and fliers with pictures of comely lasses on them, advertising their hourly rates. Even that flipping of the cards they did each time someone passed seemed in slow motion tonight. Johnny was beside me, but breathing a little hard.

"Man, would ya slow down a little, for Christ's sake," he said. "I ain't as young as I used to be."

"Neither am I."

He grinned. "Yeah, but you're in better shape than I am. All that ass-kicking."

"And jumping to conclusions," I said.

When I saw the lights for the entrance of the Monticello looming, I bypassed the side walkway and began walking up the driveway. Johnny followed me and a taxi behind us tooted twice as he shot by, coming so close that if the car had had another coat of paint he might have hit us. I considered giving him the finger, but figured it would be bad for my image. I reconsidered a few seconds later as we walked past and flashed him the bird anyway. What the hell.

The big glass doors automatically retracted sideways and the wave of noise and cigarette smoke washed over me. I looked toward the desk, trying to get a fix on Veronica's whereabouts, but Lady Luck had totally deserted me. There were more people crammed in there than a smuggler's truck crossing the Rio Grande. Then the real bad luck hit. I heard an all-too-familiar whiny voice behind me. But it called Johnny's name. His last name. I paused to see a very intoxicated Harvey Smithe stagger in front of Johnny, pointing an accusatory index finger in his face. Smithe's shirttails hung half outside his belt, and his fly was unzipped.

"I gotta talk to you," Smithe said. "Now."

Johnny smirked. "Looks like you're having enough trouble just standing, kid."

Smithe snorted. Or was it a stifled belch?

"I said *now*." The way he growled the last word set the hairs on the back of my neck on edge. I stopped looking for wayward Veronica and addressed what I perceived to be an imminent threat.

"Look, kid," Johnny said, "we're a little bit busy right now. Why don't you go someplace and sober up?"

"No!" Smithe reached out and, despite his drunken clumsiness, grabbed the lapels of Johnny's jacket. "You and me are gonna talk. Now."

I'd already stepped over next to Johnny, positioning myself to be inside the arc of any looping punches, if he felt so inclined. But then again, I wasn't about to give him that opportunity.

"Harv, you're repeating yourself," I said. "Let him go."

His head turned and his glassy eyes fixed on me. This guy was on more than booze.

"Fuck you, Blezer," he said.

"It's Belzer."

He snorted. "Get the fuck away from me, or I'll kick your fucking ass."

A sloppy drunk was one thing, but a mean drunk was something entirely different. I sidestepped slightly so I could reach over and place my hands on top of Smithe's left fist. Pushing down to break his hold on Johnny's right lapel, I pivoted as the grip broke and, with both my thumbs on the back of Smithe's palm, I inverted his hand and bent his wrist back toward him.

"Hey, leggo of me." His slurred words had a web of discomfort running through them.

I exerted more pressure and bent forward, watching Smithe's right hand fall away from the front of Johnny's jacket. Two more seconds and good old Harv was wincing quite respectably.

"Belzer, let me go. You're breaking my arm." The web had changed from discomfort to pain.

"Actually, it's your wrist," I said, putting on a tad more pressure. "And believe me, if I wanted to break something, it'd be your jaw."

Johnny's hand was on my shoulder, his face pushing close to mine. "Belz, no. Please let him go. He didn't mean nothing."

"Didn't mean nothing? He could be charged with assault and battery."

Smithe was whimpering now, little grunts that were like a Mozart concerto to my ears.

"Belz, just let him go, okay? Please." Johnny's face looked more worried than when the idiot had grabbed him. "Do it for me."

"Not till I teach this asshole some manners." I exerted enough pressure to force Smithe to one knee. "Ah, you must be a good practicing Catholic. You genuflect very well."

Smithe made two more grunts. More emphatic ones this time.

"Please." Johnny's hand was pulling at my arm. I thought about the pros and cons of releasing the wristlock. Smithe was drunk, and a mean drunk, too. That probably meant I could count on his set of beer muscles to take over when I did release him and I'd most likely end up decking him. Not good publicity for me, or Johnny, or the telethon, but I wasn't about to be accosted by this punk. I leaned closer to him. "Harv, listen up. I'm going to release you in a few seconds here, and I expect you know that if you don't behave yourself, I'll have to finish this fight."

His answer was two more grunting sounds. I couldn't tell if he was agreeing or getting ready to puke.

I stepped back and let him go. He immediately fell forward, but being on one knee already, he was able to brace his hands on the red carpet to prevent his face from colliding with it. His face might have looked better if it had. When he looked up, he had pure rage in his eyes.

"I'm gonna fucking kill you, Belzer." He started to reach inside his pants pocket and I suddenly started to see my life flash before my eyes, under the imaginary headline: "Richard Belzer Shot at Las Vegas Casino by Enraged Asshole." But I couldn't let Idiot Boy know I was shaken.

"Whatever it is you're reaching for better have 'suppository' stamped on it," I said, positioning myself to deliver a kick to his head, "because I'll shove it up your ass."

I was getting ready to launch a front kick that would send his ugly puss into orbit when I saw a hand shoot out of nowhere, fast as a black mamba, and snare Smithe's wrist.

Grady Armitage. He pulled Smithe's hand out of the pocket and shook it. A black-handled knife with a protruding metal button on the side of the handle fell to the floor.

A switchblade. Now, who'da thunk it. Good old Harvey sinking to street punkism by carrying a shiv.

Grady twisted Smithe's arm behind his back. Two uniformed security guards were there as well, one grabbing the knife and the other Smithe's arm.

Grady smiled. "Metro PD's got a place for you to stay tonight."

Johnny stepped over and placed a hand on Grady's shoulder. "Wait, Grady, no. He's actually a friend of ours. Just had a little too much to drink, is all."

"Didn't look so friendly," Grady said.

"But we don't want no trouble. Right, Belz?" Johnny's voice was plaintive-sounding.

I exhaled and wondered what this little scene had really meant. Why was he protecting a schmuck like Harvey Smithe? Especially after Smithe had threatened him. Obviously Johnny and I were also overdue for a little talk.

"Belz?" he asked again.

"It's your call," I said.

The presence of the uniforms had done wonders to give Smithe that sobering shot of adrenaline. "Hey, look, no cops, okay? I'm sorry, Johnny. Honest. You too, Belz. I'll leave outta here. Just let me call my uncle."

"Who's your uncle?" one of the security guards asked.

"I know who he is," Grady said, an expression of disgust crossing his face as he released Smithe's arm. "Take him to the office. I'll be there in a minute."

The security guard holding Smithe's other arm nodded and said, "This way, pal."

The second guard held up the switchblade. "What about this?"

Grady reached out and plucked it away. He still had that incredible hand speed.

"Go on, Jeff," Grady said. "Stay with Tony. I'll be there in a minute."

The second guard smiled and the ungainly trio went toward an unassuming office door. Grady pocketed the knife and turned to me. "You both all right?"

"Sure are," I said, grinning. "Thanks to your fast moves."

"You looked like you had some pretty nice moves yourself," he said.

"Pretty cool under pressure. Lots of people get shook up, somebody pulled a knife on them."

"Just like Bond," I said. "Shaken, not stirred."

Johnny placed one hand on my shoulder and the other on my upper arm. "This guy's my hero, that's for sure. Grady, thanks."

Grady slipped the switchblade into his pocket. "I'll save this for show and tell, in case Uncle Royce has any harsh words for us."

"Uncle Royce?" I asked.

"Royce Ocean," Johnny said. "He's the hotel manager."

I frowned. Things were becoming a little bit clearer, but I still wanted some better answers. "I hope he has the drunk tank ready."

"By the way, Mr. Belzer," Grady said. "I have a young lady in my office who was looking for you."

"Not the same office you're taking Asshole to, is it?"

He grinned and shook his head, his teeth flashing whiteness that contrasted with his dark skin. "She's in my *other* office. The one I reserve for friends of friends. A young man's with her named Barry."

"You'd better go see her," Johnny said. He turned to Grady. "I'll go help put little Harv to beddie-bye. And smooth things over when Uncle Royce gets here."

"He'll probably just send a couple of flunkies," Grady said. "This ain't been the first time this week he's had to do that."

Johnny nodded, looking embarrassed.

I touched his arm. "Why are we putting up with that jerkoff anyway?"

He pursed his lips and looked down. "Long story. Look, Belz, go see your little girlfriend and we can tag up tomorrow. Right now I got to do some babysitting of my own." He began walking toward the room where they'd taken Smithe.

I extended my hand toward Grady. "Thanks again. Can I buy you a drink later?"

We shook.

"Maybe next time," he said. "I get off in an hour or so and got a date of my own. With a pillow."

• • •

Veronica wasn't quite as hysterical as she'd sounded on the voice messages. But she was close. At least she wasn't wearing the same rag on her head this time. She'd pinned up her hair in some sort of French braid. It was pretty long and looked like it could use a good shampoo.

"Where have you been?" she said, jumping out of her chair. "Do you know what happened?"

"No, but I'm sure you're going to tell me." I motioned for her to sit down again, and turned to Barry.

"Sorry for any inconvenience this has caused," I said.

He smiled. "All in a day's work. Or in this case, night's."

Barry left and I pulled a chair up and sat across from her. The room was small and had a series of television monitors reflecting the foyer and front desk area. Grady had told the guy monitoring everything to step out to give Veronica and me some privacy. The guy's grin was from ear to ear as he got up from his desk and gave me a quick wink.

Great, I thought. They probably got my little martial arts encounter on tape. YouTube, here I come. Or maybe in this case, *America's Funniest Home Videos*.

"Mrs. Perkins," she said. "She's been murdered. Have you seen the news?"

I nodded.

"See?" she said. "I knew something like this was going to happen. I had a vision."

I held up my hands, palms facing toward her. "Can the 'I'm-a-psychic' crap."

She looked like I'd slapped her. I tried to soften it. "As the saying goes," I said, "let us not throw the rope in after the bucket."

"What are you talking about?"

I tried to appear calm. Deadpan, even. "It's from *Don Quixote*. You know, Cervantes?"

"Who's he?"

"Someone you should read," I said. "Now, look, I did see the news about the fire at the trailer park—"

"Then you *do* know."

"What I know is that there was a fire at the trailer park where we were this afternoon. We don't know that it was her trailer."

"Whose else could it have been?" Her eyes widened. "Don't you see? They must have followed us out there. We're responsible for her death."

"We don't know that for sure. We don't even know if she's the one—"

"Oh, yes I do." She brought her hands up to her face and began sobbing. "It's all my fault. It's all my fault."

I was afraid this was going to bring on another psychic vision quest. "Will you stop that?"

When she looked up her eyes looked redder than good old Harv's had, and wet tracks ran down both cheeks. I reached inside my pants pocket and took out my handkerchief. "Here."

She took it and immediately blew her nose.

"All right," I said, "let's assume that it was Mrs. Perkins's trailer that caught fire . . ."

"That poor old lady. We let her down." Another blow into the handkerchief. That one was going in the hotel laundry service bag as soon as I got back to my room.

"We didn't let anybody down. We don't know that this was anything but a real tragic accident."

"An accident? Right after we visited her?"

I shrugged. "Coincidence, maybe."

"Coincidence? What about Paul?"

"The police are investigating Paul's death. I'm sure they'll investigate Mrs. Perkins's, too."

"And we both know what they'll find." The sarcasm precipitated another blow.

"That's their job. Not ours."

"Just like Brigid."

I nodded.

More blowing. "And Constance Penroy. What about her? What about the story she was working on?"

"Constance Penroy was a gossip columnist who probably wouldn't have known a real news story if it jumped up and bit her on the"—I paused—"nose."

"That's not true. That's not true."

I stared at her for a couple of beats, then said, "Listen, kid, I remember good old Constance. I remember her columns. Fluff stuff. The kind of crap you read in the *National Enquirer* and the *Star* today. Grocery store tabloids."

"She was not."

I laughed. "And this from someone who was probably, what? Not even a gleam in your father's eye when she died?"

"I was fifteen months old."

"Bravo. You've done your homework on the dates. But you need to read up on the facts. She was, at best, a hack."

The blue eyes blinked defiantly at me for several seconds. "Oh yeah? Well, she was also my grandmother."

CHAPTER 7

Veronica's stunning genealogical admission caught me like a novice boxer's looping, overhand right. She told me that she was a small baby when Constance was found dead in her home. Veronica's mother was convinced that the death was no accident, and immediately persuaded her husband to move as far away from California as possible, as soon as possible. The family relocated to Waterville, Maine, and Constance's possessions were sold. Veronica grew up never hearing much about her grandmother's demise, until her late teens, when her mother began reminiscing about things and showed her the old diary and notes that she'd saved all these years. When Veronica returned from college with a library science degree and an insatiable curiosity, she began reading through the notes and claimed to hear "the voice" of her late grandmother talking to her. I didn't ask how she knew it was her grandmother's voice if the old doll had died when Veronica was just a baby, but I decided against it.

"That was when I became obsessed with finding the truth," she said. "And seeing that justice was done."

Great, I thought. A crusader complex to go along with her fortune-telling.

She related how she'd made the trek out to California, staying with some relatives and finding odd jobs in the secretarial field. Then one day she met Paul and something clicked between them. As the conversation progressed, I found myself agreeing to contact Las Vegas Metro PD the next morning to see if, in fact, it was Mrs. Perkins who was killed, and if there were any suspicious factors in the incident. But I had gotten a concession in the negotiation.

"All right, then," I'd said. "If I agree to do this, at least tell me how the hell Paul got my cell phone number."

She seemed to sense her imminent triumph. "Okay, that's an easy one." Bright smile. "I gave it to him."

I frowned. "And how did you get it?"

She compressed her lips and looked at me, her expression thoughtful. I knew I was on the cusp of finding out when she said, "I'll tell you what. First you carry out your part of the bargain and call the police about the fire. Then I'll tell you. I promise."

I scratched my ear. Actually, the question of the fire's origin had been bugging me, too, as soon as I saw it on the news. Especially on the same evening we paid a visit out there. It could very well have been a coincidence, but I'd never met one of those I didn't loathe. So touching base with the cops was something I probably would have done anyway. At least this way I'd be rewarded with the answer to my puzzle about how the hell she got my damn cell phone number, regardless of what the police said. Sort of quid pro quo.

We agreed to call it a night and contact them in the morning, figuring that they'd need at least that long to sort through the scene. I was worn out as it was, and frustrated by Johnny's coddling of the obnoxious Harv. Prince Punk-ass. I was going to have to press him on that, too. I could see no reason to keep the asshole on the telethon list at this point, no matter how much Johnny felt he owed that damn Elliott. The problems and frustrations of the day were like two sides of a vise closing around my head. I just wanted to get a good night's sleep and awake refreshed and ready to go. Like Grady had said, I had a date with a pillow. I was going to have to buy that guy a drink and pick his mind about the current state of the sweet science one of these nights.

• • •

The next morning I got my unwelcome wake-up call. Veronica at 6:30 a.m.

"It *was* her," she said, her voice full of triumphant rectitude, not bothering to ask if she'd awakened me.

"What are you talking about?"

"Don't you have your TV on?" Her voice was so accusatory, I had a momentary twinge of guilt. Until I rolled over and saw what time it was. "It's on the news right now. Mrs. Henrietta Perkins, dead in the mobile home fire."

The razor squeaking over glass again. It was way too early for this. But sleep at this point would be next to impossible. I told her to give me a half hour and then meet me in the lobby by the front desk.

"I thought we agreed." she said. "You were going to call the police."

"I will, once I've taken a shower, shaved, dressed, and eaten. And don't wear that thing on your head again." I hung up and swung my feet out of bed, pondering the task ahead of me. Despite the hotel down the Strip bearing its namesake, this wasn't the Big Apple and I had absolutely no police contacts out here. Outside of the slim chance that someone might be sympathetic to an actor who plays one on TV, the cops out here would probably be a bit reticent to give me any inside info on a death investigation. Plus, I wasn't sure which agency would be handling it. The trailer park had seemed pretty far away from Las Vegas proper, but since the Clark County Sheriff's Department merged with Las Vegas PD to form the Metro Police Department back in 1973, there was a possibility the investigation would fall under their jurisdiction. Clark County was pretty big. I needed to find somebody who would know.

I reached for the remote and was searching for the local news station when Brigid Burgeon, of all people, suddenly came on the screen doing a rip-off performance of Marilyn's "Diamonds Are a Girl's Best Friend." Swirling on the pink staircase, and snaring bejeweled necklaces with an elegantly gloved arm, she sang in a throaty voice that was immediately sexy and sad. Sexy because she had the charisma. Sad because I couldn't help but think hers was a life that had ended way too quickly. The scene faded and two news anchors took its place, one saying that Henri Boyer would be re-creating the famous nude photo shoot he'd done here in Las Vegas twenty-eight years ago with Brigid at the Sandstorm Casino. Current ingénue Kerri Wilson would be wearing, or not wearing, the same outfits, if you could call silk scarves outfits, that Brigid had worn. The shoot was not open to the public, but Henri and Kerri would be holding a press conference later today to answer questions and sign autographs.

I just hoped Kerri, who had spent more time lately in rehab than a recycled sweatsuit, would be able to stay awake long enough to scribble her name. But that wasn't my problem. I had plenty of my own. Like how far I was going to go in this little windmill-tilting session I was currently involved in. Of course, I'd always harbored a secret whim to star in *Man of La Mancha* and sing "The Impossible Dream" in front of an audience.

I warbled a few bars as I stood under a hot shower and let the water run over my back thinking, What to do, who to call?

Twenty minutes later I was lacing my shoes with a solution.

I'd call Barry.

He answered with a sleepy hello and I realized it was only a little after 7:00 a.m.

"Oh, man, I'm sorry. Did I wake you?"

"Yes, but that's okay. Richard? It is you, isn't it?"

"It is. And I need a favor. Two favors, actually."

"What do you need?" His voice had shaken off all the remnants of slumber and sounded full of vitality. I liked this kid.

"Can you get me the name of a local reporter, maybe from the *Vegas Star* or something? I need some info on a local tragedy."

"Sure, I can do that. What else?"

"Answer a question for me. Why is Johnny bending over backwards to coddle that jerk Harvey Smithe? Is there something about that asshole I don't know?"

"Ahhh . . ." Barry's voice had a little catch to it when he spoke. "That's a little more complicated than I'd feel comfortable discussing on the phone at the moment. Why don't you talk to Johnny about that?"

"Fair enough," I said. "But if you could help me with the other matter, I would appreciate it."

He said he would and I told him to call my cell with the info, adding that I was going to have to start calling him Sancho. I don't think he got my allusion, and I was a bit unsure of it myself. Sancho Panza didn't strike me as particularly adept at finding information, especially on a laptop.

I stood, stretched, and prepared to meet the day. When I got downstairs, there was no sign of Veronica, so I took a few minutes to stroll out the front doors and walk to the sidewalk.

The Strip has a completely different look during the day, especially in the early morning. Gone are the throngs of people, the sidewalk kiosks, the endless flow of traffic, even the legions of street-stationed Hispanics handing out the cards with sex trade advertisements. The bright lights are all off, and the buildings look almost like regular structures set against the backdrop of the far mountains. You can walk down the street and appreciate the superficiality of all the façades . . . You can see the gas jets on the fake rocks in front of the artificial volcano . . . The underwater track for the pirate ship in front of Treasure Island . . . Appreciate the calm reflection in the water where the fountains will begin dancing in the evening. It's the time I like best in Vegas: when it's stripped of all its pretentiousness and shows you what it really is: a big, artificial city plunked down in the desert designed to separate you from your money in as many ways as possible, and look dazzling while doing it. Everything's about as real as a huge, sparkling chunk of cubic zirconia.

But I had no time for ruminations about Sin City or a morning stroll. I turned and went back inside, catching sight of Veronica standing with her back to the doors, watching the elevators. But I almost didn't recognize her. She'd gathered her long brown hair into a ponytail, and switched from the long, seventies-style hippie dress to some dilapidated blue jeans and a washed-out tan blouse. From this angle, she looked almost presentable. At least you could tell she had legs. I moved up behind her and said, "Good morning."

She turned with a start. "Oh my God, you scared me."

"Good thing I wasn't the real boogeyman. And if you want to be a real conspiracy theorist, you need to be more aware of your surroundings. That means never standing or sitting with your back to the door."

She frowned slightly at my admonishment. "Have you called the police yet?"

I held up my arm and tapped my index finger on my watch. "It's not even eight yet. Let's go get some breakfast."

Barry called my cell just as I was finishing off my last bite of scrambled eggs and toast. The way I was polishing off a couple of egg yolks every morning, I was going to have to switch to oatmeal when I got back to New York until my cholesterol went back down.

"Richard, I managed to get a hold of one of their reporters," Barry said. "His name is Kevin Goather, and his column is called Got Your Goat. 'Clever, eh?"

"You are the best, kid. I'd give you a hug the next time I see you, but people would start to talk."

He laughed. "A promise not to call me again before eight in the morning will suffice." He read off the number. I motioned for Veronica to give me something to write with and jotted it on the back of a paper napkin.

"What's that?" she asked me after I'd disconnected with Barry.

"The beginning of our deal," I said, looking down at the scrawl on the napkin. I couldn't help but be reminded of how Paul and I used to write down our jokes. "But first, you promised me last night that you'd clue me in on how you got my cell number."

She compressed her lips. "Well . . ."

"And don't even think about giving me that 'I'm a psychic' BS."

Her eyes shot downward, and when they looked up, the aura of honesty was in them.

"All right, I'll tell you," she said. "I got it from Mr. Gardner's office."

"Eric's office?" I felt stunned. Eric had been my manager for as long as I could remember, and I couldn't see him giving anybody my personal cell phone number, much less this flako. "Huh-ah. No way. He wouldn't do that."

"Well, he didn't. Not exactly, anyway." Another glance at the tabletop. "His administrative assistant was out for a bit on a medical leave, and he used the temp service I worked for. I saw in the files that he was your manager, and I'd heard Paul talk about you all the time . . . how smart you are, how you always can see through the cover-ups."

"And leap tall buildings in a single bound." I shot her as stern a look as I could muster. "What you did was totally unethical and you should have been fired."

"I was," she said. "But not for that. Mr. Gardner never even knew I took it. He was so nice to me, I feel bad."

"As well you should. So what did you get fired for?"

She shook her head and her eyes welled up. "I'm really sorry, but we were just desperate to get in contact with you."

"We? You and Paul?"

She nodded. "We were so desperate . . ."

Desperately seeking Richard, I thought. At least it all was starting to make sense now. Plus, I had firmly established the rectitude in my tone now that would probably scare her all the way back to L.A. After I made a few phone calls. That was the deal, and, admittedly, I had more than just a little curiosity about this whole situation.

"Kevin Goather, please," I said to the gruff voice that answered.

"Speaking."

All business, this guy.

"This is Richard Belzer. I need a favor."

"Richard Belzer? The TV star?"

"The same."

His tone was guarded. "And how do I know this is really him?"

"You'll have to take my word for it," I said. "But I'm not just somebody trying to get your goat."

He laughed. "Okay, it is you. I recognize your voice." His tone had warmed up but kept a trace of skepticism. "So what can I do for you, sir?"

"Three things. First, call me Belz. Second, I need information on that fire at the trailer park last night. And three, I need the name of the police detective who's working the case."

"The fire where the old lady was killed? What's your interest in it?"

Typical reporter. Always wondering about the angles.

"I knew the lady," I said.

"Oh, Jesus, I'm sorry to hear that. Let me look into things and I'll call you back. There a number where I can reach you?"

"Call me on my cell. Everybody's got it." I gave Veronica a hard look as I rattled it off. To her credit, she almost blushed.

We finished eating and went back up to her room, where we spread copies of Constance Penroy's notebook on top of her bed. It was like trying to make sense of an enormous jigsaw puzzle when you didn't have any idea what the finished product was supposed to look like. Finally, after about forty minutes or so, Goather called me back.

"Belz? This is Goat. You copy me?"

I couldn't resist. "Affirmative." It almost sounded like we were reciting hackneyed lines from a bad sixties spy flick.

"I got the name of the detective handling the investigation. It was standard newsroom, stringer stuff, so I had to do some digging."

He was obviously fishing for one of those metaphorical pats on the head, so I gave him one. "Excellent, Goat. I appreciate you going above and beyond for me."

"Not a problem," he said, basking in the glow of my compliment. "But I can't help wondering if there isn't a story in this somewhere for me."

"At the moment I have to check a few things out myself, but if it turns into anything, you'll be the first person I call."

"So you're saying there is more to this, then?"

"I didn't say that." I tried to keep my voice even, but with an implicit coyness that he might interpret as a vague possibility. "But, like I said . . ."

He laughed. "Good enough, Belz, good enough. I'll hold you to that, though." I could hear some papers rattling. "The man you want is Detective Scott Kirby. He works out of their south satellite office." He read off a phone number and added that it was Kirby's direct line.

After thanking him and assuring him I'd give him a call with more details, I disconnected and looked at the number he'd given me.

"Well, are you going to call him or not?" Veronica asked.

"If I were you, I'd relax and enjoy the view." I pointed to the red and purple mountain range visible out her hotel room window. "Don't forget, if this turns out to be an accident, you'll be on your way back to L.A., as you promised."

She nodded. Her face had a pinched look.

I glanced at my watch: 9:15. Time enough for any self-respecting cop to have had his morning coffee and obligatory donut, finished the newspaper, and checked his personal emails. I set my cell down on her bedside table and studied the array of notes on the bed.

"Why aren't you calling him?" Veronica asked.

"In a minute." I wanted to read through Constance's notes about Mrs. Perkins first. The only problem was they were handwritten and in a mixture of French and English. My French is good enough for restaurants and getting stuff at the local market in France, but reading and understanding this stuff was just a little beyond my capabilities. "Why didn't she write in plain old English?"

"My grandmother was from Montréal. She was fluent in both languages. I wish I could read French. Can you?"

"No, but I know somebody who can." Two words jumped out at me: *L'Indien.* "Did Paul ever mention anything about somebody called 'the Indian'?"

Her face tightened some more. "He was an assassin. Paul knew he killed Brigid, and Mark Kaye Jr,, and my grandmother."

Busy guy, I thought. "And he knew this how?"

"I had a vision. My grandmother told me."

I frowned. "I thought we'd agreed to can that psychic crap."

She bit her lip. "I had all these notes translated on my laptop. Paul had all of his notes on it, too. He'd done several interviews with people, including some old guy who lives here in Las Vegas who supposedly told him the Indian did it."

"This old guy have a name?"

Her head slumped downward. "Yeah, but I can't remember what it was. Lennie or Freddie or something. It was on the laptop. Paul had it. He'd started writing everything up so I gave it to him to use. I tried to get the police in L.A. to let me look for it, but they wouldn't even let me in his apartment, claiming it was a crime scene and I wasn't a relative."

"Did they recover the laptop?"

Her hands jutted outward. "I don't know. That's just it. He was only giving me pieces of the information he found out." Her eyes drifted downward again. "He was . . . drunk a lot of the time."

"I'll bet he was," I said. "What type of computer was it?"

"An HP. I painted a red flower on the top lid."

"You have the serial number?"

She pursed her lips and began digging in the magic carpetbag again. "I think so."

Just when I figured she'd never be able to find it, she came up with a folded receipt with some numbers scrawled in looping scribble on the back.

"Great," I said. "Write down your California address for me, too." I handed her some of the hotel stationery while I was scrolling down my call contact list on my cell. When I found the number I wanted, I hit the speed dial.

"You're calling the Las Vegas police now?" she asked.

I shook my head just as LAPD's finest, Officer Pearsol, answered on the third ring. "This is Belz. I thought you were going to call me yesterday."

"Hey, man, sorry about that. Got kind of busy, you know?"

"No problem, buddy. What's your first name, anyway?"

"Jacob, but everybody calls me Jock."

I wasn't going to touch that one. "You have time to check on that autopsy report for me?"

"Ahhh, not yet. The ME's office was pretty snowed under yesterday when I talked to them. Sorry. I'll hit them up today, okay?"

I made a mental note to take my time if and when he ever sent me his screenplay. "Sounds good. Say, I need another favor."

"Name it. For you, anything."

Eager to please. I figured to capitalize on his largesse before it faded. "What happened to all of Venchus's personal possessions?"

"After the ETs went through and processed, they told the landlord he could bag it and hold on to the stuff until next of kin could be located."

"Next of kin . . . You find anybody?"

"I don't think so. I can check on that, too, if you want, and get back to you."

"That'd be great," I said. "Could the stuff be released to his girlfriend?"

He barked a laugh. "The psycho chick? I don't know if they were really an item or not. He was a lot older than she."

Proper grammar, once again. Maybe Pearsol did have the literary

background to write a good screenplay. "About his property . . . You remember if a laptop computer was located in the apartment? One that had
a flower design on it."

He snorted. "Psycho Chick was ranting about that. Said it was hers.
Demanded to be let in to look for it. Like we were going to let her run ram-
pant in an active crime scene."

"As if," I said, doing my best valley girl imitation while watching Veronica. Maybe I could shame her into going back to L.A., if for no other
reason than to reclaim her laptop.

"Say," Pearsol said, "she ever show up in Vegas looking for you?"

"As a matter of fact, she did. And ironically enough, the laptop was
hers. Any way of checking to see if it was located?"

"Yeah, I can do that," he said. "In fact, let me look into this right now
and I'll give you a call back in about a half hour. Sound like a plan?"

"Sounds great."

When I disconnected, Veronica was staring at me. "Who was that?"

"My buddy Jock from LAPD."

Her brow furrowed. "Oh, okay, as long as it wasn't that creep who
manhandled me and shoved me in the back of his squad car. The fascist."

I grinned as I dialed the number Goather had given me. A masculine
voice answered with a crisp, "Investigations."

"Detective Kirby?" I asked.

"Speaking."

Maybe the guy had a thing about one-word responses.

"Are you the person I should speak with?" I tried to keep my tone
peppered with the proper mixture of pathos and reverence. "I need some
information about the fire in the trailer park last night."

"Okay."

Another one-worder. Maybe he was going for a new record or something.

"I knew the victim. Mrs. Perkins."

No response this time. We'd gone from one-worders to no-worders.

"I was wondering if her death appeared to be an accident?" I asked. "Or
if there was anything suspicious."

"Why?"

Ah, progress. We were back in the one-word category.

"As I said, I knew the lady. In fact, I'd just visited her yesterday afternoon."

After a few seconds he asked, "What was your relationship to her?"

I tried to stay honest and noncommittal. "An acquaintance."

"Why would you think there was anything questionable about her death?"

"Well, I just told you, I'd stopped by to see her a few hours before."

"What did you talk about?"

"Her daughter was Brigid Burgeon. The old movie starlet."

Silence again.

I continued. "Mrs. Perkins was convinced that her daughter was murdered twenty-six years ago."

"Murdered?" Before I could answer he jumped back in with, "I don't think I got your name, did I? Your voice sounds very familiar."

"You may have seen me on TV. This is Richard Belzer."

"Richard Belzer." He repeated it in a flat tone. "You mean the same Richard Belzer that your TV partner is always accusing of seeing strange conspiracies around every corner?" he asked.

At least he was a fan.

"Only in a rerun," I said.

I heard him exhale slowly. "What exactly are you fishing for here, sir?"

"Please, call me Belz." I gave him a quick rundown of everything, capping it off with my unease that Mrs. Perkins was killed shortly after I'd spoken with her. "That's why I was concerned."

"Well, if it'll allay your concern, it appeared to be a tragic accident. Not a conspiracy."

"I'm assuming the ME did an autopsy?" I asked.

"Of course."

"Well, were there any traces of smoke in her lungs?"

"Smoke in her lungs." His repetition sounded flat, bordering on the edge of sarcasm.

"Right," I said. "To indicate if she'd been breathing when the fire occurred."

"As opposed to having had a heart attack or a stroke and having dropped dead first?"

"Exactly."

Another long breath. This guy wasn't interested in the case or in humoring me. "Well, the matter is under investigation at this time, sir. I'm afraid I can't really discuss it."

"Can you at least give me some info on the autopsy?"

"Sorry. Active investigation. If you have any pertinent information regarding this incident, I'd be glad to discuss it with you another time. You have a number where you can be reached?"

He was blowing me off, but was at least attentive enough to get a recontact number. I told him my cell number, closing with, "I'd appreciate it if you wouldn't give that out to just anyone."

Veronica averted her eyes again.

"Yes, sir," Kirby said. "Very good. I'll make sure to be in contact if we need to speak with you again."

Frustrated, I hit the disconnect button and tossed the phone down on the bed. It rang again, almost immediately. I answered it.

"Belz? It's Jock."

It was good to know we were on a nickname-friendly basis. Of course, I wasn't too crazy about the "Jock" part. Brought back too many old memories of gym class.

"I got the info for you, buddy," he said.

I felt like I was caught in a rotating phone version of good cop, bad cop.

"In fact," he continued, "one of the dicks asked me to contact you because they couldn't find anyone."

"Me? Find who?"

"Any immediate family for Mr. Venchus. I'd listed you as a personal friend of the deceased, and since they've been unable to find any next of kin whatsoever, they wanted to know if you'd like to take possession of the decedent's property." He never seemed to run out of breath. Maybe he was in training to become an opera singer. "Otherwise, it'll be disposed of after six months by the landlord."

I compressed my lips. "Were you able to find out about the laptop?"

"No laptop on the inventory. The ETs photographed everything and did a pretty thorough listing, too."

Shit, I thought. I glanced at Veronica, who was staring at me intently. "Could I prevail upon you to have it entered in NCIC if I give you the serial number?"

"Yeah, not a problem. I'll just do an addendum to my report. What's the make, model, and serial number?"

I picked up Veronica's receipt and read it off to him, in addition to her address as the owner of the lost or stolen property. I reminded him again of the hand-painted flower design.

"That does sound like something she'd do," he said. "Okay, got it. As you probably know, if it's recovered and run, it'll pop up as stolen in the computer and we'll notify her."

"Great. Thanks," I said. "Now, let me ask you another question. What will happen to the body?"

I heard Pearsol sigh. "Well, since he had no immediate family, and no money to speak of, the county will have to bury him. Unfortunately, it'll be in one of those paupers' graves, if no one comes forward."

A pauper's grave. Tragically appropriate for a man who never quite got the better of this cruel world. "What's that mean?"

"Mass burial in a county field. No marker, just a lot number." He paused, then added, "Unless . . ."

"Unless what?"

"An interested party steps forward. The dick investigating it also asked if I thought you would want to spring for a regular burial or cremation or something. I told him I didn't know, but that I'd ask you. The cremation would probably be easier."

I considered the ramifications and responsibilities, of which I had none. I thought about the photo Veronica had shown me the other night. Two optimistic young men smiling and ready to conquer the world. The world had caught up to Paul too fast. "Yeah, I guess can do that . . . if they can't find any family." It was the least I could do to salvage a bit of final dignity for my lost friend. I covered the mouthpiece and looked at Veronica. "You want Paul's things shipped to your address?"

Her mouth opened, then closed. Her eyes welled up and spilled over, as she shook her head. "I'd like to say yes, but I don't have any room. I've been renting a room in somebody's house in Oxnard."

I nodded. "Jock, do me a favor and check to see if there's any personal mementos of his, especially that laptop, if it's located. I'll make arrangements to have someone pick the stuff up. Any clothes and other items can just go to the neediest charity." I figured that would probably be the closest garbage can.

"You got it, Belz." His tone sounded upbeat and sincere. "And, ah, I can still give you a call when I get this screenplay finished, right?"

"You got a deal," I said. "But I've got one more favor to ask you."

"Shoot."

I resisted the temptation to make a joke at his word choice. After all, I needed to stay on his good side. "How difficult would it be for you to find out if anyone who worked the Brigid Burgeon case is still around?"

He emitted a low whistle. "Man, that's ancient history. Long before my time."

"Well, I'm a bit closer to it than you are."

I heard him sigh. "I guess I can stop by the archives and check the file. Stuff that old has got to be stored in this musty old warehouse near the Parker Center."

"I'd really appreciate it. And I'd love to talk to anybody who worked it that's still alive."

"Okaaaay," he said. "Anything else?"

"Well, yeah, a copy of the reports would be outstanding."

His tone grew cagey. "You working on a TV movie about her death or something?"

"Or something," I said.

He laughed. "Okay, Belz, I get ya. I'll see what I can come up with and get back to you. Sound like a second plan?"

Once again, I repeated, "You got a deal."

CHAPTER 8

My cell rang again as Veronica and I made our way through the rear exit of the hotel toward the monorail. I checked the screen and saw another "Unknown" on the caller ID. Naturally, when I held it to my ear, all I heard was a crackling sound, then a disconnect. I frowned and hit the button to call Johnny. His voice sounded sleepy when he answered after about six or seven rings.

"I guess that line about the early bird was all horseshit, eh?" I said.

"Belz? What the hell time is it?"

"Ten fifteen. In the morning. Or time for you to get your sorry ass out of bed, brother." Veronica and I began walking across the cement walkway toward the monorail station that runs behind the hotels on the Strip.

"Why?" Johnny asked. "We got something going today?"

"Just organizing the telethon," I said. I pointed to the ticket machine and inserted my credit card. She pressed the button for two round trips.

"Barry's working on that now," Johnny said. "Me, I'm taking another nap unless you want me to meet you for breakfast."

"Nah, I've already eaten." A big, barrel-chested guy with sunglasses, a deep-sea tan, and long blond hair hanging from under a Yankees baseball cap stepped up, shifted a laptop to his left hand, and shoved some currency into the machine with his right. I pointed to his hat and gave him the thumbs-up sign. If he saw me from behind those dark glasses, he didn't show it. So much for transplanted New Yorkers' fidelity.

Johnny moaned. "Where's the good old Belz I used to know, who thought getting up before noon was a sacrilege?"

"Hey, it's way after noon in New York. Besides, Veronica and I are on the way to a photo shoot." I inserted my pass in the slot of the entrance gate and went through. Like just about everything else in Vegas it was superficially beautiful and brand-new.

"Yeah, who's getting shot?"

"Brigid Burgeon," I said, and hung up.

The monorail came a few minutes later, smoothly rolling into place and stopping with the precision of a well-oiled hinge. I wondered if there was an engineer behind the opaque Plexiglas of the first car, or if it was completely automated. I sure couldn't tell, but I hoped there was an engineer. To think that the whole thing was left to automation was sad. Of course, look at the great job automation does with elevators. You never have to worry if the operator needs a bathroom break.

Once inside, we sat on the molded plastic seats as the silky computer voice told us to have a seat and hold the handrails. The big blond guy also walked on board, along with a man and a woman pushing a baby carriage, and the doors closed after the voice announced they would. Veronica went over and smiled as she looked down at the infant.

"What a little darling. How old is she?"

"It's a he," the young man said with a laugh.

"And she's usually pretty good with psychic predictions, too," I said.

Veronica shot me a frown and immediately began a conversation with the young couple, asking where they were from, how they were enjoying Vegas, and all the rest. By the time they got off, two stops later, I practically knew their whole life story since high school. Luckily, Veronica had been circumspect about her own Vegas story, although she did mention we were on our way to the MGM Grand to attend a photo shoot with Kerri Wilson. That left only her, me, and the big blond guy, who seemed gassed or at least locked in the cyberworld of his computer. With only two more stops left, the last one being ours, the big guy closed his laptop and ambled out the opening doors, leaving just Veronica and me in the car.

"A word to the wise," I said.

"Yes?"

"Beware of strangers. It's not a good idea to be striking up conversations and broadcasting our destination. Especially if you're studying to be a full-fledged investigative conspiracy theorist."

She bit her lip and nodded. "I'll follow your lead."

That'll be the day, I thought. As we rolled into the MGM Grand stop, the end of the line, we got out and began walking down the long corridor that separated the station from the hotel. When we came to some clothing shops along the way, I caught her looking in some of the windows.

"At the risk of sounding crass," I said, "are you thinking of an upgrade?"

"Upgrade?"

"New clothes?"

"What's wrong with my clothes?" She was back to being her defensive self.

"Nothing, if you like—" I cut myself off. This was a girl who took the Greyhound from L.A. to Vegas to follow her quest. Nobody takes the bus anymore unless they're strapped for cash. Maybe that's why she dressed in secondhand style. No sense hurting her feelings. I cleared my throat. "I was just thinking we should get you some new outfits. We have to maintain a professional image while we're trying to sort this out."

She frowned. "Tell that to my credit card balance."

We walked the rest of the way in silence, her stealing a few surreptitious glances toward the new clothes behind the glass windows when she thought I couldn't see her, and me wondering if I could pull off a Rex Harrison accent if I said, "The rain, in Spain, falls mainly in the plain."

As we neared the lobby, one of those big, electronic, rotating poster boards alternated pictures of Brigid and Kerri Wilson in various stages of tasteful undress. Smooth skin under orange silk under the banner, CARBON COPY. To me it looked more like a silk purse and a sow's ear.

"How are we going to find it, much less get in there?" Veronica asked.

"This is where I give you your first lesson in Celebrity 101."

I collared a big uniformed security guard and asked him where the photo shoot was being held.

"I'm sorry, sir. It's not open to the public." The guy looked like he didn't have a neck. His head just grew out of his sloping shoulders. I wondered if all the HGH he was taking was affecting his perception.

I grinned. "Don't tell me you don't recognize me."

He squinted.

I increased the wattage of my grin. Just when I thought he'd mistaken me for Joe Shit the ragman, he snapped his fingers and smiled.

"I got it. You're that guy on TV, right?" He held out his hand and I shook it. "It's a real pleasure to meet you, sir. I was real sorry when your TV show got canceled, Mr. Woods. I used to really like *Shark* a lot, and I got those DVD sets of both seasons."

"Mr. Woods?" Veronica said. "This is Richard Belzer."

The guard looked a bit befuddled. Obviously he wasn't the sharpest knife in the drawer. His recovery wasn't bad, though. He kind of did an "aw, shit" shuffle and continued like he hadn't heard her. "I mean, Mr. Belzer, of course. Are you supposed to be at the shoot, sir?"

"Actually, I'm a friend of Henri's," I said. "We don't live far from each other in France." This was more or less true. I mean, compared to the States, France isn't really that big, and I did meet him once at a party. Plus, I never said how close a friend I was. Not that Mr. Starstruck Security had thought to ask.

"Okay, I'll take you up there, then." He reached and unsnapped a portable radio from a pouch on his pistol belt.

"I was kind of hoping to surprise him," I said.

He nodded and replaced the radio, telling us, "Follow me."

The guard used his special key to open a set of elevator doors off to the side. An empty car reposed inside. We all stepped in and the door slid shut. He again used his key to activate the panel and I watched the numbers light up as we ascended all the way to the penthouse level. The doors opened and we were met by another security guard, sitting at a flimsy desk in front of a solid wall of curtained glass offices. He quickly stuffed the scandal sheet he'd been reading in an open drawer and stood up.

"Joe, this is Richard Belzer, the television star," the first security guard said. "He's a personal friend of Mr. Boyer's."

The second guy gave us the once-over and smiled. "Hey, glad to meet you, Mr. Belzer. It's a real pleasure."

"Same here," I said as we shook. He extended his hand toward Veronica just as the first guy's portable radio crackled.

"Thompson, where you at?"

Thompson frowned and withdrew his radio once again. "I'm on a celebrity escort."

"Report back to the casino ASAP," the voice on the radio said.

"Roger," Thompson said. He shook our hands again. "I got to run, Mr. Belzer, but it was a pleasure meeting you."

When he left, I turned to the second guard and gave him the same spiel I'd given Thompson.

"Well," he said, "I'm really not supposed to let anyone beyond this point, celebrity or not."

"Aw, come on." I glanced at his name tag. "Murphy, I really do need to speak with Henri." I used my best French pronunciation for effect.

Murphy had beady little eyes that darted around in a fleshy face. They looked like live things trying to escape. "I suppose I could make an exception for you . . ." The price tag for this was lurking close. I could feel it in his nervous glances. At first I wondered if I was going to have to empty my wallet to gain admittance, but it turned out to be a lot easier than I'd anticipated.

Murphy leaned close and asked, "You think you could get me an autographed picture of that babe that's on your show?"

"Not a problem, Murph," I said. "How would you like it signed?"

He shrugged, as if suddenly embarrassed. Maybe he was, since Veronica was there. He leaned close again. " 'To my favorite law enforcement type'?"

I didn't need to bribe him further with thoughts of lipstick kisses, but I would have obliged. After all, New York's full of homeless women who'd jump at the chance to put on lipstick and kiss a photo for five bucks. The autograph I could forge myself.

Murph held up his open palm and stepped to the door, flashing a fob in front of the electronic monitor. He popped the door open a crack and stuck his head in. "Excuse me."

"This is a closed shoot," I heard someone say. Feminine voice, but very bellicose. "Shut the door."

I glanced down at Veronica. It was all up to how much Murph wanted that autographed picture.

He persisted. "But there's somebody very important out here. A celebrity friend of Mr. Boyer."

He murdered the pronunciation, saying it, "Boy-yer," instead of "Boy-ay." I hoped Henri hadn't heard him. The French can get very sensitive about things like that.

"I don't care who it is," Ms. Bellicose continued. "It could be the pope himself, and he still can't come in."

Murph was floundering. It was time for one of my celebrity end-run moves. I only use them when it's absolutely necessary.

Stepping to the door, I said, "Please tell Mr. Boyer that Richard Belzer is here to see him about a very important matter."

I'd used the correct pronunciation and it seemed to impress Ms. Bellicose, who didn't look nearly as formidable as I got a glance at her. But then again, anybody can sound tough when they're being an asshole behind a closed door. The power of anonymity. . . . She looked very mousy, with old-fashioned, plastic-rimmed glasses and dark hair pulled straight back into a long, graying ponytail.

"I'll tell him you're here," she said, as meek as a church mouse sneaking a bit of the cheese on the sly.

"You do that," Murph chimed in, probably worried his autographed picture was in jeopardy.

"But," Ms. Bellicose started to say, "you'll have to wait until—"

Her words were cut off by a litany of cusswords that would make a sailor blush. They were coming from farther inside the room. And the speaker was definitely young and female.

"Cover your ears," I said to Veronica.

She frowned.

Ms. Bellicose frowned as well, and motioned us inside. "Looks like we're going to take a break," she said. "Again."

We followed her inside a small, darkened corridor that led to several other rooms, the closest of which had light spilling out onto the carpeted hallway. The swearing let up a little.

A voice with a French accent said, "But Kerri, we have only a few more shots to do in this section." I assumed it was Henri's.

"You think I fucking care at this point?" It was the sailor's apprentice. "How do you expect me to look good in something as fucking stupid as this? Plus it's motherfucking freezing in here. Look at my fucking nipples, for Christ's sake. And my stomach's still bloated. I told you I needed that fucking enema."

"Ah," Henri said, "perhaps it es a good time for us to refresh ourselves, no?"

Kerri Wilson, naked except for a long orange silk scarf that she'd slung over her neck like a beach towel, strode out of the room. She stopped when she saw us, drew the ends of the scarf over her midriff, and turned back to Henri with a snarl. "What the fuck? I thought this was supposed to be a closed set. Who are you motherfuckers?"

"You actually kiss your mother with that mouth?" I asked.

She looked dumbfounded, like I'd presented her with an unfathomable puzzle. A female assistant came up behind her with a robe and slipped it over her shoulders, but too late. I'd already noticed that her landing strip didn't match the blond tresses on her head, in case that's what brought about her attack of modesty.

Henri's head appeared around the doorjamb and cast a worried glance our way, his gray eyebrows arched slightly. The female assistant with the bellicose voice went over and whispered something in his ear and his face brightened.

"Ah, I believe we are safe, my dear. I know dis gentleman and his discretion es beyond reproach. Et es a fact, he is almost an honorary Frenchman."

I was a bit surprised he remembered me from our brief meeting at the party in Paris, but apparently he did. He stepped forward with the warm smile still on his face and said over his shoulder, "Go freshen yourself, Kerri. We will resume in a little bit."

She snorted and sauntered off down the hall, probably anxious for the "medication" that awaited her. Hopefully, the room had a commode so she could wash out her mouth once she'd finished cleaning out the other end.

"Why, she's even more lovely than she is on-screen," I said, sandwiching in as much sarcasm as I could. "Has she had all of her shots? And more importantly, have you had all of yours?"

"*Oui,* she makes zee area behind zee tripod a dangerous place at times." Henri laughed as he took a camera with an elongated lens from around his neck and set it out of sight. Turning back to us, he said, "Richard Belzer. To what do I owe zis pleaszure?"

I knew Henri was from Marseilles, where the accent is strong, and he still had problems with a few of our English sounds. He made my name sound like "Reechard Balzae." But I didn't mind. In fact, I could consider using it the next time I needed an alias.

"Henri, great to see you again." We shook hands as he eyed Veronica.

"And who is your lovely friend?" He gave me a knowing wink.

"This is Veronica Holmes," I said.

Henri started to make something akin to a salacious comment to me in French, then stopped. He looked at Veronica and asked, "*Parlez vous français, mon amie?*"

She looked a bit confused.

"No, she doesn't," I said. "And she's not that kind of friend." Although my French is quasi-conversational, there are some words you just know from the speaker's facial expressions.

He gave her another once-over. "A pity. She has good lines of the face. With a bit of work . . . *très jolie.*"

Veronica began to blush.

"Save the flirting for your protégée," I said, pointing to the direction in which Kerri Wilson had gone.

A frown creased Henri's face and he sounded off with a bit of French, then held his finger to his nose. "She will return in a bit . . . refueled."

I nodded.

"But come," he said, "I have some wine and cheese over here." He took out a cigarette case, removed one, and lit up, exhaling as he spoke. "What gives me the pleasure of this visit, *mon ami*?"

I decided that as volatile as this shoot appeared to be, I'd better get right to the point. Henri would have his work cut out for him when the lovely maiden returned from whatever relaxation method she was using. He handed each of us a glass, and then filled them with wine.

"We saw the ad that you were re-creating the famous photo shoot with Brigid Burgeon," I said. "We were wondering what she was like."

He smiled as he sampled the wine, rolling it in his mouth before swallowing. "She was lovely, most lovely."

"When exactly did you do the shoot?"

He drank some more wine and motioned for us to do the same. After taking another drag, he chewed his lips. "I tink it was only a few weeks before she died. *Oui*, yes, perhaps three weeks."

"How did she seem?" Veronica asked. Henri looked at her and she added, "I mean, was she happy?"

He nodded. "But of course. Very happy. She brought her amour to zee shoot. Zee, how you say, pol-e-te-see-on?"

"Mark Kaye Jr.?" I asked.

Henri nodded emphatically as he drained his wine. He stuck the cigarette in the corner of his mouth and refilled his glass. Veronica stepped back and coughed. Henri smiled.

"Ah, zee smoke . . . et bothers you, *n'est-ce pas*?" He took a final drag and stubbed out the butt in an ashtray. "An unfortunate habit I picked up in zee French Foreign Legion."

"You were in the Legion?" I asked.

He laughed, shaking his head. "No, I was making a bad joke. Zee legion es for *étrangers*, not real Frenchmen."

"Did Kaye seem like he was in love with her?" Veronica asked.

Henri waggled his palm. "*Comme ci, comme ça*. Dey seemed very, how you say? Very *hot* for each other."

"Did you know Brigid was carrying his baby?" Veronica asked.

If I had any concerns about getting the ball rolling by letting the cat out of the bag, she was erasing them. But Henri's answer surprised me.

"Dat subject was one we discussed." He patted his own stomach with his left hand and added, "She had zee tell-tale bump. Told me I must use zee airbrush to get rid of it."

"And did you?" I asked.

He smiled and picked up a photographic album with a ring binder. Opening it to a marked page, he turned it for us to look at. Brigid Burgeon, nude under a translucence of orange similar to the one Kerri had slung over her shoulders, reclined on an artificial setting of fake rocks, her head thrown back with a laughing expression that made her look like a modern-day Helen of Troy. Kerri was going to look pale by comparison.

"She was a diamond, no?" Henri said.

"Did Kaye say anything about her being pregnant?" I asked.

Henri shook his head. "No, no, no, we did not discuss her condition. Only that I was to use zee brush to erase her . . ." He patted his stomach again. "Here."

"See? It's just like the letter says. Kaye knew," Veronica said, her voice rising to an angry pitch. "The bastard. He knew she was carrying his child. And he had her murdered for it."

Henri raised his eyebrows and looked from her to me. "She is a distaff Oliver Stone, no?"

I smiled. The kid did have pluck. If she could only learn to keep her mouth shut.

"It didn't seem awkward, Mark Kaye Jr. being here for the photo shoot?" I asked, trying to get things back on track.

Henri shook his head. "Having a mistress is not such a big deal in my country, even twenty-six years ago. So I never thought much about it. And Brigid seemed totally in love. So did he."

"Any problems come up?" I asked. "Anything out of the ordinary?"

"Well, as I mentioned, zee situation of having another lover is totally acceptable *en français,* so I did not give it any more of my t'oughts." His French accent still wouldn't allow his tongue to bridge the "th" sound. "But Kaye's father and brother came to zee hotel and were very disruptive. I had the security escort them away, and they dragged him off as well. They had with them two very large, very scary men. Dey looked like bad actors in an old Jean-Paul Belmondo *ciné*. We finished the shoot, but poor Brigid's eyes told zee story, very sad." He paged through the book some more, then showed us another photo, this one in black-and-white, untouched by any airbrush. Brigid Burgeon looking like the carpet had been pulled out from underneath her at her birthday party. She sat, legs splayed, her head in her hands, crying. Henri tapped the page. "I know, I am a scoundrel for snapping *dis* one, but a photographer seldom is able to capture zee purest of emotions. I call it *La fin de l'affaire*." He smiled and flicked his fingers.

The end of the affair. But was it the end? I wondered if the love letter poor old Mrs. Perkins had shown us had been written before or after the photo shoot blowout. Obviously Papa Kaye and brother Larry had reservations about Markie spending time with Brigid. They still had aspirations he could end up in the White House, and, after all, this was before it became fashionable prime-time news fodder to get fellated in the Oval Office.

"Henri," I said, "this photo says it all. It's pure emotion. Pure art."

CHAPTER 9

We left Henri with our thanks and good wishes before Kerri could come stumbling back to finish the session. As we took the elevator back down to the immense lobby area the vision of Brigid sitting there crying in the black-and-white photograph haunted me. I guess she'd found it was a long way from Massillon, Ohio. I studied the gold inset design in the elevator's mirrors, trying to erase it from my memory. Veronica, however, kept tugging at my sleeve, in a metaphorical sort of way, saying, "See, I told you, didn't I? I told you they murdered her. See?"

It was like trying to ignore a splinter under your thumbnail. I winced and kept studying the design, trying to decide exactly where I stood in this escalating fiasco. Or where I wanted to stand. That logical little voice kept telling me to step away, put Veronica on the bus back to Tinseltown, and get on with the telethon. But the other little voice, the emotional one, just kept saying, "Yep, that photo was pure art . . ." Plus, the sleeve tugging continued unabated.

"Mr. Belzer, why didn't you ask him to translate my grandmother's notes for us?"

I gave her a pensive, eyebrow-raising stare that has been known to strike fear into the hearts of many suspects in an interrogation scene. With her, it only elicited a questioning look.

"Well?" she asked. "He obviously could tell us what it said."

I tried closing my eyes and taking one of those deep breaths through my nostrils. "You obviously weren't paying close attention before when I told you not to talk to strangers."

"Strangers? But you two seemed to know each other so well."

"Wrong." The elevator doors opened, showing us the corridor to the expansive lobby with the wall of high-density television screens all displaying the buildup to an upcoming boxing match. It looked like a good one, and I mulled over coming back for it.

"Well?" she said again. Maybe I could get her a job as an early warning doorbell or something.

I stopped and began ticking off points on my fingers. "First of all, I don't know Henri that well. Second, even if I did, there are certain people you trust with your dirty laundry, and those you do not."

"Dirty laundry?"

"I'm being metaphorical. And third, I know somebody I trust a lot more who can translate it for me." I glanced over toward the front desk and saw the concierge's booth. "Come on." When we got there I asked where the business center for the hotel was. He pointed across the room toward a glass-walled office area. I started for the office and motioned for her to come along.

"What are we going in there for?" she asked.

I ignored the question and held the door open for her. Once inside, I asked myself, Do I really want to do this? I weighed all the options as I listened to the little voices making their final arguments. "Okay, where are those pages we needed translated?"

She patted the magic carpetbag.

"Well," I said, "get them out."

"But—"

"No buts. Do you want me to help you with this or not?"

"Of course I do."

"Then we do it my way from here on out. That means you not jumping into the middle of the conversation when I'm talking to someone."

"Jumping in? Are you saying I can't ask questions?" Her expression reflected a growing indignation.

"I'm saying that you're ruining my image." I cracked a smile. "I'm the one who's supposed to be going around pissing people off."

I saw a hint of a grin grace her lips, but she buttoned up and reached into the bag. After sorting through the pages, she withdrew three of them. "These are the ones she wrote about the Indian."

I took them and turned to the girl behind the desk. "Can I get these faxed here?"

"Certainly, sir," she said, and handed me the form. "Just fill this out with the number you want and I'll fax them for you."

I nodded and stepped to the corner, scribbling the number on the page with a brief note. Veronica was watching me.

"Who's that we're faxing it to?"

I gave her a sideways look and took out my cell phone. Harlee answered on the second ring.

"Hi, honey," she said. "How's Johnny doing?"

"Not bad," I said. We exchanged small talk for a few minutes, then I laid it on her gently. "Say, I need a favor, babe."

"A favor?"

"Yeah. Is the fax machine on?"

"I can turn it on." Her voice was starting to get that feminine wariness tone to it.

"I'm going to fax you a couple pages of handwritten French. Could you translate them and email them back to me?"

Silence, then, "Richard, what are you getting into out there?"

When we go from "honey" to "Richard," it usually means I'm getting in deep water.

"Ah, it's kind of complicated," I said.

"Well, I've got plenty of time."

"Remember last week when my old friend Paul called me out of the blue?"

"Yes."

"And I told you he was found dead the other day, right?"

"You did."

The laconic replies were a clear indicator that she wasn't going to tolerate any beating around the bush. "Well, I'm sort of looking into the story he was working on."

I heard her exhale. "Honey, please tell me you're not out there playing Nick Charles again."

At least we'd moved back to "honey" from "Richard."

"Only," I said, "if you were to play Nora."

"I'm serious."

"I'm just looking into the story, not getting in trouble. It has to do with who killed Brigid Burgeon."

"Brigid Burgeon? That was, what? Twenty-five years ago?"

"Twenty-six, actually. But these pages might tell us something. So . . . ?"

She sighed. "Say no more. Fax them. I'll email you."

"Thanks. Have I told you how much I love you lately?"

"Not nearly enough," she said. "And promise me you'll stay out of trouble, okay? Remember the last time."

"I'll do my best," I said, drawing a heart with a smiley face next to my signature on the form. I disconnected and put the phone back in my pocket. When I turned back to the girl behind the desk, her brow furrowed slightly.

"You're Richard Belzer, aren't you?" she asked.

Ah, a fan.

"I am. And I'd appreciate it if this fax number remained confidential." I slipped a twenty out of my pocket and held it on top of the pages as I handed it to her. "Will this cover it?"

Her smile told me all I needed to know.

After we'd completed our faxing and replaced the pages in the magic carpetbag, we made our way through the immense lobby toward the side exit onto Tropicana Avenue. It was getting close to noon and the Strip was starting to buzz. I felt a sudden urge to hit Fatburger for a greasy burger and fries, but I'd just finished promising Harlee I'd stay out of harm's way. My cell jangled again and when I looked at the screen, I saw it was Johnny.

"Where you at?" he asked.

"Walking the Strip. Why?"

"I was hoping you'd give me a hand writing some of this opening monologue is all." His voice sounded nervous.

"Since when does the master need his best disciple to write anything for him?"

"Since I invited him to help me out with this. I need somebody good. Somebody who knows what they're doing."

"Yeah, well, I'll check to see if Bruce Vilanch is busy."

"Come on, Belz, I'm counting on you." He hesitated. "Besides, we need to sit down and talk."

"About what?"

"About stuff." I heard him sigh. "You know how important this telethon is to me, right?"

"I do. Look, how about we meet for dinner and we can discuss the monologue then?"

Another heavy sigh. "All right. Give me a call when you get back to the hotel, okay?"

I told him I would and disconnected. Deciding to remove myself from the Fatburger temptation, I motioned for Veronica to follow me to the escalator and took it up to the bridge that goes over to New York–New York. I stopped in the middle and watched the traffic passing under us. Just below the Plexiglas shield, someone had stuck a "Kaye III for Governor" sticker on the solid white section of the wall. No matter how much things change, they somehow remain the same. I still had my cell phone in my hand, so I scrolled down until I found Pearsol's number and hit the speed dial.

"Hey, Belz," he said. "You have an uncanny ability to call me just when I'm thinking of calling you. How do you do that?"

"I'm with a psychic," I said, looking at Veronica. "You find anything out on that report?"

"Yeah." He drew the word out so it sounded more like a sigh than an affirmation. "I was right that it was buried in the archives. Getting over there to copy it is gonna be a major endeavor. I'll have to wait till my day off or something."

Red tape abounds, I thought.

"How about splitting the difference, then?" I said. "Can you give me anything on the guys who worked it?"

"That I did find out. I looked up some of the old newspaper articles online. Leo Russell was the guy who was quoted in most of the articles. I asked a couple of the old-timers and they said his partner in those days was Eddie Sikorski. Both have long since retired. I know Russell's dead. I think Eddie's still alive, though."

"Could you get me his phone number and address?"

Pearsol said nothing for a few seconds. "Ahh, that would be against departmental regulations." His reticence was palpable. Cops are very zealous about guarding their own privacy, and that of their fellow coppers. For Pearsol to break that trust, even for a retired officer, would be anathema.

"How about this, then," I said. "Can you call him and give him my info? Ask him to call me?"

"Yeah, I can do that." He seemed happy that I'd provided the out for him. "What number you want me to give him for you?"

"Give him my cell phone number," I said, glancing at Veronica, who was hanging on my every word. "Everybody has it anyway."

I thanked him, calling him "Jock," and mentioning again that I was looking forward to reading his screenplay.

Who knows, I thought. It could even be good. Sometimes cops can make pretty good writers.

We strolled across the rest of the boulevard-spanning bridge and began walking north along the fake Brooklyn Bridge in front of the hotel. I had no desire to watch the miniature fireboat spray the water at the ersatz Statue of Liberty at the opposite corner. It would only make me homesick for the real thing.

As we passed the boardwalk section between the major expanses of hotels and casinos, we walked past a row of smaller stores with full glass pane windows advertising clothes, travel opportunities, and, once again, a huge poster saying "Kaye III for Governor." A Vegas-style campaign office: here today, gone tomorrow. An idea began to cultivate on the devious side of my mind.

"Feel up to causing some ripples?" I asked.

"What kind of ripples?"

"It's just like Dino said in *Robin and the 7 Hoods*. When the guy across from you is holding all the aces, sometimes the only thing you can do is kick over the table."

Her brow furrowed. "I'm not sure what that means."

I winked. "Just follow my lead."

I pushed open the door and went in. A collection of fresh-faced young men and women sat at the desk folding fliers. Each one pictured a smiling, color photograph of Mark Kaye III. His face was also adorning several more huge posters on the rear walls above the slogan "Solid Family Values—Economic Prosperity." One of the posters had the image of him and his uncle Larry superimposed over a photograph of Mark Kaye Jr., with the caption, "Generations of Public Service."

Now, wasn't that original?

The kid behind the desk looked up at me and smiled. "May I help you, sir?"

"Yes, I'd like to make an appointment to speak to Mr. Kaye."

The kid's grin curled up a bit. "Well, sir, I can give you a list of his upcoming campaign stops, but scheduling an appointment wouldn't be possible at this time."

"What about Uncle Lar?" I asked, flashing a grin. "Would he be available?"

"State Senator Kaye is busy as well, sir. But if you'd like to look at this flier, it will tell you where they'll be over the next few weeks." He dutifully held out one of the folded papers.

I unfolded it. "These special elections come around once in a blue moon, don't they? Your elected governor was recalled, wasn't he? Some kind of scandal?"

"Yes, sir," the kid said. "That's why Senator Kaye the Third has built his campaign on family values."

"Don't forget economic prosperity." I smiled again, and thought I was getting him set up just right when the loose cannon broke free.

"Family values!" Veronica said. "What a hypocrite. After his father helped to murder somebody."

The kid behind the desk flashed a concerned look at one of his compatriots. A balding, middle-aged guy with an unhealthy paunch stood up in the back and walked forward.

"May I help you?"

Before I could speak, Veronica did all the talking. "Who are you?"

"I'm the supervisor here."

"Well, do you know who this is?" She pointed at me. The guy shook his head. I shook my head, too, but she continued anyway. "This is famous television and movie star celebrity Richard Belzer. And we *demand* to be allowed to see Mr. Mark Cover-up Kaye the Third. Right now. Or should I say, *the turd*?"

Oh, dammit, I thought. Raising my index finger, I pointed at her and said, "Stop. Now."

She suddenly looked like a sailboat in a failed breeze, her mouth open at the ready, but no sound coming out. It was a beautiful sight to behold. I turned to Mr. Paunch. His expression was somewhere between wonderment and aggravation. In other words, he looked like he had a bad case of gas.

"We're getting off on the wrong foot here," I said.

"To put it mildly," the guy said. "Are you really Richard Belzer?"

I nodded. It was too late to claim to be my handsome twin brother.

Mr. Paunch extended his hand. "I'm George Bailey. What can I do for you, Mr. Belzer?"

"George Bailey," I said. "*It's a Wonderful Life*. Great flick. I'll bet you get ribbed about that a lot, don't you?"

"Yes, sir." His smile looked as nervous as a high-wire act in a heavy crosswind.

"All right, then." One of the problems with having a half-assed plan when you walk in a place is that if you're flying by the seat of your pants, there's not much purchase left when things start to go south. "I'm staying at the Monticello and we're doing a charity telethon for autistic kids. On behalf of Johnny Leland and myself, I'd like to extend an invitation to Mr. Kaye, and Uncle Lar, as well, to appear on the program."

Bailey was breathing rapidly through his mouth. "I'll let them know. Thank you."

"My pleasure." I turned and grabbed Veronica by the shoulders, steering her toward the door. "I'd give you my cell phone number, but I'm sure they already have it. Everybody else does."

Once we'd left the comfort of the air-conditioned office, I strode away, moving in the direction of the hotel. Veronica came up next to me in a slight jog, the magic carpetbag bouncing against her leg, to keep up.

"Mr. Belzer, could you slow down, please?"

I continued my power walk.

"Please."

We came to the end of the block and had to wait for a stream of cars turning into the Monte Carlo. She tugged at my arm. I whirled and shot another baleful stare down at her. "I thought we had a deal."

"Deal?" Her voice had taken on the characteristics of a cartoon show mouse.

"That I was going to do the talking and you were going to quit pissing people off."

"I'm sorry." She appeared ready to cry again. If this kept up, I'd have to take her out to Hoover Dam. She could fill up the low spots in Lake Mead in no time.

"You're overdoing the crying game, kid. That won't work on me anymore."

She looked down and licked her lips.

Despite my anger and frustration, I still felt a twinge of protectiveness toward this impetuous girl who was intent on trying to prove her grandmother was murdered. She kept making all the wrong moves, but, I sensed, for the right reasons. I notched my index finger under her chin and raised her head so I could look her in the eyes.

"Like I said before, *I'm* the one who's supposed to be going around pissing people off. You're blowing my image." I paused to see if I'd softened my reprimand enough.

She nodded, but she still looked close to tears.

"But, I have to say," I said with a grin, "that 'turd' line wasn't bad. In fact, I may steal it at some future date."

CHAPTER 10

We went over to the Paris Casino for lunch, mostly out of nostalgia for my home in France, but that didn't do any more for me than New York–New York had. I was starting to wish that I'd never made the trek out here to the neon city in the desert and gotten involved in this crazy twenty-six-year-old conspiracy investigation. But why had I? Loyalty to an old friend I hadn't seen in three decades? The tears from a young girl bent on solving her grandmother's possible murder? A black-and-white photograph of a long-dead movie starlet crying at her last photo shoot? All of the above? Or . . . was it something more?

I pondered that as we ordered and feasted on the basket of French bread the waitress set on the table. Veronica had been pretty much silent since my last admonishment, and I was enjoying that as well. Still, it was time to reemphasize some more ground rules.

"Let's go over a few things, shall we?" I said.

She looked up all innocent eyed and nodded. Maybe the kid had a future in acting after all.

"I want you to know that I'm this close," I held up my index finger and thumb, separating them by a millimeter, "to putting you on that bus back to L.A."

"Why? We're uncovering all kinds of stuff."

I flashed her an open palm. "Let me finish, please. What we're uncovering is debatable. At the most it's fuel for a gossip column or scandal sheet, if we could even find one interested, and at the least, well, it's nothing that hasn't been tossed around for a couple of decades in those two mediums."

"With two people getting murdered for trying to tell their stories?" Her voice raised a few decibels. People at the surrounding tables started to look.

I flashed her the open palm again. "Tell the whole restaurant, why don't you?"

She glanced around self-consciously, then pursed her lips. "Sorry."

"Remember that circumspection is the mother of discretion."

Her expression turned to one of befuddlement. "What?"

"Never mind. Just keep in mind that we don't know if foul play was involved in either Paul's death or Mrs. Perkins's. And the police are looking into both of those."

She frowned and seemed ready to argue, but thought better of it and nodded.

"However," I continued, "if there was foul play involved, we have to be cognizant of the fact that we might have upset a hornet's nest."

Her face tightened. "You mean . . . this could be dangerous, right?"

"Very right. I'm especially concerned about this Indian guy."

"Paul was worried about him, too. Said the guy was like a legend."

I frowned. "He say anything else about him? Like what he looked like?"

She shook her head.

I cleared my throat so I could speak in a lowered tone. The rest of the surrounding tables had returned to a state of relative normalcy. "If we are dealing with people capable of committing murder and making it look accidental, we could be putting ourselves at risk."

"That's exactly what Paul told me. But I wasn't afraid then, and I'm not afraid now. I came all the way out here from Waterville to find the truth. To get justice for my grandmother."

I lifted my palm up again. "Great, then I'll be scared enough for both of us."

"A famous TV detective? I find that hard to believe."

"Sorry to punch a hole in your idealism, but he has a script and a fake gun to help him feel secure. Besides, he who isn't scared from time to time, in the face of real danger, usually is very brave or very stupid, or very both of those."

"So you're saying we should back off?"

"I'm saying we need to be careful. And circumspect. That means not butting in and shooting your mouth off when I'm engaged in conversations with people."

She looked down. "You already yelled at me for that, remember?"

"How could I forget? You keep reminding me all the time." My cell rang, sparing us further useless conversation. I checked the screen and saw it was Pearsol.

"Jock, my man," I said.

"Hey, Belz. Have I got a scoop for you. Like I said, Russell's long gone, but his partner, Eddie Sikorski, is living in Vegas and would be glad to talk with you. I called him a few minutes ago. I told him you were writing a book about old Hollywood mysterious celebrity deaths."

"Hey, that's great. Thanks, Jock."

"Anytime, buddy."

He gave me the number and I scribbled it down on the back of a business card.

"One other thing, Belz." Pearsol's voice sounded tentative.

"Yeah?"

He sighed. "I hate to talk bad about the dead, and especially about a fellow officer, but I got to tell you this." He paused again. "It's about Russell. Word is that he had some very unsavory friends, if you catch my drift."

"That's interesting."

"He was originally from Chicago, so go figure. He retired and was rumored to be one step ahead of a federal indictment when he dropped dead of a heart attack."

I considered this. "What about Sikorski?"

"He was clean as far as I know, but like I said, they were partners. Take it for what it's worth and forget I told you, okay?"

I told him I would and disconnected. This one was starting to get real interesting.

When we got back to the Monticello there was a message from Johnny on my hotel phone, telling me to call him in his room as soon as possible. I told Veronica to sit at my desk and plug in my laptop while I dialed Johnny. He answered with a hurried "Hello."

"I'm back," I said.

"Great, now how about swinging up here and assisting me with this opening?"

"On my way," I said.

"Oh, Belz," he said. "Don't bring the bag lady, okay?"

"Wouldn't dream of it," I said.

After I did a quick check of my emails and saw there wasn't one from Harlee, I signed off, and told Veronica to do some web surfing for a deceased LAPD copper named Leo Russell. "Check on a guy named Eddie Sikorski, too."

"Aren't you going to call that retired policeman and set up an appointment?"

"Yeah, but I want to go in prepared. That's why I want you to Google them first." I took the "Kaye III for Governor" flier out of my pocket and set it on the desk. "Might as well see what you can find out about the mighty Kayes while you're at it."

She seemed excited about having something to do, so I told her to stay here, and not to answer the phone.

"Why not?"

"Because if anyone calls me, like my lovely wife, I don't want to have to explain why a young girl was taking messages for me."

She covered her mouth with her fingertips and giggled.

I told her if she needed me, to call me on my cell, and went up to Johnny's room. When I got there he and Barry had several sheets of paper spread out on the bed, and Barry cradled his laptop on his lap.

"About fucking time you got here," Johnny said. He grinned, but I noticed an underlying nervousness in his face. Or was it just fatigue? These telethons were draining, and Johnny had a tendency to micromanage things a lot. He reached over and grabbed a glass with some melting ice cubes and took a sip. Frowning, he thrust it toward Barry and said, "Can you freshen this up for me?"

Barry nodded and gently set the laptop on the bed. When he was over at the wet bar Johnny leaned toward me and asked, "So how was the photo shoot?"

"Fabulous," I said. "Henri Boyer is a true artist with the camera."

"So who was getting shot?"

"That fabulous darling of MTV and YouTube, Kerri Wilson."

"She's outta rehab?"

"Too early."

He smirked. "I was thinking about contacting her, since she was in town, to do a song on the telethon."

"Only for the R-rated version," I said.

Barry returned with Johnny's drink. He raised his eyebrows expectantly at me, but I shook my head.

"Let's get busy with this, shall we?" I said. "I've got another meeting lined up for later on."

Johnny eyed me warily over the rim of his glass.

One of the neatest things about working with one of the modern masters is that once you get on a roll with stand-up lines, you don't want to stop. We kept it up for about three hours, bouncing lines off each other and figuring where to put in the breaks. When we had a pretty good temporary outline of the entire thing, I leaned back and stretched.

"Now I need that drink," I said.

Barry set the laptop down and asked what kind I wanted.

"You got any Snapple?" I asked. "Or maybe some iced tea?"

He went to the refrigerator and gave me a cold glass bottle of peach-flavored tea. I twisted the cap and took a long pull.

"You want something stronger than that?" Johnny asked. Barry had just finished mixing him a new one, his third since I'd been there.

"Looks like you're drinking enough for both of us." I grinned. "Bet you could give old Sal a run for his money."

Sal Fabell had carefully cultivated his reputation as a heavy boozer, but those who knew him laughingly insisted it was all an act.

Johnny shook his head. "Good old Sal. He sure was good last night, wasn't he? Still got it, after all these years."

"Speaking of those who have it and those who don't, did you get rid of Mr. Harvey Shit, with an E?"

Johnny took another quick sip and shook his head. "I can't, Belz. I promised Elliott."

"Then why don't you tell Elliott to put the son of a bitch on a leash? Or maybe even in a cage?"

His face looked pinched. "I'll talk to him."

I drank some more of the peach-flavored tea and relished its slow, icy descent down my esophagus. "You do that, boss." I stood. "Mind if I borrow Hector for a little evening drive?"

"Where you going now?"

"I've got to see a guy about a murder."

"Murder?" Johnny sounded almost panicked. "Belz, what the hell are you getting into?"

"Relax," I said, draining the last of the tea and setting the bottle down on the table next to the bed. "We're talking ancient history here. Brigid Burgeon and Mark Kaye Jr. Hector? You got anything going for him?"

He shook his head, but the worried look persisted. "You gonna have any time for rehearsals?"

"Sure," I said as I made my way out. "Just let me squeeze in a little time between checking out murders."

Back in my room, Veronica was still busily surfing and typing. She smiled as I came in and said, "Gosh, I forgot how much I missed my laptop. I had a ton of emails to answer. I hope you don't mind."

"You get to any of that stuff I asked you to do?"

She gave me what could have passed for an injured expression. "Of course I did. I did that immediately." Turning, she poised herself above the keyboard. "Who do you want to hear about first? Russell or Sikorski?"

I stretched as I thought about it, then pulled up a chair next to her so I could see the screen, but the print was too small and the effort too great. I massaged the top of my nose and said, "Let's go with Russell. Break it to me gently."

She began reading. "Here's his obit. Leo Russell. Born in 1949. Joined the Chicago Police Department in 1970 after a hitch in the marines. Served during the Vietnam War during something called the Teet Offensive."

"That was 'Tet,' " I said.

"Whatever. Left Chicago in 1978 and came out to join the LAPD. Served with distinction in various capacities including vice and robbery/homicide. He also handled some famous cases, including the Brigid Burgeon death investigation. He retired in 1999, when he went into the private sector. Began his own security company, which specialized in dignitary protection. Died suddenly of a heart attack in 2003."

"That's all you got?"

Her expression changed to one of indignation. "No, I have more. That was just the preliminary round."

I grinned and nodded, leaning back and closing my eyes. I was starting to visualize this whole thing. "Proceed."

"Now, guess what some of the columns said about Detective Russell?"

"That he was rumored to have mob ties?"

Her mouth dropped open. "How did you know?"

I shot her a wry grin. "I'm in the presence of a psychic, remember? Maybe it's rubbing off."

She blinked twice, then went back to the screen. "This columnist named Norman Perona wrote a column in the L.A. Times about how Russell was one step ahead of a federal indictment. Here's a quote. 'Leo Russell's sudden accidental death ends the hopes of U.S. Attorney Alex Powell, the power slugger out of Washington, D.C., who's vowed to break organized crime. Russell, who served for almost thirty years as a cop in our fair city and in Chicago, was long rumored to have had close ties with such mobsters as Vinnie "Meatballs" Messina and Dario "Iceman" Capacaza.' "

"Alex Powell, huh? What ever happened to him?"

She shrugged. "I don't know. Want me to Google him, too?"

"Maybe later," I said. "Keep going on Mr. Russell."

"That's really about all I found. He was quoted as saying, 'Brigid Burgeon's death was another example of the tragedies that often befall the young and beautiful in this town.' Meaning Hollywood, I guess." She frowned. "The asshole."

"You shouldn't speak ill of the dead," I said. "Anything on his partner?"

"That Sikorski guy? Not really. I guess he was the lesser of the two evils."

I chuckled. "That's a good line. Hold on to it, but also try to keep an open mind about people and things. One of the worst things it to proceed into an investigation with preconceived notions. It creates an unconscious tendency to bend the facts to fit your own template."

She nodded and looked down. "I guess I have been doing that, haven't I?"

"We all do from time to time. Let's concentrate on what else we know. Sikorski's a wash. How about the Kayes? There had to be a lot on them."

"There sure was." She smiled and rubbed her finger over the mouse pad. "I came up with tons of them and put them in a document. Mark Kaye Sr. is now in his eighties, but still considered the patriarch of the family. They live in Reno. Have since the seventies when his son—" She paused to mimic placing her finger in her mouth to simulate self-purging. "Mark, ick, Kaye Jr. won a seat in the House as a congressman." She frowned again. "No wonder this country's in so much trouble, electing idiots like him to Congress."

"It's easier than thinking for yourself," I said. "What else did it say about Old Man Kaye?"

She adjusted the mouse some more, pressed the cursor button. "Only that his family had been in industrial research and that's how he made all his money. Especially during the sixties, apparently. They expanded to international status in the following decades."

"Industrial research," I said. "Probably a euphemism for arms dealing. I remember him being mentioned in a couple of those really boring Capitol Hill sessions that they televised during the Reagan years. Maybe when Ollie North was on the hot seat."

"Didn't he make that movie about Vietnam and JFK?"

"That was Oliver Stone. Anything about the current incarnation of Kaye?"

She flipped to another document. "Mark Kaye the Third, son of the late Mark Kaye Jr.—who was killed in a car crash a bit more than a year after Brigid and the same month as my grandmother was murdered—was born in 1975. He's served on the Reno city council and then in the state legislature. He's now, as we know, the front-runner in the special election they're having for governor here."

"Sounds like he has all the qualifications," I said.

"What?"

I leaned forward and tapped the political flier alongside the laptop. "Solid family values, economic prosperity."

"What a joke," she said.

I massaged the bridge of my nose, then took out my phone and the number Pearsol had given me for Eddie Sikorski. It rang five times, then went to an answering machine. The voice sounded gruff on the recording: "Leave a number and a message."

Short and to the point. Maybe Mr. Sikorski would be amenable to giving me the inside scoop on anything he remembered about Brigid's demise. I left a brief message saying who I was and that Officer Pearsol had told me it was all right to call. I ended by reciting my cell phone number and saying, "Please call me back. I'd like to speak with you about one of the cases you might have worked."

"Do you think he will?" Veronica asked as I disconnected.

I shrugged. "I think so. At least that's what Jock told me. I don't think he would have given the okay if he was opposed to the idea."

She made a few more adjustments on the laptop, saving the documents. "So what's our next move?"

"Wait for Sikorski to call back. I'd like to talk to him face-to-face. He lives in the area. I've got Hector lined up for that."

"You *are* planning on taking me along, aren't you?"

"As long as you behave yourself and follow my lead."

"Haven't I done that already?"

"No comment."

Veronica sighed and stood up. "Well, I really need to go back to my room and brush my teeth." She shoved some papers back into the magic carpetbag and headed for the door, pausing before she went out. "You weren't really thinking of going to talk with that Sikorski guy by yourself, were you?"

Only in my dreams, I thought. I smiled and shook my head. "Of course not. I'll call you if anything breaks."

Actually, she was the one who called me about ten minutes later. Her voice sounded confused. "Did you call my room before?"

"What? When?"

"Before. When I was in your room."

I was beginning to wonder if she was trying to reenact a scene from *Alice in Wonderland*. "What are you talking about?"

"Before. When I was in your room and you were up with Mr. Leland."

"Yeah?"

"Well? Did you call my room, telling me to meet you in the lobby?"

"No."

Silence.

"Veronica?"

"Mr. Belzer, I'm kind of scared. I came back here to brush my teeth and saw the message light flashing. When I checked there were two calls from some man saying you were down in the lobby waiting for me and for me to go right down to meet you." She stopped and I could hear her almost panting. "I mean, at first, I thought they were from you, but then something told me that it wasn't. I mean, I'd just come back and there were two, so I listened to them again, and the times they were left were like an hour and a half ago. Ten minutes apart."

I didn't like the sound of this. I'd been working hard at taking the view that while this whole conspiracy thing was possible, and maybe even probable, the imminent danger to anyone was based mostly on Paul and Veronica's overactive imaginations. Paul's death, after all, had been ruled natural, and as far as I knew, it was. Mrs. Perkins had died in a fire. An older lady living in a trailer—excuse me, a mobile home—on oxygen and with some health issues. . . . Stuff like that happens every day. . . . But someone leaving messages on Veronica's hotel phone, saying I wanted her to meet me down in the lobby when I hadn't even called her. . . . My alarm meter went into overdrive. "Stay in your room, and deadbolt it," I said. "I'll be right there."

CHAPTER 11

"Ms. Holmes," the male voice said on the message tape. "I'm contacting you for Mr. Belzer. He's down by the front desk now and wants you to meet him there as soon as possible. Thank you."

The second message was more of the same, adding that he was trying to contact her again. Male voice, deeply resonant, slight nasal quality. . . . Other than that, it was hard to tell much else. I watched Grady Armitage, who was standing next to the sliding glass door leading to the small cement balcony, talking on his cell phone with that serious look on his face. Johnny sat at the table, nursing the drink that room service had brought, with Barry next to him, and Veronica sat on the bed staring up at me. Or at least I think she was on the bed. There were so many various items covering it—clothing, hair dryer, papers, the magic carpetbag—that I had to check twice to be sure. How could she cram all that stuff into just one suitcase?

I thought about asking her, just to break the tension, but Grady disconnected from his cell and stepped over.

"Not much to tell," he said. "The calls came in at 1604 and 1615. That's four o'clock in civilian time."

I nodded. The same time I was in Johnny's room and Veronica was in mine surfing. And she'd said the phone hadn't rung at all in my room.

"Came in from outside the hotel," he continued, "the caller asking for Ms. Holmes by name, and rerouted to her room."

"Any other conversation?" I asked.

He shook his head. "Nothing the clerks can remember. We don't give out guests' room numbers anyway."

"That's great to hear," Veronica said. For the first time since I'd known her, she looked, as Elvis would say, all shook up.

"Maybe it was somebody looking for a date," Johnny offered, but his expression looked about as genuine as that of a three-card monte hustler.

"What you wanna do, Belz?" Grady asked me.

"Yeah, Belz," Johnny echoed. "What *do* you want to do?"

I knew he was alluding to cohosting the telethon, but couldn't he see that I had a real problem here? I gave them a stalling grin and held up my hands. Bowing my head in what looked like a prayer, I actually raced through the facts and options, thinking everything through.

What *did* I know?

An unidentified male caller, pretending to represent me, had called Veronica's room and told her I wanted to meet her in the lobby . . .

Totally false.

The caller had known Veronica's name, but not her room number. That information is confidential. Thank God for small minds and privacy policies.

But he still knew she was staying at this hotel and was friends with me. Okay, "friends" was maybe too strong a word. Associated. But he couldn't know she was in my room, under strict orders not to answer my phone under any circumstances.

But there were no corresponding calls to my room, so the caller wasn't trying to trick both of us into going down to the lobby. He was only after her . . .

The calls came after 4:00 p.m., or sixteen hundred, as Grady said. After we'd returned from our morning jaunt and lunch. That meant the caller probably knew we were back.

Had he been watching us? And if so, why? And, more importantly, who?

The answer was one that I didn't want to consider: *L'Indien* . . . the Indian.

Paul had mentioned he'd been worried about talking to me because of him. Had his concern been based in fact, or had it been just one more of his boozy illusions?

Constance Penroy's notes had mentioned something about him, too. Could that have been where Paul had gotten the idea? Another paranoid delusion of an alcohol-addled brain? But what kind of an Indian? Someone from India, or a Native American?

Maybe I was the one being paranoid . . .

"Belz?" Grady asked. "You still with us?"

I was, and I had a lot of unanswered questions. But first things first.

"Veronica." I said. "What would you say to going back to L.A. and letting me look into this from this end?"

"That's right, kid," Johnny said. "No sense staying around here if things are uncomfortable. It would be a lot easier on all of us if you did go back home."

She looked like she was considering it, then shook her head. "Mr. Belzer, I think you know I can't do that. I can't give up on catching my grandmother's murderer when we're so close."

I probably could have once again argued that we weren't close to much of anything, but on the other hand, the strange calls had tipped the scale enough for me to realize that we had caused some untoward ripples on a pond a lot of people wanted to remain still water. I turned to Barry. "Can we reregister her under another name in a new room? Preferably close to my room. Like next door."

He looked to Johnny, who nodded. Barry went to the hotel phone and began punching digits.

I glanced at Grady. "Champ, can we have a notation put in at the desk that Veronica Holmes is no longer registered at the hotel?"

"Totally doable," he said. "I'll have an extra security watch put on her new room, too."

I hedged. "Let's not make it too obvious. Maybe just extra patrols on the floor?"

"Okay."

"And on all our floors," Johnny said. "Who knows what this creep was after?"

"Roger wilco, Mr. Leland."

"Grady, puh-leeze, call me Johnny."

"You got it, Johnny."

"And you've got to let me buy you a drink later," I said. He nodded and I turned to Veronica. "Pack up your stuff. Barry will take care of the rest."

He waved to us and smiled, still talking in hushed tones on the phone.

Johnny stood up and slapped my shoulder. "Can I talk to you outside for a sec?"

We went out with him and he walked down the hallway, about twenty feet away from the door. I followed him and he turned toward me abruptly. His eyes had a glassy look to them and I could smell the booze on his breath.

"Look, Belz, this is getting more than a bit distracting, ain't it?"

"What do you mean?"

He sighed. "Look, I kind of like the kid, too, but hell, we're getting a little far away from our primary purpose, running all over playing Columbo. Ain't we?"

"As Tonto said to the Lone Ranger when they were surrounded by Indians, what you mean 'we'?"

"Don't fuck with me. You know what I'm talking about, don't you?"

"Suppose you lay it out for me." I knew exactly where he was going with this, but I still wondered why.

"Well, what I mean is," he was speaking more slowly now, like he was tiptoeing through a briar patch, "maybe you ought to see if you can try a little harder to convince her to take that one-way ticket back to Tinseltown and get back to business."

"And 'business' means?"

He shrugged and shot me that famous Johnny Leland grin—the same one that had been endearing him to audiences around the world for forty years. "I mean, you are going to cohost the fucking telethon with me, ain't you?"

He was overusing the F word, and he was drinking too much, and he was being borderline insulting, but he was still my mentor and best friend. I placed my hand on his shoulder. "That's why I'm here." I knew he was waiting for me to agree with him, but I didn't feel right about sending Veronica back at this point. Even though I had no official responsibility for her, I was concerned about her well-being. And sending her back to L.A. after having been stalked in some fashion by the mysterious calls, and after all the coincidental deaths that had occurred recently, didn't seem prudent. I was just about to say I'd be there totally for him when my cell phone rang. I looked at the screen. It was the same number I'd called earlier. Everything Johnny had said seemed to linger in the air in front of me for a split second, but I knew what I had to do.

"Sorry," I said, " but I have to take this." I pressed the button and said hello to Mr. Sikorski.

"Mr. Belzer?" His voice sounded old and crotchety. "I got your message. Some copper named Pearsol from my old department said you been trying to get a hold of me. What can I do for you?"

It suddenly dawned on me that the way things had been going, the real reason I wanted to talk to him might not measure up. I reviewed my options and decided the best course to follow would be to use that tried-and-true principle of persuasion: MSU, better known as "making shit up."

"I'm working on a book," I said. "The mysterious deaths of Hollywood. I heard you might have worked one of the cases I'm interested in."

It sounded like he blew his nose. "What case would that be?"

Again, I had to move cautiously. I was baiting the hook. "We're going to touch on the old standbys, of course. Virginia Rappe, the Black Dahlia, Marilyn . . . we wanted to do George Reeves, but they beat us to it a couple years back with that movie version."

"All those were way before my time. And that movie was pure horse-shit, too."

"That's what we're trying to avoid," I said. "Did you see *Auto Focus*? That movie about Bob Crane's demise?"

"He was another shitbird, but he was killed in Arizona."

This guy sounded like he had enough crankiness to scare off a colony of carpenter ants. "What about Brigid Burgeon?"

I heard the slight catch in his breathing.

"Yeah, I'm familiar with that one."

"Great," I said. "How about we get together for a chat?"

He didn't answer immediately. When he did, it was slow and unsure. "You're that guy who plays the cop on TV, right?"

"I am."

"Yeah, I seen your show. Not bad, and you guys don't portray coppers in a bad light like some of them assholes do." He made a sound like he was either clearing his throat or getting ready to spit up some mucus. "I guess we could do that. My young brother in blue, Pearsol, told me you're in my town right now, huh?"

"I'm in Vegas. We're doing a telethon here Sunday and Monday. When would be a good time for us to talk?"

"Come by tonight, if you want." He gave me his address and I grabbed a pen from Johnny's pocket and wrote it on my hand. After thanking Mr. Sikorski and telling him I'd be out there around 6:45, I disconnected.

Johnny took his pen out of my fingers. "What? No napkins to write on?"

"Left them in my tux for the telethon."

"Okay, Columbo." He grinned. "So I take it you're not sending Miss Ditz back to whence she came?"

I shook my head. "Like I said, I'll be there for the telethon, and for you. This I promise. But I have to make sure things are stabilized for her first."

He raised his eyebrows, then his smile turned to a smirk. "I knew you liked to play detective, but didn't know you'd started another career as a fucking social worker."

"Yeah, the pay's lousy, no benefits, I'm underappreciated, but every once in a while I get to kick someone's ass."

We both laughed as we headed back to Veronica's soon-to-be-vacated room.

Eddie Sikorski lived in Henderson, which is a little bit south of Las Vegas. Hector said we could take Boulder Highway and he'd have Veronica and me there with time to spare. I kept my eyes peeled for anyone following us, and remembered that black Hummer that I'd seen when we'd paid our visit to Mrs. Pearsol. Everything looked clear. The only glitch in the trip came when my cell phone rang with another one of those "unknown" calls with no number listed on my LCD. I wasn't going to answer it, but curiosity got the better of me and I did, but heard only static. Frowning, I put the cell back in my pocket. I knew from past experience that hitting *69 wouldn't do any good.

"Who was that?" Veronica asked.

I shook my head and shrugged.

Her eyes widened. "Do you think it's the same person who called my room?"

"Maybe, maybe not. I'll have to look into it. But first, let's review our agreement."

"Agreement?"

"Right. That you keep your mouth shut and let me do the talking. Remember?"

She started to say something, but thought better of it and just nodded.

I turned and watched the sun setting over the mountains as we sped south, then tapped the screen. It lowered and Hector grinned.

"What's up, boss?"

"You know where this place is at?"

"GPS, remember?" he said, tapping the device on his dash.

"Okay, do something else for me. Keep your eyes peeled for anyone following us. Especially when we're inside this guy's house. Could be a black Hummer."

I caught a glance of his furrowed brow in the rearview mirror.

"Black Hummer, huh? *No problema.*"

We arrived at Sikorski's place shortly thereafter. It was typical Nevada real estate. Ranch-style stucco with one of those curved tile roofs. Attached garage and a driveway. It was set about fifty feet back from the street and looked pretty much like all the rest of the houses on the block. A cream-colored Caddy sat outside the garage door.

I held the door for Veronica and we strolled up and rang the bell. An older guy I assumed was Sikorski opened the door and gave us a cop's once-over. He was thin with a fringe of white hair around his ears and nothing on top but baldpate. From the looks of his skin, he didn't spend much time in the bright sunshine. His grin seemed friendly, though.

"You Belzer?"

"Yes, sir." I extended my hand. "And you must be Eddie Sikorski."

"Right." We shook and I introduced Veronica as my assistant.

Inside, it was apparent he lived alone and it was the maid's day off. Stacks of newspapers, magazines, and DVDs sat on a coffee table in the small living room. A three-foot plasma-screen TV adorned the opposite wall. Sikorski motioned for us to sit on the sofa and plopped himself down in a nearby easy chair. It looked like it got a lot of use.

"Oh, pardon me all to hell," he said. "You two care for something to drink?"

Before I could decline, Veronica asked for some water.

He nodded and raised himself from the chair with considerable effort. He grimaced as he straightened. "Damn knee's shot. Supposed to have a replacement, but I been putting it off."

"They can do wonders with those now," I said. "But I'm sure Veronica would be glad to give you a hand."

"I never turn down an offer from a pretty girl," he said with a grin.

She smiled and stood as they went toward the kitchen. "Are you sure you don't want anything, Mr. Belzer?" she called over her shoulder.

"Maybe some Snapple would be nice," I said, standing. I wanted to look at the numerous plaques hanging on his wall next to the TV. "Peach is my favorite."

Sikorski snorted. "Snapple? Not unless it has 'Budweiser' pasted over it. You'll have to settle for good old Lake Mead H_2O."

The plaques commemorated his thirty years on the LAPD. Several were from private organizations thanking him for participatory or contributing gestures. Pretty much standard stuff for a retired copper. Several framed, eight-by-ten photographs hung next to the plaques that traced his career. An old black-and-white shot of him graduating from the police academy, a photo of him receiving letters or awards from various dignitaries, and a group that piqued my interest even more. The first was of Sikorski and a heavyset guy, who looked like a human salamander, standing side by side and flashing grinning leers toward the camera. The next was a picture of Eddie with a movie starlet, and then one of him and the salamander again. In this one they were standing alongside Sal Fabell, and it looked like Sal had even autographed it. The handwriting was almost indecipherable, but I could make it out: "To my two good bodyguarding cop buddies and honorary paisans, Leo and Eddie. Go ahead and stay drunk next time. It's easier that way. —Sal."

I sat down as they came back, with Veronica carrying a metal tray with three glasses on it. When Sikorski had settled he grabbed his glass, the one with the foamy head on it, and sipped a copious amount.

"Ahhh," he said, wiping his lips with the back of his hand. "King of beers. Sure I can't get you one?"

I sipped my water, pretending it was peach-flavored iced tea, and respectfully declined.

He took another long sip and leaned forward. "So tell me about this book you're writing."

I gave him a brief repetition of the MSU that I'd used earlier on the phone, ending with, "I'd be glad to mention your participation in the acknowledgments section."

He drank some more beer and shook his head. "No, thanks. I got enough problems without somebody else wanting to sue me. You know how many times I was sued when I was on the department?"

"Way too many, I'll bet."

"You're goddamn right." He snorted and drank some more, then wiped his mouth with the back of his hand. "Forty-three lawsuits in my thirty years. Most of them in the goddamn eighties when the judges were so intent on screwing Reagan that they were letting everybody off. Shitbirds like Johnnie Cochran made a mint. The scumbags would get arrested, then go to court and get acquitted because of the judges, then they'd march over to their lawyer's office and they'd file suit. They all knew it was a money-making proposition. It cost the city more to fight the suit than to pay them off." He shook his head and took another drink. There was only a little bit left in the glass. He held it up and said to Veronica, "Hey, sweetie, get me another one, would ya? You know where they are now."

Instead of exploding into a tirade, like I expected, she merely smiled and took his glass back into the kitchen.

"So, you see, Mr. Belzer, I got no need to be mentioned in anybody's book. Get it?"

"Got it."

"Good." He belched just as Veronica returned with his now-full glass, the foamy head blooming out of the top like an effulgent flower. Sikorski sipped at the foam and grinned. "You stay around here long enough, sweetie, I'll show you how to tilt the glass when you pour so you don't get so much foam."

Ah, the beer drinker's art. Figuring he'd been lubricated enough, I got right to it.

"Eddie, I'm really interested in what you can tell us about Brigid Burgeon's death. You were there, right?"

His mouth twisted into a lopsided grin, like an adolescent admitting to his first taste. "I was there. First patrol officer on the scene, in fact. The maid found her and called the cops. I happened to be on patrol in the area and jumped the call."

"So you saw the body?"

The smile disappeared. "Barely. I went in there, but Leo had somehow beaten me to it."

"Leo? Leo Russell?"

He pointed to indicate I'd gotten it right as he tilted the glass. "He was in dicks, of course. That's why I couldn't figure how in the hell he got there quicker than me." He shrugged. "Not that it mattered much. Being in patrol, I knew that I'd pretty much get stuck guarding the crime scene anyway. But I'd seen her movies and she was a fox."

"What exactly did you see?" I shot a warning look toward Veronica. The last thing I needed now was for her to break my rhythm.

"It was like they said, she was nude. On top of the covers. Leo let me sneak a peek. Not that she looked sexy or anything at that point. I could tell she was dead. Lividity had set in. That's where the blood settles to the bottom of the body and causes discoloration."

"Postmortem lividity," I said.

His expression brightened. "Oh yeah, I almost forgot. You play that cop on TV, don't ya?"

"As realistically as I can." I smiled at him.

"Damn glad to hear that." He swallowed some more of the amber liquid, then exhaled loudly. I could smell the beer from here.

"Was the lividity on her back or her front?"

"She was facedown." He held out a flat palm to illustrate. "So it was on her front. Her boobs were—" He stopped and recoiled as he looked at Veronica. "Sorry, miss."

"That's okay, Eddie. I've heard of boobs before."

I gave her an approving look. If she kept this up, I might even consider letting her ask one or two questions later on.

He shrugged and glanced downward, a grin spreading across his face. The beer was loosening him up. "Anyway," he said, "her breasts showed the discoloration and were compressed. She didn't have no implants. Didn't need 'em, as far as I could tell." He cupped his hands in front of his chest and gave me one of those guy-to-guy looks and a wink.

I returned it. "So did Leo ever tell you how he beat you there?"

"Lemme tell you something about Leo, God rest his soul. He had an almost supernatural ability to know things. When things were gonna happen."

"You and he were partners a long time?"

"Yeah, he was impressed with me that day of the Burgeon thing." Eddie's eyes got that full-of-pride look. "You see, I didn't want to jump in and act like I was in charge. He was the dick, I asked him real polite what he wanted me to do. He told me later that he appreciated my attitude. Put in a good word for me, and kind of took me under his wing. Got me into plainclothes and then grabbed me as his partner on a lot of stuff."

"That him?" I pointed to the pictures on the wall.

"Yeah." He made an attempt to get up, fell back, then tried a second time and made it. "Lemme show ya something here." Sikorski removed the picture of him, Russell, and Sal and wiped the glass with his sleeve before handing it to me. "See that? That's me, Leo, and Sal Fabell. The singer."

"You know him?"

He barked out a quick chuckle. "Not like Leo did, but we did a couple gigs bodyguarding him. Shit, we made some good bucks doing that, lemme tell ya."

"I'll bet." I mustered a concerned expression of reticence to make it look like the next part was difficult for me. Sometimes it pays to be an actor. "Eddie, I'd be lying to you if I didn't tell you that I'm a bit curious about all those allegations that Leo was tied to the mob."

His face soured like he'd just sucked on a rotten egg, and he waved his hand dismissively. "Horseshit, that's what I say. Leo had friends, sure. Were some of those friends less than reputable? Sure. But he was from Chicago. He knew a lot of them guys from his old neighborhood. Growing up. I never seen him take a dime, and that's the gospel."

I nodded.

His face froze. "Wait a minute, you ain't insinuating that I was a bagman, are ya?"

"Not at all. I know better."

"Damn straight. I mean, Christ, would I be living like this if I'd been on the take?" His hand fluttered toward the substellar surroundings.

While he was still loose, I tossed him a curveball. "The reason I asked, I heard that some reporter was saying that stuff about Leo. Constance Penroy. Ever hear of her?"

His head shot back as he barked a laugh. "Hear of her? She was a pain in our asses for months. Months. Calling and asking all kinds of stupid questions. It finally got to the point Leo wouldn't talk to her. Shoved the calls to me, and my job was to keep repeating that I didn't know nothing."

"What did she ask about?"

"Stuff." His head waggled a bit.

"Stuff?"

"About Burgeon's death. We told her it looked like an accidental OD, but she wasn't buying it. She was hot about Brigid and some politician, too."

"Mark Kaye Jr.?"

"Yeah." His face twisted into a smile. "Leo danced a jig when we heard she'd kicked the bucket." He was obviously loosened up quite a bit by the beers. Maybe this would be fruitful, after all.

I noticed Veronica stiffen.

"We ended up catching that case, too, believe it or not." He laughed at his recollection. "What a fucking mess that crime scene was. Shit and vomit and blood all over the place. Like she just exploded inside." He chuckled again. "Leo said she shit herself to death and fell out her asshole. The old bitch."

That was all Veronica needed. "Don't you dare call her that."

Oh no, here we go again, I thought.

"Huh?" Sikorski said. The smirk faded as his face slid into the perfect picture of inebriated befuddlement.

"I said, don't you dare call her that, you pathetic old drunk."

"What did you say to me?" His mouth dropped open, his fists balled up.

"You're a pathetic old drunk," Veronica shot back. She'd gotten to her feet. I got to mine, too, and began moving her toward the door.

"Eddie, it's been a slice," I said over my shoulder. "We got to get going."

"Take this hippie bitch with you." His face became beet red. "The nerve of it. Coming into a man's house and insulting him. Don't you know a man's home is his castle?"

"What are you going to use for a moat?" she yelled. "Beer?"

I leaned close to her and whispered, "Now is not the time to get stressed out."

"I am *not* stressed *out*." She enunciated each word, like a heavy-duty stamping machine crushing tin cans at the scrap factory. "I knew that man was going to be a pig. I *knew* it."

It looked like her "psychic abilities" were beginning to manifest themselves once more. But this time, I had to agree with her. I managed to extricate us from the castle and get her into the limo. Hector lowered the screen, his white teeth gleaming under his mustache. "Where to now, boss?"

"Back to the Monticello." I stared at Veronica and wondered if I should stop and get some duct tape for the next interview.

CHAPTER 12

"You have a way with conversation that ends conversation," I told Veronica as I escorted her to her new room. Unfortunately, it was right next to mine, just like I'd requested. I was so POd that I could have used some wiggle room. We'd ridden back most of the way in silence, with her occasional attempts to apologize. I'd cut her off each time. Not that I thought we were going to get much more out of old Eddie anyway. My guess was that Russell had seen Sikorski as someone stupid enough not to ask too many questions, and grateful enough to appreciate all the perks Russell, Johnny-on-the-spot death investigator of the rich and famous, could throw his way. Someone who would keep his mouth shut and accept the chaff as pure gold. As it was, I had promised to meet Grady for that drink. I admonished her to stay in the room, deadbolt the door, and not answer the phone.

"If I want you, I'll call your cell," I told her. "You do the same for me."

She nodded, completely subservient again. It was hard to stay mad at her, but she was giving me a lot of reasons to practice.

"Where are you going?" she asked.

"I promised Grady I'd buy him a drink when he got off. Plus, I've got three voice messages from Johnny on my cell that I haven't listened to."

"Ah, could I borrow your laptop?"

"My laptop? For what?"

She shrugged. "I thought it might be a good idea to start writing down what we've learned so far."

"You're right, it is a good idea." I didn't feel right about giving it to her, especially since I hadn't checked my emails yet, but on the other hand, if it kept her out of trouble . . . and my hair. "All right, you can use it. But I'm coming by when I get back in an hour or so and I want it back, understand?"

She nodded, all smiles again. I glanced at my watch: 8:15. "Are you hungry?"

She shook her head.

"Good. Stay in the room, use my laptop, rent a dirty movie if you want, but don't leave, understand? If you get hungry later, order room service under the name we reregistered you under."

"What's that?"

I smiled. "Mary Goodnight."

She assured me she would. I gave her my computer and I checked the hallway as I left. Empty. I figured she'd be safe enough. She seemed to have little taste for excursions, unless she was with me. Maybe she just liked making my life miserable. I dialed my voicemail and listened to Johnny's first call. It was listed at two hours ago.

"Belz, we got problems," he said. "Give me a call."

Number two, ten minutes later: "Belz, where you at, man? Call me."

And finally, after another seven minutes: "Okay, Columbo, I guess you're still out playing detective or whatever. Anyway, I'm up to my knees in troubles. Our second opening act, that group the Loners, canceled on me. Canceled with two days left before the fucking telethon. We got to figure something out, bro. Like I said, call me. Please."

So I did. And I got his voicemail. I left messages on both his cell and his hotel phone, mentioning that I was going to be in the second-floor bar buying Grady a drink. I called the champ next. He answered on the third ring.

"You still on duty?" I asked.

"Been off duty for a couple hours now," he said. "Just catching up on some time sheets in the office."

"Got time for that drink now?" I asked.

His chuckle was deep and resonant. "Sure. Where you at?"

"On my way to the Marebello Room."

"Meet you there," he said.

And ten minutes later, he did. We settled into a booth with two drinks. Red wine for me and a B and B for him.

"Thanks again for helping me out with the kid."

"All part of my job." He raised the glass and took a tiny sip of the amber fluid.

I grinned. "So how did you get to be in charge of security here, again?"

"I used to be a deputy sheriff in Santa Fe County. I retired from the force and came down here. But I'm not totally in charge. I'm just a lieutenant."

"You juggled a full-time police job while you were a contender?"

"Most boxers do." He grinned.

"Most boxers never get a shot at the title, either."

"Just like most of us never see that big money we dreamed of." He had a wistful look in his eyes. "Couldn't afford to quit my day job. Or my night one, neither. But back in the day, when I was a cop, they'd let me train at the academy for free when I had a big fight coming up."

A big fight . . . I wondered what Grady's reaction would be to the MMA bout. Maybe Johnny could get another ticket somehow.

"Speak of the devil," Grady said, "there's Mr. Lessing now. He's in charge of things."

I glanced across and saw three men coming into the bar. One of them was Elliott Collins. "Who's who?"

Grady picked up his drink as he spoke, his lips barely moving. "The guy on the left's Otto Lessing, chief of security at the hotel. Gave me my job here, so I can't say much bad about him." He brought the glass to his lips and drank. "The one in the middle's Royce Ocean, the hotel general manager, and the last guy's—"

"I know the last guy," I broke in. "Elliott Asshole, Harvey Smithe's agent."

Grady chuckled, then said, "Mr. Collins ain't such a bad guy."

"Easy for you to say. He's been strong-arming Johnny to put that jerk Smithe, with an E, in the telethon, even after the guy made such an ass out of himself last night."

"Yeah, I know. We see a lot of Mr. Smithe at this hotel."

"You do? Sorry to hear that."

Grady chuckled again. "They book him a lot for the lounge act at the bar downstairs. The Region. We usually have to assign a couple extra men to the security detail because he gets in so many fights with the patrons."

"Fights? Easygoing Harvey?" I laid the sarcasm on as heavy as I dared. "That's hard to believe. Can he deal?"

Grady smirked. "Only from the bottom of the deck. Swings like a cheerleader. No chin, either."

"Well, I hope his stand-up has improved since I saw him get booed off the stage in Jersey."

That got another chuckle from Grady. "He thinks he's a white Chris Rock. Insulting people in the audience, flirting with girls on dates. We got to keep him from getting his ass kicked."

I watched as the trio ensconced themselves in a booth that a waitress had hurriedly cleared off for them. "Why do they keep booking him if he causes so many problems? His clout?"

"Exactly. He's related to Mr. Ocean. A nephew, or cousin, or something."

"Ah, nepotism. Almost as original as a name like Ocean. And for a minute there I was worried it was cronyism."

At that moment, Elliott's eyes happened to lock with mine and he excused himself from the other two men.

"Oh, joy of joys," I murmured as it became clear he was coming over to talk to me.

"Richard," Elliott said. "How's Johnny?"

"I don't know. Why don't you ask him?"

His nose twitched and he tilted his head to the side. "You have heard, haven't you? He was taken to the emergency room a couple of hours ago."

"What?" I glanced at Grady, who looked as dumbfounded as I did. "What happened?"

"I don't know. I just heard about it from Royce. He sai—"

"What hospital's he at?" I asked as I got up.

Elliott shrugged. "How the hell should I know?"

I ignored him and pulled out my cell, hitting the speed dial for Johnny's number. It rang once and went directly to voicemail. "Dammit," I said, disconnecting.

I felt a calming hand on my shoulder. Grady's. He was talking quietly in hushed tones in his own cell. When he disconnected, he said, "He's over at Garden Star. It's on Maryland. I'll drive you."

Grady got me there in record time, taking a few side streets and pulling up in front of Garden Star Hospital and Medical Center. The place looked ominous at night, but what hospital didn't? He dropped me at the ER entrance and told me he'd catch up as soon as he'd parked. I rushed through the retracting doors and went right to the information desk.

"A friend of mine was—," I started to say when I heard someone call, "Richard!"

I turned and saw a very worried-looking Barry jogging toward me with a cell phone in his hand.

"I was just going outside to try and call you," he said. "They won't let us use these inside here."

"Never mind that. Where's Johnny?"

He motioned for me to follow him and turned back toward the hallway he'd just come out of. During a trip through a couple of corridors, all painted with an eerie white and tan design, Barry explained what had happened. He and Johnny had been trying to get a hold of me when Johnny started having chest pains. At first he waved them off, then they got suddenly worse. "His color was awful, just awful," Barry said. "He was white as a ghost. I insisted we call the paramedics, and they transported him right away, after hooking him up to one of those machines."

He turned into a room and I saw Johnny lying in a bed, IV lines in his arm, an oxygen tube hooked under his nose, his bare chest sprouting wires from white sticky patches, and several telemetry machines showing a moving parabolic line, punctuated by a steady beeping sound. I drew some measure of comfort from it, having been indoctrinated by countless episodes of *ER,* where all you hear is the flatline buzz when the protagonist walks into the hospital room. He smiled as I approached, the oxygen line looking like some ludicrous plastic mustache.

"Look who's here," Barry said.

Johnny waved and said in a whisper, "I guess this is one way to get you to return my fucking phone calls, huh?"

"Johnny." I grabbed his hand in both of mine, and then, because I couldn't think of anything else to say, asked, "How you doing?"

He laughed a little. I took that as a good sign.

"Felt like one of them MMA guys had me in one hell of a bear hug and wouldn't let go. Feeling better now, though."

He didn't look "better," but I smiled and nodded. "What are they saying?"

"What's who saying?" He managed a weak laugh. "You know those fucking doctors. The first question they ask is what kind of insurance you got."

"They're not sure what exactly it is at this point," Barry said from the other side of the bed. "But they are recommending he stay overnight and take some tests tomorrow."

"Which he's going to do," I said.

"The horse's ass I am," Johnny said. "Did you get my voice message? I got a huge gap to fill in—"

"Which Barry and I will take care of for you," I said. Had it been my imagination, or had the steady heart monitor sound just skipped a beat? I looked back to the telemetry screen for reassurance. The erratic orange line continued its normal regularity. At least I hoped it was normal regularity.

When Grady got there, I gave him a quick briefing and thanked him again for driving me. I took out my wallet but his big hand closed over mine.

"Not necessary, Belz."

I told him I wanted at least to pay for the parking. He grinned and shook his head. As I was repocketing my wallet, I heard Johnny's voice behind me.

"Ya cheap bastard. You had to strong-arm poor Grady into driving you over here so you didn't have to pay for a fucking cab, huh?"

His tone was still weak, but I figured if he could at least crack a joke, albeit a questionable one, he might not be as bad as I'd feared. I whispered a silent prayer that it would be so.

"You and Johnny are pretty tight, huh?" Grady asked as he was driving Barry and me back to the hotel.

"We go back a long way. He was a star and he stopped in at one of my stand-up routines in Jersey once when I was just starting out." I smiled at the memory. "After the show, he came by my dressing room, if you could call it that. More like a janitorial closet they'd cleaned out."

"Sounds like some of the places I fought at."

"Here was the king of comedy coming into my little penny-ante room, saying how much he liked my routine." I shook my head. "Sometimes I still can't believe it. It marked the beginning of things taking off for me. Before that my friend and I used to meet at McDonald's every day and write jokes on napkins, trying to come up with a winner."

"People think just 'cause you got there, it was easy."

I shot him a sideways look. "Since you won't take any of my money for helping me out, how's about going to the MMA fights with me on Saturday?"

"MMA? The one at the hotel?"

"Yeah. Johnny got me tickets. What do you say?"

"Sounds good. Thanks."

I turned and looked to Barry in the backseat. "You got that?"

"Not a problem." He made a few moves on his laptop. "I'll take care of that right now."

I thought about asking him if he was joined at the hip with that thing, but decided not to look a gift horse in the mouth. I glanced at my watch and saw it was now closing in on 11:30. Time had stopped for me when we were in the hospital, and now I realized it might have stopped for us, but it had gone right on ticking for everybody else. Hopefully Veronica would be fast asleep by now, and the thought of waking her from her slumber, and hearing her razor-over-glass voice after the evening I'd been through, was hardly appealing. When Barry stopped fiddling on the keyboard, I asked if he had an Internet connection on that thing.

"Of course." He tapped the broadband card.

"You think I might use it for a moment to check my emails?"

"Sure." He made a few more deft moves and handed it over the seat.

I signed in and listened for the familiar voice telling me I had mail. At least I hoped I did. From Harlee.

My heart jumped when I saw her familiar screen name. I quickly fingered the mouse into position and clicked it.

> *Hi,*
>
> *I'd be lying if I said I wasn't a little bit concerned after translating this. It's very hard to decipher. Like some kind of code or something. And, I'm hoping you aren't involved in something like last time. Honey, please leave the never-ending pursuit of truth and justice to your TV show and just come back home safe.*
>
> *That said, the translation's attached. I hope it helps, whatever it is you need it for, but I mean it: stay out of trouble . . . In other words, don't make me come out there. ;-)*
>
> *Love you,*
>
> *Harlee*

That's my one and only, I thought as I smiled. I was one lucky guy.

I didn't really want to download the translation on Barry's laptop. Who knows what it said, and I was honestly feeling too beat to make sure I deleted it afterward. I closed the email, re-marked it as unread, and signed off. Tomorrow would be another day.

CHAPTER 13

Early the next morning I figured I'd be the one waking Veronica up for a change, but some people follow directions with an exacting literalness that drives me up a wall. The phone in her room rang fifteen times before it went to voicemail. I left a quick one, saying I hoped I wasn't disturbing her beauty rest, but I needed my laptop back as soon as possible.

As soon as I hung up, my phone rang.

"Did you just try to call me?" she asked.

"Ah, yeah. Were you in the shower or something?"

"No, I've been up for a while."

"Then why the hell didn't you answer the phone?"

"You said for me not to, remember?"

My instructions from yesterday were a distant memory, caught in a fog. It had been after midnight by the time we'd gotten back from the hospital, and despite being awash with fatigue, I'd found sleeping problematic at best. I glanced at my watch: 7:38, and here I was all showered, shaved, and dressed for action. The business center wouldn't be open for at least another twenty minutes. I asked if she wanted breakfast.

"I guess so. Are we going out?"

I pondered the wisdom of this. If someone was stalking her, and most likely me as well, it might be better to keep a low profile for a while. And to make some appearance changes. I asked what she wanted and told her I'd order it on room service. In the meantime, I needed my laptop back.

"Oh, sure," she said. "I figured you were going to come for it last night, but you didn't and I fell asleep. Sorry."

"No problem. I had a rough time last night."

"Is something wrong?"

I considered needling her about being a self-proclaimed psychic, but didn't want to open that can of worms again. "Johnny's in the hospital."

"Oh my God. What happened?"

"They're not sure. Running some tests today, which is where I'm heading after we eat."

"Can I go, too?"

"Unh-uh, I've got something else for you to do."

"What's that?"

Better to break it to her gently. "I'll tell you later, while we're enjoying breakfast."

She started to protest, but I cut her off by reminding her of her latest round of promises to do whatever I said from last night. I figured it would be good until at least 8:30 or 9:00. Besides, what I had in mind for her wasn't at all unpleasant for a girl. I told her to hand the laptop out the door when I knocked the old "shave and a haircut" on her door.

"The what?"

"Never mind, I'll be there in about half a minute." I hung up.

I took the laptop from her, slipped back into my room, and hooked up to read my email. I couldn't resist rereading Harlee's email from last night, but her underlying concern and her request that I "leave the never-ending pursuit of truth and justice to my TV show" stuck with me like an undigested hunk of bread in my stomach. Was that what I was doing? Chasing justice? Playing a cop in real life?

I told myself I was merely seeking to stabilize things. Of course, that's what Bush and Cheney kept saying about Iraq.

I downloaded the attachment and read it. Harlee had put an epigraph of sorts at the top:

This thing reads like a fragment from someone's
personal diary. A lot of it didn't make sense, so I tried to
translate it as best I could. You'll have to tell me all about
it soon.

DMMCOT.

Love,

Harlee (your obedient wife and expert

translator) ;-)

I smiled as I read that last part. If the gossip columnists ever got hold of that, forget it. Of course, I wouldn't have to worry about any embarrassment. Harlee would kill me first. DMMCOT—don't make me come out there.

I suddenly thought about calling her and telling her to take the first plane west, but thought better of it. Although I wasn't totally convinced that there was an imminent danger, enough had happened that I didn't want her to be in harm's way. Veronica, either. The kid could be blindsided very easily with her naïveté and hair-trigger temper. If only she could learn to keep her mouth shut. Of course, telling her to follow my example in that department was like asking my dog not to jump on the sofa after I'd plopped down on it.

I read the translation.

> Freddie has told me very little about him. The
> Indian. Only that he's the one. And that he's a
> legend already. Very dangerous man. Bragged
> about being in a lot of places south of the border
> as "a freelance employee." That means assassin.
> Fits with KSr <sic> taking down Salvador in '73,
> and planting the gun in his hand. Talked about a

Panama assignment that he was contracted for at
some future date. One for the Gipper. He wouldn't
say much else, but I'll get it out of him. Pillow talk
will do that. Brigid knew that. If only her little
black book hadn't vanished that night, but Freddie
shook his head and said it was gone. Irretrievably.
More pillow talk will be scheduled for that. Mmm,
he may be Freddie the Fox, but he's my fox. And
he is kind of sweet. I have two of the whos. What
I have to figure is the why and how. Why would
a G/freelancer take the time out to kill a movie
starlet? And who took the diary? What secrets were
in it? Was KSr worried about adverse publicity for
KJr? Or did he tell her too much? Maybe some
pillow talk of their own? And I can't wait to learn
more about his video productions. Once I have
those whys and hows, I'll blow the lid off this
whole thing. Mr. Pulitzer, I think I'm ready for my
close-up now . . .

I read it again, not liking it much better the second time. The word
"assassin" added a whole new dimension to the game. And the mention of
Salvador '73 and the G/freelancer . . .

Salvador Allende, the president of Chile, who died in a coup instigated
by the CIA in 1973? The reports said that Allende had committed suicide,
but the rumor was that the CIA had placed the last nail in his coffin. Or
was it his temple? And the Panama allusion . . . If Constance wrote this in
'77, that was after the '76 election when Reagan, aka the Gipper, had made
such a big deal about the U.S. "giving away" the Panama Canal. Omar
Torrijos, the Panamanian strongman, was killed in a mysterious plane
crash right after Reagan took office. One for the Gipper? Could someone
connected to Reagan in '76 have promised the Indian gainful employment
south of the border if the "Great Communicator" won the presidency in
1980?

Why would a G/freelancer take the time out to kill a movie starlet? The "G" obviously meant the government, but Constance's question still remained: Brigid had been involved with Congressman Mark Kaye Jr. Maybe he'd confessed some top-secret things to her . . . pillow talking . . . but it still seemed a stretch. Theories had been plentiful about Brigid's death, and most of them involved theories that Old Man Kaye, Junior's father, had bumped her off because he felt she was detrimental to his son's political career. The old man, who'd made his fortune as an arms dealer, was rumored to have had ties to the mob and the CIA. And if the Indian had bragged about doing Allende . . .

Obviously, I was going to have to find out more about this Indian dude, most specifically what he looked like, and, if possible, make sure Veronica and I both steered clear of him. And what the hell was she referring to with his "video productions"? I'd never heard of them.

My cell phone rang and I checked the screen: unknown. I answered it and got a lot of static. Disconnecting, I scrolled my list for cell phone service and called, asking for their security department. After answering a slew of dumb questions, including verifying my first pet and my mother's maiden name, I finally got through to someone.

"This is Bernie from security. How may I help you?"

"Bernie, this is Richard Belzer. I've been receiving harassing phone calls over the past couple of days. I wonder if you could check the records and give me the number so we can find out who it is?"

"When was the last one, sir?"

"About five minutes ago."

Bernie took my cell phone information and put me on hold. I waited what seemed like an interminable time, and he came back on.

"Mr. Belzer?"

"Bernie?"

"Yes, sir. I checked the number. It's the first time it's called you."

I thought about telling him I was reasonably certain the number hadn't called me at all. It was someone using a phone with that number. But I didn't. Instead I rattled off times, as close as I could remember, when the other calls had come.

"Well, it's pretty hard to find them unless you have specific times for me to look for, sir."

"Can you email me a list of all my incoming calls in the past week?"

"Yeah, I guess I can do that." He sounded uncertain.

"Good." I told him my email address, then asked, "Out of curiosity, who does that last number come back to?"

"It's unlisted."

Figures, I thought. I ended by reminding Bernie that I'd be expecting that email sooner rather than later. After disconnecting, I downloaded Harlee's translation to a separate document and stored it on my laptop's hard drive. Then I went down to the business center where I asked the girl to hook me up to a printer. She did, and I printed out the translation and stuck it in my pocket. After disconnecting my computer, I turned to the girl behind the counter. She was staring at me with big blue eyes.

"Are you Richard Belzer?" she asked.

"I am."

"Cool. Could I, like, get your autograph?" She tentatively held out a pad of paper and a pen.

Ah, the life of a celebrity. I flashed her one of my medium-wattage smiles and asked, "And how do you want this signed?"

" 'To Hank,' please."

"Hank?"

"It's for my boyfriend," she said, beaming. "He just loves your show to pieces."

To pieces? I scribbled something illegible and asked her if there was a beauty shop in the hotel.

"Fifth floor. Do you want me to make you an appointment?"

I almost asked if she thought I needed one, but I shook my head and left. I stopped on five and saw an arrow pointing the way to the Monticello Salon. Inside, I slipped the receptionist a hefty tip and set up an appointment for Veronica in an hour and a half. I figured that would give us enough time to eat, and plan the day's activities.

On the way back up to my room, I called Barry's cell.

"Any news?" I asked him.

"Nothing. I'm getting ready to go over there in about an hour. You have any ideas about what we can do to fill the opening void?"

"Yeah, I got an idea. Tell you what. I'll meet you over there in a bit. I have a couple things to take care of first."

After looking up and down the empty hallway, I knocked the "shave and a haircut" on Veronica's door. She opened it up and I slipped inside. She looked like she'd scrubbed her face and washed her hair and put on a duplicate outfit from yesterday. New clothes were in the picture, also.

"Time to order breakfast," I said.

"And then what?"

"And then you've got an appointment at the fifth-floor beauty parlor. It's under the name of Mary Goodnight."

"Beauty parlor?" She shook her head. "No way."

"Look," I said, "you need a makeover. A complete makeover. You might have some badass dude stalking you, and remember, for all practical purposes Veronica Holmes is no longer staying at this hotel."

"So?"

"So, we need a little wiggle room. Throw him off, if he's still out there. A new look for you."

"But won't he know it's me when he sees us together?"

"We'll travel a ways apart, with a couple of Grady's guys tagging us."

"Tagging?"

"It's a cop term, okay? Following."

She sighed and nodded. "And after my makeover, then what?"

I held up my fingers, ticking off each point. "First, the new hairstyle. Keep it the same color if you want to, but I've always had a thing for redheads." She frowned. I continued. "Second, I've got two of the makeup gals from the telethon coming up to the parlor to show you new ways of putting on your makeup."

"But I don't wear makeup."

"Exactly. And three, new clothes. You're going from the fifth floor to the boutique on level one. They're going to fix you up with some new, dynamite outfits."

"What's wrong with this?" She held her palms outward.

I studied the washed-out blouse and oversize blue jeans.

"Everything," I said.

"Why are you doing this?"

"I just told you," I said.

"Come on. What's the real reason?"

I shrugged.

"That's not good enough. Do you expect me to roll over like some trained poodle?"

"Listen, I can't even get you to sit and shut up." She looked offended, so I softened it. "Sorry. Look, I know it looks like I've got this *My Fair Lady* thing going, but I actually have several good reasons."

"Oh yeah? Name one."

"Well, you're a very pretty girl, and I need you looking like a knockout for something later this afternoon."

"And what's that?"

I raised one eyebrow. "A guy who likes pretty girls."

After escorting Veronica to the beauty shop, and making sure the makeup girls would follow in about an hour, I called Grady's cell and advised him of the situation.

"No problem, Belz, I'll have one of the guys keep an eye on that floor."

"Most inconspicuously, right?"

He laughed. "Exactly."

I thanked him and called Barry. Luckily, he hadn't left yet, and I told him I was going to accompany him to the hospital. He seemed pleased.

"Great, Johnny's already been threatening to check himself out this morning," he said. "You can help me convince him to stay a bit longer."

I told him I would, but wondered if even I would be able to convince Johnny of anything. The man's stubbornness was legendary.

When we arrived at the hospital, I figured Johnny was feeling better because he was arguing with the doctor.

"What's this fucking test gonna prove anyway?" I heard his distinctive voice saying as I neared the door.

"Mr. Leland, please—"

"Please, my ass," Johnny's voice bellowed.

Barry and I exchanged glances. His appeared totally distraught.

"Where do I sign to get outta here? I got a goddamn telethon to run."

I stepped around the doorjamb. "Not till the day after tomorrow you don't."

"Belz." His head recoiled slightly, like he'd been clipped by a quick jab. "Man, am I glad to see you." He still had the plastic hoses running along his cheeks to the coupling under his nostrils.

"Likewise. Now quit giving these people a hard time and take the damn tests."

"Easy for you to say. You know what they want to do to me?" He sounded serious, but I thought I saw a hint of the old Johnny Leland smile beneath the plastic hookup. "They're talking about putting some fucking camera thing up a vein in my leg to check my heart."

"Actually, we use an arterial vent," the doctor said. He didn't look old enough to shave every day. Sort of like a slightly older Doogie Howser with a fraternity pin and a fledgling goatee that looked more like somebody's armpit. Maybe Neil Patrick Harris had a much younger twin brother. "The procedure is not that high-risk."

"Oh no?" Johnny said. "How high is it?"

"Ninety-five percent of all patients undergoing an angiogram have no complications whatsoever," Doogie the Second said.

Johnny's mouth curled into a half smile. "So what you're saying is, five people out of every hundred do have complications, huh?"

Doogie looked ready to spout off some more reassuring statistics when I raised my hands between them. "Doctor, is there a less invasive procedure available?"

"Well, we could use magnetic resonance imagery. However, if an obstruction is found, it would require a subsequent, and possibly more intrusive, surgery."

"And are any of these tests necessary?" Johnny asked.

"I wouldn't recommend it if I didn't think it necessary. Plus, it provides immediate access to any blockages, should an angioplasty be prudent." Doogie had gone from young and perspicacious to a tad surly and condescending. It served to remind me why people hate and fear doctors. Plus, I wasn't sure if Johnny was arguing because he was scared of what they'd find, or just for the sake of arguing with this young whippersnapper.

"Doctor," I said, "may I have a moment alone with Mr. Leland?"

Doogie pursed his lips, then nodded. He turned and walked out of the room. I watched him go, then turned back to Johnny.

"You need to get checked out, you know."

He lowered his eyes and cocked his head to the side a couple of times. "Yeah, I know, Belz. It's just that . . ."

"Go with the MRI scan if you don't want them to put the probe up your leg," I said.

"I'm thinking of telling Dr. Chinwhiskers to go fuck himself," Johnny said.

"He's probably good at it," I said.

Barry broke in. "Will you two stop? Johnny, you were white as a ghost. You collapsed, and I was so scared I didn't know what to do. Please, let them do their tests."

Johnny frowned, but still wouldn't look me in the eye. "What about the telethon? We still got to fill that new void in the opening."

"Why don't you leave that to me?" I asked.

His lips shifted into a pucker. "You saying that you'll quit playing Super Columbo and take care of business?"

"I guarantee you, I'll make it my first priority."

His eyes seemed to brighten and his face looked like a load had been lifted from it. "Hell, if I'd known that, I'd have had the damn test yesterday." The full grin flashed at me now. "Call Junior Dr. Kildare back in here and tell him to get his fishline and flashlight ready. This is the best I've felt all week."

After a more lengthy discussion with the doc, Johnny was leaning more toward the MRI instead of the new millennium version of *Fantastic Voyage*. "Since Raquel Welch isn't available," he added. Naturally, Dr. Doogie made a nodding gesture, but we both knew Johnny's joke had perplexed him. Maybe I'd explain it to him later and he could watch the old flick the next time it hit Turner Classic Movies.

Barry and I were relegated to the waiting room while Johnny was prepped, and I decided to step outside and give Grady a call and check on Veronica. I stepped out and the hot desert air hit me like a wallop in contrast to the ice-cold air-conditioning of the waiting room. I took out my cell and called Grady. After I got through to him, he told me to hold on.

Over the phone I could hear his radio conversation: "Thirty-one from Command One."

"Command One, go ahead." It sounded like a female voice answering. Smart move, having a girl watch a girl. That way, who'd be suspicious of another woman, even one in uniform, hanging around a hotel beauty parlor?

"How's the project coming?" Grady asked.

"Super, boss. Shouldn't be too much longer."

Grady ended the radio call and came back on the line with me.

"I heard," I said.

"Good, 'cause I hate to repeat myself." His deep chuckle sounded reassuring. "What's next on the agenda?"

"Can your security girl take her to the boutique? Get her fixed up with some dynamite outfits? Casual as well as dressy?"

"You got it, but who should I say is paying?"

"Put it on Johnny's tab," I said. "No, wait. On second thought, put it on mine." Although the joke would have been good for a laugh, and I would have paid him back, I realized it might not be the best time to pull it. I'd wait until after these tests were finished. Grady and I chatted a bit more and he asked how Johnny was doing.

"He's getting checked out now," I said. "Keep your fingers crossed."

"Will do," he said.

I suddenly became cognizant of a guy in a gray suit with a black-striped power tie and a dark leather valise-type briefcase standing off to the side watching me. Anybody who wears a suit in this kind of weather in Vegas is either a lawyer or just plain stupid. Of course, this guy probably picked his wardrobe from some 1970s *Dress for Success* book. Or maybe this was cold for someone who lived out here. In New York, this would have been a February heat wave to end all heat waves. I mentioned to

Grady that I had to get going and that I'd call him later. When I'd disconnected, the guy made his move.

"Mr. Belzer, a moment of your time?"

I checked my watch and snapped a picture of him with my cell all in
one smooth motion. It was a move I'd practiced almost as much as the
wristlock throw I'd learned in the *dojang*.

"I'm really kind of tied up," I said, but I was curious as to who this
overdressed guy was. And how he knew to find me here.

"This won't take long," the guy said. "I guarantee it." His flashy, artifi-
cially enhanced teeth made me revise my initial estimation from slimy to
unctuously slimy. "How's Mr. Leland doing?"

I shook my head. No sense giving this guy any information, especially not knowing who the hell he was and who he was working for,
although I had a sneaking suspicion on the latter. "How did you know I
was here?"

"Well"—he paused momentarily—"I merely assumed you'd be here
with Mr. Leland in the hospital."

"And you know what happens when you assume." I grinned. He did,
too, until I added, "So who told you about Johnny being here?"

He made an attempt at a congenial shrug. "Heard it through the
grapevine."

"I didn't like either version of that tune," I said, "and I like it even less
now."

"Can I buy you a cup of coffee?" Mr. Unctuous asked.

My immediate reaction was to tell the guy to scram, but I was just
curious enough to wonder what his angle was. "It's your dime. Better
make that several dimes. There's a machine down this way." I pointed as
the doors retracted to allow us entry. "I don't believe I got your name."

"Joseph Patrick Nolan," he said, shifting his briefcase to offer me his
hand and a politician's smile.

He had a good, solid handshake that he probably spent hours practicing. The dip of the shoulder, the slight inversion to allow my hand to
assume the upper, and hence dominant, position . . . very practiced. The
move of a guy who kissed major-league ass for a living, all right. He took

out a business card with his name and "Attorney at Law" printed in bold, black letters. The address was local.

"Now," he said, "about that coffee . . ."

I watched him reach into his pocket and withdraw one of those small, oval-shaped, plastic change purses that were popular in the sixties. He squeezed the ends and the slit down the middle peeled open like an excited clam. As his fingers punched around in the purse for some change, I wondered if his parents should have used "Parsimony" for a middle name instead of "Patrick." I dipped into my own pocket and took out two one-dollar bills.

"Name your poison," I said, inserting the first dollar. He shot me a half-assed look as his mouth formed an oval to match the purse.

"Oh," he said. "Let me pay for those."

I made a dismissive waving motion. "Not a problem. Say, did you know that Frank Sinatra always carried around a pocket full of dimes after his son was kidnapped?"

He blinked twice and I pointed to the array of buttons.

"You want to choose a blend while the day's still young?" I asked.

He opted for cream and sugar, then hit the extra sugar button to add more. After the machine had stopped its semitoxic dribble, I chose hot and black for mine. Coffee machines are usually so bad that it's the only way to drink it. Puts hair on your chest and parts it down the middle.

We sat at a nearby table, the only other occupants of the small room. He rummaged around in his leather valise. I sipped my coffee, if you could call it that, and set the cup down in case Joseph Patrick Nolan needed a paperweight. He looked up and flashed me another one of his ingratiating grins. I wondered if he practiced in front of a mirror.

"Thank you for taking time out of your day to sit down and talk with me," he said.

I nodded, resisting the temptation to take another sip of the dark brew.

He cleared his throat and set a white, business-size envelope on the table and pushed it in my direction. I looked down at it but didn't touch it. Our eyes met. His were obviously trying for a reading, which I wasn't about to offer, thanks to my photochromic lenses.

"Nice envelope," I said.

He flashed another smile, more nervous-looking this time, then cleared his throat. "I represent the Picardus Corporation in this endeavor."

"That's nice." I kept my tone flat.

He cleared his throat again. The cool air must have been having an effect on him. "We're aware that you're in Las Vegas with Mr. Leland's tele- thon, and would like to make an offer of a contribution."

"An offer of a contribution?"

"Yes."

"I take it that's a convoluted way of saying you want something in return?"

He flashed the porcelain veneers again and forced out a half-assed laugh. If he could bottle and sell it, he'd be a hit for a television comedy's laugh track.

"Of course," he said, "our intention is primarily altruistic."

"Of course."

The smile again. This guy was really getting on my nerves. I wondered if he was Harvey Smithe's cousin.

"However," he said, "the Picardus Corporation does have a vested in- terest in . . . certain political issues."

I gave him a serious nod, like we were two insiders on the same side of the fence. This seemed to buoy his optimism.

"Thus, the check, of course, is not contingent on any conditions. Picardus is very interested in worthy causes." He smiled again. "And few of them are more worthy than this telethon."

I wondered if he even knew what worthy cause the telethon was rais- ing money for, but I didn't want to throw him off pace by asking. Instead, I wanted to soften him up before delivering what I figured would be the zinger. "I certainly appreciate your generosity, Joe." I stopped and raised my eyebrows. "May I call you Joe?"

He showed me the veneers clean back to the molars. "Why, of course, Rich."

I didn't tell him I hated people calling me "Rich." Instead, I asked, "So what is the quid pro quo you've been hinting at?"

He paused to inhale deeply, planning his words carefully. This guy must have been a hungry juror's worst nightmare. "Rich, I'll be blunt. You stopped in a campaign office yesterday."

"Did I?" I tried to look perplexed.

"You and a young lady."

I snapped my fingers. "Right, we did."

"We couldn't figure out exactly what your motivation was," he said. "And the young lady made some rather spurious allegations in a rather bellicose manner."

I smiled with a little nod of my head. "She can be bellicose, can't she?"

He nodded. "Exactly. We at Picardus would like to avoid any future incidents of this nature, for the sake of the political process." He paused and scrutinized me for a reaction. "You do understand, don't you, Rich?"

"I understand the First Amendment."

The expression of expectant success dropped from his face. "Am I . . . do you . . . I think there may be a misunderstanding of sorts."

I shook my head. "Who's your client?"

"I already told you. The Picardus Corporation."

"Which is a dummy name for who? The Kaye family?"

He licked his lips. "I'm afraid it wouldn't be ethical for me to divulge any information about my clients without their explicit approval."

"Yeah, I'm sure." I glanced down at the envelope. He must have followed my gaze.

"Go ahead," he said, "open it."

I reached down and picked up my paper cup of coffee. It didn't taste any better the second time. "Why don't you tell the Picardus Corporation they're welcome to call in the contribution once the telethon starts on Sunday."

"Come on, Rich. Let's not make this difficult. We can't negotiate unless we establish a baseline amount, right?" He pushed the envelope closer to me.

I toyed around with the idea of doing a Bogie imitation and saying something like, "I don't negotiate with flunky lawyers." But I didn't. Instead, I opted to stand up and walk away.

"Next time, Joe," I said, "tell them to send the A team."

I went back inside to see if Barry wanted to get something to eat. He shook his head. The kid had such a worried look I wondered if it would be contagious. I plopped down beside him on the vinyl couch and thought about the day's developments. My trip to Mark Kaye III's campaign office had stirred the pot, thanks to Veronica's timely outburst. My visit to Leo Russell's ex-partner had confirmed my suspicions that they were probably both dirty, with Eddie Sikorski being the Stan Laurel to Russell's Oliver Hardy. Judging from his picture, he even looked a little bit like Ollie. First dick on the scene, beating even the marked patrol unit there. . . . No small feat, considering how fast you can fly in a marked squad going to a death investigation of a movie star. And they both knew Constance Penroy . . . and didn't like her very much. I frowned and wondered how much more old Eddie would have loosened up if Veronica had been able to keep her mouth shut and I'd plied him with another Budweiser.

So the connecting line starting with the untimely death of Brigid Burgeon extended to Mark Kaye Jr., to Constance Penroy, and all the way to Russell and Sikorski. Draw in tangential lines to the present to include Paul and poor old Mrs. Perkins. I was going to have to rattle that LVMPD detective's cage again in reference to her death investigation. I wondered where the Indian fit in and if he was actually following Veronica and me. The phone calls could have been from Joseph Patrick Nolan. Maybe an attempt to approach Veronica with a "scholarship fund" or something. Maybe I was jumping the gun by assuming it was the Indian . . . Maybe he was a long-gone figure who cropped up in Paul's imagination after he saw the name in Constance's notes.

I'd come close to the realization that this whole thing could be dismissed as a series of unfortunate coincidences when Dr. Doogie walked into the waiting area. He looked grim. Barry and I stood simultaneously.

"What have you found out?" Barry blurted.

Doogie stared at him, as if he were going to admonish him not to speak unless spoken to. "At this point, we've got him sedated so we can do the insertion."

"You're going for the angiogram?" I asked.

The imperious gaze turned to me. "Yes."

I hate monosyllabic answers, especially from a young guy who thinks his shit doesn't stink but is really just a schmuck.

"So what does that mean?" I asked. "That we've been here for over three hours and you haven't done anything yet?"

He blinked twice. Slow blinks, a grammar school teacher getting ready to address the class clown. "No, that's not true. We were waiting for certain lab results to come back. We've ruled out pericarditis."

"Latin was never my best subject," I said.

"A viral inflammation of the heart muscle."

I nodded. "So how long before we know something?"

"It's hard to say. We're waiting on Dr. Pecolar. He's our resident cardio specialist and we usually like him to do the angiograms."

"He have a midmorning golf engagement?"

Barry put his hand on my forearm. "Doctor, can we see Johnny?"

Doogie frowned a bit. "We normally don't like to disturb the patient while the sedative is taking effect. The nurse is shaving him, also."

"He'll love that. I know I would." I felt Barry's fingers dig deeper into my arm. "Of course, that would depend on the nurse, I guess."

Doogie obviously didn't appreciate good humor. I wondered if he'd sat on a Popsicle stick when he was a kid and forgotten to have someone remove it.

"Regardless, you're both welcome to wait," he said, "but it's going to be at least a few more hours before we can make any determinations." With that pronouncement, he turned and walked away, saying over his shoulder, "If you want, you can leave a contact number with the nurses' station and we'll call you."

"Call us what?" I said, but if he heard me he didn't let on. We watched him disappear through the swinging doors labeled Authorized Personnel Only.

"Richard, what are we going to do?" Barry appeared to have aged considerably over the past fourteen hours. "Johnny's counting on us to fill the vacancy in the programming, but I can't even concentrate on anything while he's like this."

I placed my hand on his shoulder. "That's because you care about him. We both do." I nudged him over to the couch and made him sit. "You want to go back to the hotel and get some rest? I'll stay here and call you if anything breaks."

He shook his head. "I couldn't sleep. Barely got any rest last night, worrying."

I looked at my watch. As much as I'd been dreading it, I knew Veronica must be nearing the end of her makeover, and I had to get back to keep her out of trouble. Plus, there was a little matter of my promise to Johnny. I had to fill the program. I told Barry what I was going to do, and he agreed to call me with any updates. As I was walking out, I turned on my phone and called Grady to let him know I was on my way back.

"Want me to send someone to get you?" he asked.

"Nah, it'll be easier for me to grab a cab. That way your guys can stay on the job and not be catering to some fucking celebrity asshole."

He chuckled. "And who might that be?"

As I hung up I looked at my caller ID screen. The "unknown" listing gnawed at me, and I remembered Bernie from my cell phone security department was supposed to be emailing me that list of incoming call numbers. I went back inside and tagged up with Barry again, using his computer to check my emails. Sure enough, good old Bernie had come through. I quickly found the number in question and scribbled it on the back of Joseph Patrick Nolan's card. Then I went to the front desk and asked them to call me a cab. While I was waiting, I decided to call Pearsol and see what he'd been up to. He answered with the usual, "Hey, Belz. What's up?" I was getting to like the guy and I'd never even met him.

"You got any contacts that can run down an unlisted number for me?"

"Not a problem. What is it?"

I read it off to him.

"L.A. area code," he said. "Shouldn't be too difficult. Can I call you back?"

"Sure."

"Ahh, this isn't some chick's number, is it? I mean, I'm going out on a limb here a little, and if it's something that's gonna come back to bite me on the ass, it'd be best if I knew about it."

"I don't know whose it is, but they keep making these hang-up phone calls to my cell and it's driving me nuts."

"Well, that's different. Hey, I wonder if it's that psycho chick from your buddy's death investigation."

"No," I said. "I know her number." Did I ever.

"Okay. Call you back."

I disconnected and no sooner than I did, the cell rang again. I couldn't believe it was Pearsol, unless he was wearing a blue suit with a big red S on the front. The number looked vaguely familiar. Las Vegas area code, unless I missed my guess. I answered and was surprised as hell.

"Mr. Belzer? This is Detective Kirby, LVMPD."

"Scott, right?" I silently hoped I'd gotten his name right.

He laughed. "Yeah. I'm flattered you remembered."

"What can I do for you?"

"I was wondering if I could speak with you in person," he said.

"Concerning?"

"A couple matters. Are you at the Monticello?"

"Actually, I'm at Garden Star Hospital waiting on a cab."

"Great," he said. "Cancel the taxi and I'll swing by and pick you up. I'm coming up 215 now. Be there in ten."

I wondered why, after practically blowing me off when I'd inquired about Mrs. Perkins, he was so all-fired eager to talk to me now. "Is this about the Perkins case?"

"No, actually it's about another one I caught," he said. "An ex-LAPD copper named Eddie Sikorski turned up dead."

CHAPTER 14

Detective Scott Kirby was a slim, Hispanic-looking guy with wavy black hair and light blue eyes. He didn't fit a name like Kirby. A man of contradictions, I thought. He'd pulled up in a blue Chevy Caprice and parked in front of the doors. A security guard barked an order to move it, but Kirby flashed his badge and came over to shake my hand.

"Mr. Belzer, I recognize you from your TV show." His grin seemed genuine, but that wasn't surprising. I have a lot of cop fans.

We shook and he pointed to the passenger door, saying, "It's open," as he went back around to the driver's side. After settling in and buckling up, he glanced over to me and told me to do the same.

"Departmental regulation," he said.

"All passengers must wear seat belts?"

"Unh-uh." He grinned and put on some wraparound sunglasses. "Only celebrity passengers who might stop production of a popular television show if they hit the dash."

I smiled and complied, and I was glad I did. Kirby hit the gas and practically launched us out of the drop-off zone. He shot back onto the street and wove in and out of traffic with the accomplished ease of a NASCAR driver. After popping a stick of sugarless gum into his mouth he held the pack toward me. I declined. I didn't want some hospital tech probing my gullet for it if we had to stop fast.

"So you were saying Eddie Sikorski's dead?" I asked.

"Yeah." We were on a four-lane highway now but the racetrack moves didn't cease. Up ahead I saw a traffic signal and prayed it would turn red to slow us down. "How well did you know him?"

"Not very. I only met him for the first time yesterday."

"What did you talk to him about?"

"A couple of his old cases."

"Which ones?"

"Before I answer that one, may I ask a question?"

He nodded. His attention shifted back to the traffic around us.

"How did you know I talked to him?" I asked.

"Your cell phone number." We shot from the right lane through a half-car length into the left lane and cut back around a slower-moving semi. "I hate to be behind trucks."

"Me, too. Ah, my cell phone number?"

"Right. I pulled Sikorski's phone records. Saw the number. It was the same one you called me on."

"Indeed it was," I said. "A lot of people have it."

He changed lanes again. Ahead, the expansive skyline of the Strip loomed like friendly territory.

"How did Sikorski die?" I asked.

"You already had your question. Now, which cases were you interested in, and why?"

I considered my options. I knew if I wanted any information, and his co-operation on getting any more of it, I'd better not play the wise-ass. "I asked him about his former partner, Leo Russell, and the Brigid Burgeon case."

"Russell?"

"Ex-LAPD as well. Sikorski's partner and mentor on the force. Died in a car accident a few years ago."

"Brigid Burgeon?"

"Oh, come on. You must remember Brigid. A beautiful actress. Blonde. Played in a handful of hits in the seventies. Died tragically."

He slowly nodded. "Okay. 'Diamonds Are a Girl's Best Friend,' right?"

"She did sing that," I said. "In *homage* to Marilyn."

"*Homage?* Is that, like, French?"

"Only if you pronounce it that way." I gave him a quick thumbnail sketch of the entire situation, from Paul's phone call to Veronica Holmes's unexpected arrival in Vegas. "Did Sikorski call anybody after me?"

"Nope." We whirled around an intersection and were suddenly approaching the Strip from the eastern side. "You said you were staying at the Monticello, right?"

"Right."

"That Veronica chick there, too?"

"She should be."

"Good," he said. "I'll need to interview her as well."

"Fine," I said. "But I don't think we can tell you much. It was a pretty short interview with old Eddie."

"Got to touch all the bases."

"So now that I've practically told you the story of my recent life, how about telling me what happened to Sikorski?"

"He drowned."

"What? Where at?"

"In his bathtub. Looks like he slipped and hit his head first. One of his neighbors called when they saw water running from under his front door. They also said some guy and a dowdy-looking girl pulled up in a white limo earlier. That was you, right?"

"It was." I then did my best for the next six and a half minutes to convince Kirby that there must be a connection between the deaths of Sikorski and Mrs. Perkins, ending with, "After all, the only thing those two had in common was that I talked to both of them and they subsequently turned up dead."

"You're right," he said. "That fact's not lost on me, either. Which is why I need to verify your alibi for last night. Where did you go after you talked to Sikorski?"

The question, which was one that I'd asked in hundreds of television episodes to other actors, stunned me. Where *did* I go? It took me a few seconds. "Let's see . . . we went back to the hotel and I had a drink in the bar with a buddy of mine. He works security at the hotel. Then I went to the hospital to be with another friend who'd been admitted."

"For what?"

"They're checking his heart."

"Who is he?"

This I did have a problem talking about. It was one thing to provide a verifiable alibi for myself, but another one entirely telling the world about Johnny's medical woes. Still, he probably had ways of finding things out. "Johnny Leland."

Kirby rounded a turn and we were zigzagging through the rear parking area just as easily as we had on Maryland Parkway. "Johnny Leland had a heart attack? No shit?"

"I didn't say that. I said he was admitted for some tests. And I'd appreciate it if you kept that between us for the moment."

We pulled up alongside the building and Kirby shoved it into park. Before we got out, he reached down and stuck a red light on the dash. "Don't worry, I won't tell anybody."

"In that case, you can call me 'Belz.' " I called Grady and arranged for him to bring Veronica to an office section on the second floor. Kirby and I took the elevator and she was waiting for us when we got off.

Veronica's new look stunned both of us. Me more so than him, because I'd seen "the before." They'd woven some soft waves into her iron-straight hair, and lopped off at least half of it, so it hung just below her jaw line, in an attractive but relaxed-looking flip style. Her makeup accentuated her cheekbones with just the right amount of foundation and blush, and for her eyes they'd used a brownish shadow that matched her hair. The dress fit snugly in all the right places, with a circular cut in front to advertise a hint of cleavage, and a hemline short enough to show off some pretty decent legs. She must have liked it, too, because she had that prom queen confidence about her. George Bernard Shaw would have approved.

"You look fabulous," I told her. Certainly not "dowdy."

She demurely glanced downward and smiled. For the first time since I'd known her I saw a full smile and realized she had very nice teeth.

"I owe it all to you, Mr. Belzer," she said. "I never thought I could look like this."

"I'm glad you feel that way," I said, "because I need an alibi, and men always believe a pretty girl. Now, without any coaching on my part, please tell Detective Kirby here exactly what we did after we left the Sikorski place."

"That old creep," she said, the smile vanishing. "I wish he were dead." Kirby raised his eyebrows.

"Actually," I said, "he already is. That's why I needed an alibi, but I guess we both need one now."

Veronica's mouth stayed in an O shape for several seconds, and I wondered if she was going to lapse into a rendition of "Oops! I Did It Again." Instead, she went into a rapid discourse about how we came back and she stayed in her room while I went to the bar and then, she assumed, the hospital. Kirby made notes in his small notebook. I called Grady and he gave another recounting of our trip to the bar and then to Garden Star Hospital. Kirby took more notes. When we all had finished, he asked for contact information from all of us. After we'd given it to him, he politely thanked us and turned to walk away.

"Is that it?" I asked.

He stopped and glanced over his shoulder. "No, I forgot to tell you, Mrs. Perkins . . . no smoke in the lungs. But they're still calling it accidental. Looks like she must have had a brain hemorrhage and died on the spot. Probably just after she'd turned on the stove."

I smirked. "And if you believe that one, I got a piece of Hoover Dam I'll sell you."

He lifted his eyebrows again, as if in salute, and began walking.

"Like I said," I called after him, "there's a lot of dead bodies popping up around here."

"Yeah," Kirby said over his shoulder. "Especially right after you get finished talking with them."

Just for safety purposes, we had one of Grady's guys escort us to the side entrance where we met Hector. I told him to take the long way around to the Mirage.

"Make sure no one's tagging us," Veronica added, then smiled at me. "It's a cop expression."

I nodded in approval. Maybe the makeover had worked more wonders than I figured. She did look like a whole new person. Hector dropped us off at the front entrance about twenty minutes later, which, considering Vegas traffic, wasn't half bad. He asked me if he should wait, but I told him to take off and that I'd call him when we wanted to be picked up. I told Veronica to move ahead of me and I hawked the crowd around us, which, considering I didn't know who I was looking for, didn't make too much sense. But it made me feel a hell of a lot better.

I normally would have had the ever-capable Barry grease the way for me, but the poor kid had been so preoccupied with Johnny's health woes that I'd handled this one myself. I grabbed the first security guard I saw, introduced myself, and told him I was a friend of Sal Fabell. The guy recognized me immediately and called on his radio.

"Is Mr. Fabell still in rehearsal?"

"Ten-four," came the reply.

"Be advised, I have a celeb friend I'm bringing by."

After another "ten-four" acknowledgment, our guard led us through the casino and through some back office areas marked AUTHORIZED PERSONNEL ONLY. I wondered how much simpler life might be with a special name badge that said, "I'm Authorized Personnel." The hallway narrowed and we made a right turn and then a left one. A faint hint of a tune—Sal's mellifluous baritone—floated in the air and got progressively louder as we walked. Finally, the hallway opened into a massive ballroom. A uniformed security guard stood at the entrance and nodded to us as we passed.

"This is Richard Belzer," Veronica said.

The guard smiled and nodded.

"Celebrity 101," she whispered to me.

Sal was on the stage finishing up "These Foolish Things." He was dressed in a sweatshirt and dark pants, and had the same twenty-member band behind him as when Johnny and I had seen him the other night. The enhanced lighting and dark backdrop were missing, but the effect was still mesmerizing.

He saw us coming and immediately stopped in midsong and uttered, "Finally, they found those people that skipped out on their checks. I was wondering if they were gonna get 'em." It caused a ripple of laughter in the band. His rehearsals and recording sessions were legendary for the jokes and clowning, and the microphone was amplifying every word. We were still too far away for him to recognize us. He finished with the song and did a quick foot shuffle, then started with another joke.

"Oh, I like the one where the woman asks the psychiatrist what a phallic symbol is, and the psychiatrist unzips his pants and says, 'My dear, this is a phallic symbol,' and the woman says, 'Oh, it's like a prick, only smaller.' "

More laughter. Veronica looked at me with her mouth in a simper.

"Heyyyy, it's my pally, Richard Belzer," Sal said. "How you doing, buddy?"

I smiled and waved as the guard seated us at the table closest to the stage. I knew Sal fairly well, having met him when he guest-starred on an episode of one of my TV shows, but we weren't what you would call close friends.

"Finally, after all this time," he said, still cutting up, "we have an audience. How much did you have to pay 'em?" He flashed us that famous smile—salacious yet with a twinkle of innocence—as he made a show of checking out Veronica. "Hey, Belz, who's your pretty young friend?"

"This is Veronica Holmes," I called up to him.

"Veronica . . . ," he sang. *"We can pretend you're eighteen . . ."*

She smiled up at him. It was one of the brightest smiles I'd ever seen.

"You know, Belz," Sal said, looking totally relaxed, holding the microphone, "I'm really glad you two showed up today. I always sound better when I'm singing to a pretty girl."

"I hope you're talking about her," I called back.

He smiled and turned back to the band, saying something I couldn't understand, then the music started. "Can you lean on those marimbas a little bit more?" Sal said as he brought the microphone back up. He caught the rhythm and launched into a beat-driven version of "Baby-O," pointing his free hand at Veronica as he belted out the lyrics.

She put her fingers over her mouth to cover her laugh, or her embarrassment. I wasn't sure which, but one thing I was sure of: she was totally starstruck. Go figure. Sal was not only old enough to be her father, he could have been her grandfather. But then again, give or take a few years, so could I. But you don't really have to be that old to be a grandfather nowadays.

He stopped after the song and waved to the band, telling them to "take five." He placed the microphone in its holder and stepped off the stage, coming to join us at the table. I stood and we shook hands over the tabletop. Veronica stood and offered her hand, but Sal shook his head with a grin and gave her a tight hug instead. "Make a dirty old man's day, gorgeous."

I worried this would set her off, but instead she smiled and, as unbelievable as it sounds, giggled. Giggled! I was wondering if they'd permed more than her hair during the makeover. Maybe somebody had slipped some Prozac into her shampoo. And it penetrated.

An attendant came and set a glass of amber-colored liquid in front of Sal and he asked us if we wanted anything to drink.

"Too early for me," I said.

"For me, too," he said with a sly grin. He held up the glass and added, "Apple juice. The same thing I drink onstage during my act."

Veronica giggled again. I sat in stunned silence. She was watching him more closely than her favorite reality show.

I was thinking of asking Sal to accompany us on the rest of our interviews, since his charm was obviously the key to lock down her mouth. But first things first.

"I caught your show the other night, Sal," I said. Better to ease into things.

"Oh yeah? Why didn't you stop by the dressing room afterwards?"

"Well, it was me and Johnny."

That seemed to stop him like a punch. His brow furrowed. "Johnny? My old ex-partner Johnny?"

I nodded.

Sal smiled. "How's he doing?"

Here's where things got delicate. Did I tell him Johnny was in the hospital, and that we needed his help, or should I lay more groundwork? His smile looked wistful. I figured the direct approach was the best.

"He could be better," I said. "He's over in Garden Star Hospital."

"No." Sal's brow furrowed. "What's wrong with him?"

"They're thinking maybe it has something to do with his heart."

Sal shook his head slowly. "Poor kid. He always had more heart than he knew what to do with. Always a sucker for a good cause."

"Speaking of good causes," I said, flashing my version of a Sal-type grin, "I'm here to ask you a favor."

He said nothing, but raised one eyebrow.

It was now or never. I wouldn't get another opening like this.

But before I could speak, Veronica butted in. "Oh my God. You're going to ask him to be on the telethon, aren't you?"

"Telethon?" Sal said.

I sat there with my mouth wide open, unable to figure out what to say. Since the cat was out of the bag, thanks to Veronica. What a time for her "psychic abilities" to manifest themselves. I figured straight up the middle was the best tactic. "Actually, the reason I came out to Vegas this time was to help Johnny cohost this telethon . . ." I went into the long, sad tale of how we'd been working on the program, had everything set, then how a last-minute cancellation of our major opening musical number had sent everything into a tailspin. I purposely left out any mention of my other activities during the past few days. "So you see, Sal, we could really use your help on this. I know you and Johnny go way back—"

"Way back," he cut in. "We ain't talked in twenty-five years."

"Which is why," I said, "this would be a great opportunity for you two to have a reconciliation."

Sal snorted as he took a quick drag, then stubbed out his cigarette. "You want to contact a couple of my ex-wives while you're at it? He send you over to talk to me?"

"He doesn't even know I'm here. He wouldn't have allowed it."

"Oh no?"

"Sal, Johnny bought the tickets the other night, but insisted we sit far enough back so you wouldn't see us."

Sal shook his head.

"Look," I said, "I know this must be hard—"

"Hard?" He caught himself, paused, and let the anger dissipate, then got a reflective look on his face. "Johnny ever tell you why we broke up?"

I shook my head.

"Some things are better not remembered." His eyes got a real distant look. "But if it's one thing I've learned, it's you can't embrace the past."

"Sometimes you regret it if you don't," I said.

He squinted at me. "Meaning?"

My eyes searched the tabletop. It was Formica over wood. Like everything else in Vegas, nobody would notice once the decorative tablecloth had been spread over it. "I had an opportunity to reunite with an old friend this past week, but I didn't. We used to be close, but I hadn't seen him in about twenty-five years plus, either." In my peripheral vision, I saw Veronica stiffen slightly. I continued. "He died unexpectedly, and now embracing that part of the past is something I wish I would've done."

Sal straightened up with an expression of concern. "You aren't telling me Johnny's dying, are you?"

"No, no, I'm pretty sure he's going to be okay."

He relaxed a bit, nodding. "So you're saying I got a second chance here? To embrace the past."

"To make things right," I said.

He looked contemplative. "Oh, hell, why not." The famous Sal grin reappeared. "When is it?"

"It starts tomorrow night at seven. I was hoping to have you on at eight."

Sal took out his cell phone. After hitting a button, he spoke into it. "Rog, we got a show scheduled tomorrow night at seven?" He listened, then said, "Cancel it. I've got a conflict. Yeah, I'm sure. And tell Bill and the boys I got a gig for them across the street. On my dime." He flipped the phone closed. "That's that. I guess every end has a new beginning. Maybe it is time to reconcile with my other ex."

I reached across the table and placed my hand on his arm. "Thanks, Sal. I really appreciate it."

Veronica jumped up and gave him a hug. "You're just as wonderful as you are in the movies."

"Heyyyy," Sal said. "This is turning out to be worth more and more all the time." After milking the hug for as much as he could get, he added, "But I doubt you were even born when I did my last movie."

"Oh, don't be silly," she said. "I've seen a lot of your movies. Like the one you made with Brigid Burgeon, for instance."

I caught a quick flutter of her eye. Almost a wink. And here I'd had her pegged for being totally starstruck.

"Brigid? *Two to Tango?*" Sal shook his head. "No, that one we never finished. Poor kid."

"What was she like?" Veronica asked, obviously knowing she was pushing the envelope. I wasn't sure how I felt about that. I mean, it was great she was actively taking part to get information in a subtle and positive way, instead of charging in with her saber rattling. But my primary purpose here was to get Sal to do the telethon. I owed that to Johnny.

"She was a sweet kid,' he said. "I liked her."

"Was she really in love with that senator?" Veronica asked.

He shrugged. "That was her business. She didn't talk much about her personal life, and believe it or not, at night I went home to my family."

"Do you think she committed suicide like some people say?"

He shrugged again. "Possible. She seemed pretty down. Don't think she was on any kind of drugs, except maybe the prescription kind. It was around the Elvis era, after all."

"Sal," I started to say. "We've—"

"What about Constance Penroy?" Veronica said. "Did you know her?"

Oh no, I thought. This could be like a bull walking into a yard with sheets on the clothesline.

"Say—," I said.

"Constance?" Sal said, smiling. "She was what we used to call one gutsy lady. I always liked her. And she was real nice to me, too."

I loosened my white-knuckle grip on the chair.

"Did you know her well?" Veronica asked, the picture of well-coiffed innocence.

"Not real well," he said. "She used to come by the sets in the old days when we were making movies. Like I said, she was always square with me. Never took any cheap shots, always asked me straight-out about any rumors. Gave me a chance to tell my side of things. I appreciated that."

"She sounds nice," Veronica said.

He nodded. "In a way, she kind of reminded me of me. Said her dream was to break some real big story someday. Get the recognition that she never got. Maybe win the big one."

The ending line in the page Harlee had translated for me: *I think I'm ready for my close-up now.*

Sal picked up his glass and drained it, then stood up. "I got to get back to work."

I figured not to press our luck. I stood up, also, and we exchanged cell phone numbers. "I'll have Barry, that's Johnny's personal assistant, call you to work out all the final details."

He nodded. "Just do one thing for me. Don't tell Johnny. I want to surprise him."

"Sure, Sal. We can do that."

He grinned. "I owe that *facocktason* a good shocker after you told me you guys were here the other night and didn't even tell me."

On the way out, as soon as we were alone, Veronica canted her head as she looked at me. "That went exactly the way I knew it would."

"Puh-leeze," I said. "No 'I'm a psychic' crap right now, okay? I'm just pleased as punch that everything went as well as it did."

She nodded, then leaned close to me and asked, "But why didn't you press him some more? I tried to give you the openings."

"Press him about what?"

"That Sikorski and Russell thing."

"Because my primary concern in coming over here was to get Sal to agree to do the telethon. I owed that to Johnny."

"I know, but—"

"No buts. We already know Russell and Sikorski had contact of some sort with Sal from that picture, but it doesn't mean they were barroom buddies."

"But—"

"Like I said, no buts. Good job of restraining yourself back there, by the way. This is a whole new you in more ways than one."

She tucked her lower lip between her teeth and canted her head. "Thanks. I am feeling different. I feel like I could conquer the whole world."

"Just make sure you do it one step at a time," I said. "And your next step tonight is back to your room."

"My room?"

"Right, unless you want to arm-wrestle Grady for his ticket to the fights."

CHAPTER 15

As Hector was taking us in another roundabout way to the rear entrance of the Monticello, my cell phone rang. For a split second I was worried that it was Sal calling me to say he'd changed his mind, or Barry with bad news from the hospital. To my relief, however, the familiar L.A. area code of my favorite cop popped up. I answered with, "About time you called. I thought you were going to get back to me right away."

"Sorry, Belz," Pearsol said. "I kept running into dead ends on tracing that number you gave me. Plus, I do have a life, you know. And a job."

"And I hope you're putting it in that screenplay for me. What's the scoop?"

He laughed. "The number's a disposable. That's why we couldn't trace it."

"A disposable?"

"Yeah, it's a tried-and-true trick by drug dealers. I heard the CIA is even using it."

"How does it work?"

"The party who wants to use the phone buys a bunch of those phone cards, then gets a cell phone and has all the calls forwarded to the phone card number. Since they're disposable, and practically untraceable, bida-boom, bida-bah."

"Don't you mean 'bada-bing, bada-boom'?"

"Whatever," he said.

Apologies to Francis Ford Coppola, I thought. "You say dealers and spooks use it?"

"Right. Leaves no paper trail. The cards your caller used were purchased here in L.A. Not too far from the Farmers Market."

"Any chance you could pull surveillance tapes where they were bought?"

He laughed again. "Who do you think I am? James Bond?"

"Ever hear of a guy called 'the Indian'?"

"As a matter of fact, I have. He hung around with a guy wearing a mask and riding a white horse, right?"

"Very funny. Jock, I owe you."

"And I'll collect," he said. "Watch yourself."

After I disconnected, I realized I hadn't pressed for new info on Paul's death, but figured he would have told me if there was any. Veronica asked me about the conversation and I gave her the rundown.

"So those 'unknown caller' ones you keep getting," she said. "Do you have any idea who's doing them?"

I shook my head. "All I know is we're ordering dinner through room service tonight."

Hector pulled in to the rear parking lot area and stopped by a set of doors even I didn't know existed. The screen separating him from the rear portion of the limo lowered and he turned and smiled.

"Safe and sound, boss. No tails."

I patted his arm and moved across to open the door. As we were getting out, the most popular cell phone in town rang again. A Las Vegas area code this time. It looked vaguely familiar, too.

"Mr. Belzer? Joseph Patrick Nolan."

"Most people are satisfied to just use their middle initial, you know."

A forced laugh. "I'll have to remember that. We're at the hotel and would like a moment of your time, sir."

"We?"

"My client and I. Last time you said to send the A team, remember?" His voice was laced with a trace of resentment. My jab had struck deeper than I'd realized. I could have told him to blow it out his ass, but I was curious to meet "his client." If anything, it had all the trappings of a scene in a John Grisham novel.

"Great," I said. "I'll meet you in the Marebello Room in ten minutes. It's on the second floor."

"I know where it is. We'll be waiting."

He disconnected. I immediately called Grady's cell and asked him to meet us by the back elevators. When he showed up, I asked him to escort Veronica to her room and then shadow me in the bar.

"Who you meeting?" he asked.

"Some slimy lawyer type named Nolan."

His face twitched. "Joseph Patrick Nolan?"

"Yeah. You know him?"

"He's friends with Mr. Ocean. And your other boy, too. Came by earlier to take old Harv out of the hotel. Word is they took him to rehab to dry out. Again."

"They've got their work cut out for them. Let's hope he doesn't make it back in time for the telethon."

"I guess that's why they took him. So he could make it. At least that's what they said."

"Ah well, I knew it was way too early for my Hanukkah gift. See you in the bar." I pointed to Veronica. "I'm only going to say this once. Stay in your room. I can only handle so many worries at one time."

She nodded and Grady hit the button for the elevator. As they went up, I quickly called Barry's cell to see if there were any updates, but it went to voicemail after one ring. A sure sign it was still off. I left a message for him to call me when he got this, and disconnected. I had an appointment to keep, and I was more than a little curious as to what Nolan would offer this time. I walked through the back corridor, past a nice wall that simulated an exotic waterfall, and went up an escalator that put me on the same level as the casino. I walked through, keeping my eyes peeled for anything or anybody suspicious. How did the Secret

Service handle crowded scenes for dignitaries and politicians? With a lot of help, I reminded myself.

I walked into the Marebello and found Nolan waiting for me at the entrance. He called my name sotto voce.

"I've taken the liberty of reserving one of the private rooms," he said. "I hope you don't mind."

I did, but didn't want him to know it. I paused at the bar and told the bartender to tell Grady which room I was in when he got there. This seemed to cause Nolan a bit of distress.

"You're bringing someone else?" he asked.

"I was supposed to meet a buddy here. Lead on, Macduff," I said, intentionally bastardizing the line from *Macbeth*.

"It's Nolan. Joseph Patrick Nolan," he said. His nervous meter was working overtime.

"You've got enough names for two people," I said.

The private room was off toward the back, in the section that was furnished with a Japanese motif. Sliding doors and walls of opaque paper. An ornate design had been printed on the one he opened. He motioned for me to step in and I saw a thin figure hunched over a table with a drink. The man's hair, what he had of it, was slicked back and he wore dark glasses. His head swiveled as we entered and it took me a moment to realize who he was. He looked quite a bit different than he had on the poster in the campaign office. But then again, that's politics—all smoke and mirrors . . . and image . . . and hairpieces.

I moved to the table and took a seat opposite him. "I didn't recognize you without your toupee." I raised an eyebrow. "You are Lawrence Kaye, brother of the late Mark Kaye Jr., and uncle of the current Kaye running for governor, aren't you?"

Uncle Lar whipped off the glasses and stared at me with intense blue eyes. "Cut the shit, Belzer. You know goddamn well who I am and why I'm here."

I smiled. "Well, just so we're both on the same sheet of music, why don't you tell me anyway?"

"You and that crazy bitch seem intent on sabotaging my nephew's campaign." Bits of spit gathered at the corners of his mouth. I almost felt obligated to hand him a napkin, but figured that was Nolan's job.

"So I take it that freedom of speech isn't part of the gubernatorial platform?" I asked.

His mouth twisted into a scowl. "Don't be crass. How much do you fucking want?"

"How much do I want for what?"

"To leave us alone. To make you and her go away. Permanently." His eyes looked glassy as he tossed down the rest of his drink. Shoving the glass across the table, he said, "Joe, get me another one."

"Larry . . ." Nolan's voice was cautious and restrained. "Don't you think you'd better wait?"

"Get me another fucking drink. Now!"

Nolan compressed his lips and slid out, taking care to display a worried expression before closing the door after him.

I turned back to Uncle Lar. "Alone at last."

He wasted no time in leveling an index finger at my face. "You're stupid, Belzer, if you think you can get away with this. I've heard about you. I know what you're all about."

"I'm flattered."

His cheeks shook. "We're prepared to make a substantial contribution to this telethon thing of yours. Plus an added bonus to you, personally. In cash."

"Then it wouldn't be tax-deductible for you."

"Quit playing games. What exactly do you want?"

"The truth would be nice," I said.

"The truth? About what?"

"Brigid Burgeon, for starters," I said. He smirked, but it faded when I added the next part. "And how it all ties in to Paul Venchus being murdered in L.A. and Mrs. Henrietta Perkins being killed here. And let's not forget good old Eddie Sikorski. There are a lot of dead bodies piling up lately. Your family made its fortune in the arms business, didn't it? Supplying weapons systems to the military? I imagine your old man had significant connections to the Company, right? And the Indian?"

"Shut the fuck up!" He slammed his palm down on the table. "My family had nothing to do with any of that. And listen, my father's eighty-seven years old now, and he doesn't need any of this bullshit being jacked around again." He gave the tabletop another slam.

"Nice hand slap," I said. "Too bad you didn't have that move perfected when that group of thugs attacked your friend outside that Reno bar."

I let the statement hang there. His face blanched, then reddened with rage. He pointed the "lethal" index finger at me again. "You make any spurious allegations and you'll find yourself buried in a lawsuit. We'll sue you for everything you have, you . . ." He let that one trail off, but I caught the meaning with his next statement. "After all, money is something you people understand, isn't it?"

Nolan came in carrying two drinks. His face twisted when he saw Uncle Lar's preapoplectic condition.

"You'd better put your boy back on the leash," I said. "His anti-Semitism is showing."

Nolan set one of the drinks in front of Kaye and said, "Larry, let's not make this counterproductive." He held out his hand, offering me the second glass.

"No thanks, but that idiot could probably use another one."

The corner of Nolan's mouth tugged downward. "Then I take it we have not come to an agreement as yet?"

"That son of a bitch wants more money," Uncle Lar said, tossing back half the amber liquid in the glass. He muttered something about "just like a Jew" under his breath.

"Larry," Nolan cautioned.

"Hey, don't worry about it," I said. "He's obviously trying to water his backbone. Say, what really happened outside that bar in Reno? And what about the theory that you're actually gay?"

Uncle Lar practically choked on the swallow he'd just taken. His eyes were vivid as he fixed them on me.

I stood and calmly faced him down. "Come on, Lar, in this day and age it's a new time of enlightenment. Nobody's going to hold it against you. It's not like you got caught in an airport washroom stall or anything."

"You go fuck yourself, Belzer."

Far too many assholes had been swearing at me lately, and I wanted to change that. I gave them both a little hand salute and moved toward the door.

"Belzer, wait," Nolan said, the desperation edging his words. "We need to work this out."

"Go ahead," I said, "but start without me." I shoved the paper door to the side and started to step through, Uncle Lar's vituperative warning calling out after me.

"You don't know who you're messing with, Belzer. You ain't even got a fucking clue. They'll bury your ass."

I paused at the opening and smiled. "You know, I really hate stupid conversations with mean drunks. Especially when they're assholes."

As I entered the main bar area, Grady nodded to me from the other side. He'd situated himself so he could watch the door of the private room. I walked over and sat on the stool next to him and said, "Whatever you're drinking, I'm buying."

He held up a glass of clear liquid. "Soda water does me just fine when I'm working."

I ordered a shot of tequila. The bartender set it on the bar with a lime and packet of salt. I skipped the ceremony and just took a straight sip, feeling the burn all the way down, not wanting to admit to myself that I'd let some petty insult from a drunk get to me as much as it had.

"You get her safely up to her room?" I asked.

He nodded. "And then I hightailed it back down here."

"Thanks, Grady. I appreciate everything you've done."

"Don't worry 'bout it. I will say that things have livened up a bit since you got here, though. Maybe we ought to have you come out every so often just to keep us on our toes. Run some scenarios by us."

I swallowed some more of the tequila. "The only scenario I want to run right now is grabbing a quick bite to eat in my room and heading to the fights."

We agreed to meet at the elevators next to Betty's All Night Cafe at 7:00. As I finished off my drink I saw Nolan leading a staggering Uncle Lar, replete with the baseball cap and dark glasses, down the corridor toward the rear exit. I tapped Grady's arm. "Can they get out that way?"

"They can if they have a special key. And they come here a lot. Know the way real good."

"Let me guess, friends of Mr. Ocean?"

"You got it," he said.

CHAPTER 16

After dining in and giving Veronica my laptop to keep her occupied, I once again admonished her to stay in the room unless she heard from me directly, and only from me.

"Yes, sir," she said, making a mimicking salute. At least she used her right hand.

"I'm serious," I said. "This thing's starting to heat up, and we could be dealing with some really bad people."

"I knew that already," she said. "That's what I've been trying to tell you."

I started to go over safety precautions again but she shooed me out, saying she was a big girl and wouldn't get into trouble. I thought about telling her that she got me in enough trouble for both of us, but decided not to press my luck.

In the hallway I tried Barry again and finally got through to him.

"Belz, I'm sorry," he said. "I've been meaning to call you, but the heart specialist just finished talking to Johnny."

"What did they find?" My own heart felt like it was in my throat.

"Nothing."

"What?"

"But that's good," he said. "They found no significant blockages with the angiogram, and no arrythmias. The fact that the angina was temporary has led them to believe the whole incident was stress-related."

"Stress-related," I repeated. You got to love doctors. They tell you you're on death's door, insist on all the precautionary tests, put you through all the hell, worry, and anxiety, and then tell you it was nothing. Just stress. No shit? It was enough to make Sherlock flatten Dr. Watson. "Is he ready to be discharged?"

"It'll be at least another hour or two. They put a special dissolvable stitch in the artery in his leg, and they want to make sure it's not going to rupture."

I glanced at my watch. "You want me to come by to pick you guys up?"

"No, no, no," he said. "I've got Hector on standby for that. In fact, Johnny told me to give you specific instructions to go to the fights tonight. I told him we gave Grady the other ticket, and he's thrilled."

"I'm glad. By the way, I filled the telethon spot."

"Really? Who?"

"Promise to keep it a secret?"

"I will."

"Sal Fabell." I heard Barry gasp and I gave him Sal's cell number. "I told him you'd call and give him the specifics."

"Richard, this is wonderful. Johnny will be so thrilled."

"You can't tell him yet," I said. "Sal wants to surprise him."

"It'll certainly do that. You're the best, you know that?"

I reminded him to call me when they were back, no matter what the hour, and went to meet Grady.

They'd transformed the center ballrooms of the hotel into a massive arena. Seating went well back and there were balconies all around; our seats were right up front. In the center was the eight-sided cage, with the ten-foot-high cyclone fencing that has become standard for Mixed Martial Arts contests. The mat in the center had exotic designs and advertisements on it, making it so colorful I wondered if they did that to mask the blood that would inevitably be spilled. But then again, no one was forcing the athletes to climb inside the cage, and they could stop whenever they wanted. Too bad racehorses and greyhounds didn't have that same option.

I realized the tequila had affected me more than I thought, so I waited for the burn-off and just had a bottle of water. I offered to buy Grady a beer, but he made a joke about being "partially on the clock," and just drank water as well. Who'da thunk it, thirty years ago, that we'd be paying for the privilege of drinking plain old tap water out of a plastic bottle with a label saying it was from some distant mountain stream? It made me think about investing in some company that would bottle that same mountain air for sale in the near future. But the way things were going, we might need it.

The first two fights on the undercard didn't get past the first round. Of course, since the rounds were five minutes long, it ate up the better part of an hour with the buildups, interviews on the big-screen TVs, and the announcements. One guy got clocked so badly he went to his knees and his opponent did a savage follow-up, bashing him until the ref stepped in. Grady shook his head.

"Makes me glad the old Marquess of Queensberry made them rules for the boxing ring," he said. "Hitting a man when he's taking a knee is poor sportsmanship in my book."

"Mine, too," I said. "Too much like a street fight."

The camera guys were panning and zooming around between matches, shooting footage of the crowd, focusing on the celebrities in attendance. One of them finally noticed me and mentioned something to one of the commentators. I didn't know the guy, Stan Something, but he came over and introduced himself.

"Richard Belzer, here for the fights?" he asked.

As they say, any publicity is good publicity, I thought, as I watched my image on one of the big screens posted overhead. "If I'm not, I sure as hell made a wrong turn at the roulette wheel, didn't I?"

He laughed. "It's well known that you're a big boxing fan, but it's good to know you're interested in MMA as well." His voice sounded like it was covered with three coats of lacquer. "Who do you like in our main event tonight?"

"Actually, I like them both," I said, grinning into the camera. "I wouldn't want to make either of them mad at me by picking a favorite."

"Wise move," he said. The camera shifted away and focused on some more of the rich and famous.

"Is it like this everywhere you go?" Grady asked.

I shook my head. "Only in Vegas and New York. When I'm home in France, I'm just another spoiled, ugly American."

He chuckled and drained his water. I set mine down on the floor and told him to save my seat. "I'm going to hit the little boys' room before the big one. I'll grab some more water for you."

He nodded.

The signs marked RESTROOMS, complete with crude pictures of male and female forms, directed me down a long hall. I pushed the door open and joined about five other males in the process of relieving themselves. As luck would have it, several urinals opened up and the occupants left. Without washing their hands, I might note. This didn't bother me so much as the two squirrelly guys hanging out between me and the door. They were both kind of swarthy-looking, in a greasy sort of way. One was good-sized, the other one small, but wiry. When I went up to the sink, I noticed out of the corner of my eye that one of the guys, the bigger one, had stationed himself at the door with his foot against the bottom. He must have tipped the scales at close to three hundred, and evidently was considering a job as a portable doorstop. I hoped nobody had a case of the runs.

The little guy, whom I had dubbed Greaser Number Two for lack of a better term, made his way to the end wall and started kicking open stalls. A couple were apparently occupied, because I heard some yelling, but they left after some hurried flushes. I continued to wash my hands, keeping an eye on the big greaser, who was still standing with his foot against the bottom of the door. Someone banged against it from the other side, but Doorstop didn't budge. The person tried again. OAB, most likely, or, in layman's terms, overactive bladder. Doorstop still didn't move his foot. Little sympathy from this end.

"It's temporarily closed," he yelled out. "Go someplace else."

I heard a muffled reply from the other side of the door, and was just about to comment as I reached for a paper towel.

"We been waiting for you, Jew boy."

I turned. The little guy, leaning against the wall that separated the sinks from the rest of the toilet apertures, had spoken.

"That's good to know," I said. Mentally, I was trying to figure out my initial moves against the two of them. They were spread out far enough that it wasn't going to be easy. They also looked like the types who'd done this before. But then again, exactly what were they going to do?

Doorstop must have read my mind. "Hey," he said.

I glanced as he tapped something heavy and metallic in his coat pocket against the side of the door. "Don't you try nothing now."

"Wouldn't dream of it," I said. "Taking on two tough greaseballs in a public washroom isn't my idea of fun. Especially if one or maybe both of them has a gun in his pocket."

"We been waiting for you to get away from the nigger," Greaser Number Two said.

"Better not let him hear you call him that." I turned sideways so I'd present a narrower target to the one with the gun. It was all I could think of doing at this point. I had no weapon of my own, no course of emergency egress, and no Chuck Norris or *Walker, Texas Ranger* script to rescue me from this situation. "I suppose you're going to tell me you're armed as well?"

Greaser Number Two pulled open his jacket and let me see the butt of a pistol stuck in his waistband. He grinned like a happy little weasel.

"You think I'm afraid of some fucking shine, no matter how big he is, kike?"

I sighed. "Another anti-Semite. I already met one of you guys today. And you're a racist to boot." I looked toward Doorstop. "I guess it's hard to find good help these days, isn't it?"

Greaser Number Two moved forward and gripped my arm, saying, "Come on, asshole."

I immediately grabbed his wrist and doubled him over. Above his squeal, I heard a distinct clicking sound and froze. I held Greaser Number

Two's arm in a *kimura,* causing him to bend over at the waist with his head pointing down toward the floor. He was swearing a blue streak, but Doorstop had removed the item from his pocket, which I now saw was one of the biggest revolvers I'd ever seen. The end of the barrel stared at me like a third eye, and appeared to be about three feet in circumference.

"Let him go now, Mr. Belzer," Doorstop said.

At least he'd called me "Mr." It was a step up from "Jew boy" or "asshole." I released Greaser Number Two, who stumbled back a few steps, then cocked his arm back like he was going to take a swing.

"Rocco," the big guy said, stopping the smaller one with his tone. "The boss don't want him roughed up yet, remember?"

Rocco straightened up, swearing. His dark eyes met mine for a moment with a glare of pure hatred, then he clipped the underside of his chin with his index finger and pointed toward the door.

"Know that if you try to make a break, or try any more of that kung fu shit," Rocco said, "Vito will cut you down before you go two steps."

Vito and Rocco. Two goombahs. It was so nice to be on a first-name basis. The offhand comment that "the boss" didn't want me roughed up sounded a tiny bit encouraging. And if their intent was to do serious bodily harm, they could have done it and left already. But he'd also said "yet." I figured feigning compliance until we were in a public area was my best, and only, option at the moment.

"Lead on, Macduff," I said.

"That ain't my name," Rocco muttered.

"Don't worry, Shakespeare got it wrong, too." I hoped I sounded more insouciant than I felt.

Big Vito opened the door and peered out. He glanced back inside and cocked his head. He exited with me following and Weasel Rocco bringing up the rear. The corridor was pretty much deserted. Where are the obnoxious autograph seekers when you need them? But as they ushered me away from the hallway leading back to the arena, I heard someone call my name. We stopped and turned.

Grady was jogging toward us. "Hey, Belz, where you going, man?"

"Buzz off, shine," Rocco said, then motioned for Vito to stop Grady.

Vito looked like a refrigerator with arms as he positioned himself in the middle of the aisle. His voice was a low growl as he muttered, "You heard him. Get the fuck outta here."

Grady stopped a few feet in front of him and grinned. Before Vito could react, Grady's jab, a total blur, shot out three or four times, popping the bigger man in the face. Vito snorted like an angry bull and reached out, but Grady sidestepped, giving him an angle, popped a double jab, right cross, left hook to the big head. It sounded like someone smacking a watermelon with a ball-peen hammer. Vito stopped and staggered. Grady stepped inside and did the shoeshine to the huge body, culminating with a solid left hook to the liver, then a right uppercut just as Vito's knees started to sag. The big man collapsed in sections, like a slow-motion demolition job, first to his knees, then plopping forward on his hands, and finally curling into a ball on his left side. It was a beautiful thing to behold.

A rustling movement caught my eye and I saw Rocco pulling out a six-inch barreled revolver. My left hand shot out, catching his wrist and pushing the gun upward as I gave him a backfist to his hooked nose. It exploded in a spray of blood under my knuckles, accompanied by a horrendously loud *boom* as the gun in his other hand discharged. An acrid odor filled the air and my ears completely shut down with two school bells ringing overtime. I used my right hand to grab Rocco's gun and twist his wrist back toward me, peeling the weapon from his grasp as I did. I clopped him on the temple with the butt and he fell to the floor like a bag of yesterday's dirty laundry.

I shook my head, trying to clear the ringing out of my ears. I saw Grady kneeling on Vito's head and patting him down. He pulled the big guy's jacket up so that both his arms were pinioned behind him. Grady slipped the big revolver from Vito's shoulder holster and grinned.

"A three fifty-seven," he said. "Nice weapon and it don't leave no shell casings."

I realized that my hearing was starting to return. The bells had diminished to a faint noise now. I gave Rocco a quick pat-down search and pulled his jacket back to trap his arms like Grady had done. I was going to have to show that move to my instructor, Jimmy Lee, when I got back to the

dojang. Plus, it would probably impress the shit out of the show's techni-
cal advisors. I stood, keeping my foot on Rocco's head, a good resting place
for it, and gazed up to see where the errant bullet had struck. It took a few
passes, but finally I saw a small, black hole near the juncture of ceiling and
wall. I silently hoped that no one on the other side of it had been injured.

Grady had his cell phone out and was talking to someone. I assumed it
was the police. When he disconnected he said, "Cops are on the way." Vito
was still out for the count, but Rocco had begun to stir slightly. "Las Vegas
Metro gonna love talking to you two goombahs."

"Fuck you, jig," Rocco said. I felt a sense of satisfaction as I noticed his
teeth had a coating of crimson.

"Don't feel bad," I said. "He was calling me 'Jew boy' inside the washroom."

The only bad thing about the police arriving when they did was after they
saw the recovered guns, and the hole in the ceiling, they invited us all
down to headquarters to sort things out. It was an offer we couldn't refuse.
They even took Grady's piece from the holster on his belt for the transport,
despite his proper security guard IDs. After placing Grady and me in separate rooms, they proceeded to take our statements. It goes without saying
that the room I was in was eerily similar to some of the ones I've worked in
on the show, but I knew there was no camera crew and soundstage beyond
the one-way glass. After telling my account for the third time, and request-
ing they contact Detective Kirby for verification purposes, I was delighted
when he finally walked in.

"Belz, what the hell happened?" he asked. He gave the person who had
been taking my statement a dismissive wave and the guy left.

I gave Kirby the rundown, ending with the two goombahs' mention of
"the boss."

"Any idea who that might be?" I asked.

"Yeah, I do," he said.

I waited, but he didn't offer anything more. "They say anything about
what this was all about?"

Kirby shook his head. "Nah, they both lawyered up. We'll hold them overnight and get them into court in the morning. Hopefully, the judge will give them remand, but our damn jail's so crowded they may get out on bond."

"Ah, the wheels of justice turn slowly. But I met a real scumbag Las Vegas lawyer recently, if they need one. The always sleazy Joseph Patrick Nolan."

Kirby's eyes narrowed. "You know him?"

"He was trying to get me to lay off asking questions about all the recent accidental deaths cropping up around here. I take it he's well loved by the LVMPD?"

"Oh yeah." Kirby smirked. "But first things first. I'll get you two guys out of here in a couple minutes. I'm assuming you'll want to sign complaints against these two goons, right?"

I shot him a sly smile. "If I do, does that mean Clark County will pay for a free trip back to Vegas?"

He laughed. "I'll see what I can do."

"If not, I suppose I could force myself to fly out for altruistic reasons," I said. "Like helping out your local economy at the tables."

By the time Grady and I walked out into the cool desert night, it was close to 10:00 p.m. Kirby said to wait in front and he'd have a marked unit take us back to the Monticello.

Grady shook his head. "Looks like we missed the big fight."

"That's okay," I said. "I got to see a better one. You ever think about making a comeback?"

He grinned. "Sheeeit. You sure that was only water you was drinking?"

CHAPTER 17

Needless to say, by the time Grady and I got back to the Monticello, the main event was history. Reeves had taken a split decision, but from all accounts it had been one hell of a fight. They were already screaming "rematch." I told Grady I'd have to catch that one. I then called Barry, who said he and Johnny were upstairs and that Johnny was fighting off the effects of a sedative while waiting for me.

"I'll be right up," I said.

"Uh, Belz, I have something else to tell you." Barry's voice sounded sodden with guilt.

"Okay, you going to spill it or make me wait?"

"I . . . told Johnny that Sal agreed to fill in at the telethon. He was so worried about it, and when I told him that you'd gotten it covered, he wanted to know, and I didn't know what to do, and I—"

"Barry," I said, cutting him off. He was like a runaway train once he got started in confession mode. He was an unethical cop's dream. Once he got going, he'd confess to killing John Kennedy if he thought it would please you. "It's okay that you told Johnny."

"It is?"

"Yeah." I pressed the button for the elevator. "As long as you don't tell Sal."

• • •

Johnny looked worn out when I got to his room. Barry had fluffed up the pillows behind him so he could lean back comfortably. I wondered how many rooms he'd raided to get all those pillows. Either that, or he'd promised the maids a big tip. I gave Johnny a quick hug.

"It's good to see you without your oxygen hoses," I said.

"Yeah. I was getting kind of attached to those things." Even his voice sounded weak, deflated. He shook his head and smiled. "I can't believe it. Sallie coming to do my telethon . . . how'd you do it?"

"To quote Mickey Spillane, 'It was easy.' " I grinned. "Actually, he was all for it. Just don't let on that you know. He wanted to surprise you."

"That *facocktason.*"

"He called you the same thing," I said. "What's it mean?"

His shoulders hunched in a shallow shrug. "Some kind of Italian thing, I guess. He used to call me that all the time. I never did ask him . . . maybe he just made it up."

He looked like his eyelids were getting heavy.

"Why did you two split up anyway? I've always been curious."

He shrugged. "Don't want to go there. Bad memories. Lots of bad memories. Too many."

"No problem." I stood and patted his arm. "Why don't you try to get some much-needed rest and leave everything else to Barry and me?"

"Sounds like a plan, partner." He closed his eyes, seemed to doze for a few seconds, then snapped awake. "Belz. You okay? Where you at?"

"I'm right here, Johnny."

He grinned. "You ain't still going 'round playing cop, are you? That stupid Brigid Burgeon thing? Please tell me you ain't."

"No, Johnny." I didn't want to tell him things had evolved way beyond poor Brigid, the trio of mysterious deaths, and the possible Indian stalker, with the two goombahs accosting me in the restroom.

"You swear?" He grabbed my arm. "Swear to me."

"Relax. I am not a cop." I felt his grip slacken. "Get some rest."

His eyelids looked heavy. He blinked once, looked up at me with an almost drunken expression, and closed his eyes again. His breathing slowed to a sonorous pace.

I stepped out and pulled the door shut, motioning for Barry to move over to the balcony. I slid open the glass door and stepped outside. The night air was cool and the myriad of lights, in varying colors and brightness, looked practically endless.

"I know he sounded kind of out of it," Barry said, "but the doctor suggested he be given the sedative as soon as we got back. He refused to take it until he saw you, so I put it in some juice."

I grinned. "You slipped your boss a mickey?"

Barry seemed disturbed by the remark. "It was for his own good. And he kept saying he wasn't taking anything until he knew you were all right, so what choice did I have?"

"Relax, I was just kidding." I studied him for a moment. He looked almost as worn out as Johnny had. "You had any rest since this thing started?"

He shook his head. "Not much."

"Why don't you get some sleep, too," I said. We started to go inside when something else hit me. "Why was he worried if I was all right?"

Barry smiled. "He cares about you, Belz. He always says you're the illegitimate son he wishes he had."

I chuckled. "That sounds like vintage Johnny, but we'll have to think of a better title than that."

His neck muscles tightened. "Belz, I'm sorry about telling him about the Sal thing. He just wouldn't let up."

I waved off his explanation. "What do you know about why him and Sal broke up?"

"Johnny never talks about it."

"He ever talk about a couple of L.A. cops named Russell and Sikorski?"

He considered the names and frowned. "They don't sound familiar."

"What about Elliott Collins? How's he fit into this picture?"

Barry rolled his eyes. "He used to represent Johnny. Sal, too. Maybe he still manages Sal. But he's the go-to guy around here. Approached Johnny about doing the telethon at the Monticello months ago. Said he could set it up with the owner."

"Elliott approached Johnny?"

He nodded. "Why?"

Things were starting to add up in a way I wasn't sure I liked. But I had to play this close to my vest. "We might have another gap in the performance schedule. Word is that everybody's favorite comedian, Harvey Smithe, was taken to rehab yesterday."

"Oh, shit. Johnny wanted him on at ten."

"Ten? I thought we'd agreed to relegate that asshole to the three a.m. spot?"

"That's what I suggested, but Johnny said he'd have to at least be close to prime time. It's what Elliott wanted."

And what Elliott wants, I thought. But any arguments would wait until tomorrow. There was no sense upsetting Johnny with trivial matters tonight, even if we could wake him up.

Sleep wasn't on my mind when I got back to my room. I poured myself a glass of wine from my refrigerator and sat down at the circular table with a pencil and paper. There were too many variables in this one for me to make sense of things. It was like some kind of patternless crossword puzzle with no spaces or numbers and only rows of blank squares. I had to come up with the overall structure. I scribbled the names of the original principals, Brigid and Mark Kaye Jr. I added Constance Penroy and the Indian, off to the side, and drew a line from him to each of them.

On the other side of the paper, figuring it would represent twenty-six years, I wrote in Paul's name and Veronica's. I added in the rest of the Kaye family: Mark Kaye Sr., grandson Mark III, and good old Uncle Lar. Old Man Kaye had made a mint selling weapons systems, and who would have been a better customer than the Company? I wrote "CIA" underneath the Indian. Next, I jotted down Mrs. Perkins and Eddie Sikorski. Parallel to Eddie, I wrote in Leo Russell's name, then just for the hell of it added Joseph Patrick Nolan and the mysterious Mr. Ocean.

The thing was beginning to look like the cast of a half-assed comedy of errors. Who was I missing? Elliott Collins and Harvey Smithe, with an E, obviously. And the two goombahs, Vito and Rocco. Those two acted like a couple of refugees from *The Sopranos*.

I went back to the top and used a heavy line to circle Brigid, then drew the line down and circled Mark Kaye Jr. and Constance Penroy, connecting those three to the Indian. I drew a separate line to Paul, and then one to Mrs. Perkins and Eddie. And Eddie to Leo.

The inscription on the photograph I'd seen on Sikorski's wall, "To my two good bodyguarding cop buddies and honorary paisans . . ." I wrote down Sal's name and then, after a moment of contemplation, put Johnny's name on the paper as well. I didn't have to draw in the rest of the lines. It already formed a big circle, each party connected in some way to the other. Russell, the dirty cop doing business with the mob, bodyguards Sal, who was partnered with Johnny, both of whom were managed by Elliott . . .

It was shaping up to be something I wasn't going to like. Johnny was like a second father to me. My hero, my mentor, the man I'd do just about anything for . . . and him for me. . . . *You ain't still going 'round playing cop, are you? That stupid Brigid Burgeon thing? Please tell me you ain't.*

I set the pencil down.

Okay, Johnny, I won't tell you.

CHAPTER 18

I awoke early when the probing morning sunbeams found their way in the sliver between my drapes, casting a bright, vertical line on the wall of my room. I'd tossed and turned most of the night, not wanting to believe the only thing that was making sense: Johnny knew more about this whole thing than he had told me. That's why he'd been so adamant about me dropping my "Columbo routine" and concentrate on helping him with the telethon. And every time Elliott insinuated himself into the scene, Johnny either shooed me away or looked like he was about to have a stroke. Or a heart attack.

I'd worked it over in my mind until it made as much sense as I could make of it. Elliott had approached Johnny about the telethon at the behest of Mr. Ocean, aka the Outfit. Obviously, the mob is always looking for a way to launder a few extra million. Pledges to a charity that go to a specific "charitable organization . . ." Like the Picardus Corporation or the old widows and orphans fund that strictly benefited bachelors . . . But how would someone with mob ties get a gaming license, especially after the feds made such a project of cleaning this town up after things got out of hand in the late seventies?

Perhaps he got approved with a little help from his friends . . . like

Joseph Patrick Nolan and a sympathetic state senator named Lawrence Kaye . . . whose lawyer, Joseph Patrick Nolan, once again, approached me when I happened to kick some dog shit into the Kaye campaign center office. But what would Kaye have to gain by getting in bed with the mob? An exchange for long-ago help for taking care of the "Brigid problem" by having Leo Russell take care of the crime-scene investigation? But to protect whom? His brother? His father? The Ocean–Uncle Lar union was a tenuous lineage at best, and looked even thinner when it was stretched over twenty-six years. Fodder for a conspiratorial tabloid maybe, but a couple quarts low on provability for real newspaper standards. Still, there were a lot of recently dead bodies popping up. Or rather, falling down. And if Ocean was part of this arabesque, how safe would Veronica be, staying in this hotel? How safe would I be?

The question remained: was the threat of a tabloid conspiracy enough to start making people in high places so nervous that they'd dust off the Indian and dispatch him to start eliminating people? Maybe not people so much as loose ends. Loose ends that could tie them to a couple of old murders. And maybe some new ones. The exact whats and whys were the parts of that "patternless crossword puzzle" that weren't quite clear yet.

But did I have anything solid to bring to the authorities? As of the moment, Veronica and I were like to two flies buzzing around a horse's ass. I smiled at my imagined metaphor. It fit good old Uncle Lar to a T. But we were still horseflies, and they tended to end up one of two ways: either swatted out of existence or up to their knees in a pile of shit.

I heaved a sigh. I'd worked with a lot less to figure out a mystery, but none where the stakes were so high. Not only were Veronica's and my physical safety at risk, but I couldn't keep delving into things and run the risk of somehow hurting Johnny. Plus, with so many pieces of the puzzle missing, I'd pretty much run out of options to explore and people to interview. You can only overturn so many rocks before the tide comes in and washes all your discoveries away. And the tide was the telethon. The clock was running and once it was over, I'd leave Vegas and go back to my life in New York. Maybe it was time now to put Veronica on that bus back to L.A. and tell her that the police had enough leads on things to do their own follow-ups. It sure beat jumping at shadows and trying to outthink some mythological assassin whose face was one of the crucial missing pieces.

Plus, it was 7:00 a.m. on Sunday morning, and the countdown for the launch of the telethon had reached the final twelve hours.

After a hot shower and a cup of coffee in my room, I dialed Barry's cell. He picked up and sounded wide awake.

"How's Sleeping Beauty?" I asked.

"Still asleep. I've been up getting everything set with the hotel arrangements. They're already downstairs setting up the ballroom, and the camera and sound techs are there, too." He paused. "What time do you think I should call Sal?"

"He always bragged that he never got up before ten, so I'd wait till at least eight thirty."

He laughed. "I'm so excited about that. You did great, Belz. Thanks."

"You mentioned last night that Johnny got approached by Elliott to do this one?"

"Right."

"Johnny told me that he owed Elliott one. Any idea what he was talking about?"

"Not really," Barry said. "Elliott had dropped Johnny way before I became his assistant."

"Yeah, I forgot you're still in your tender years. Was he Sal's manager, too?"

"Yeah." He drew out the word. "I know he managed Sal for quite a while, up until about five or ten years ago. But why are you asking me all these questions?"

"I was up most of the night working on a patternless crossword puzzle."

"Huh?"

"Never mind. I've got a few loose ends to tie up this morning, but I'll be there for the opening, come hell or high water."

I disconnected and called Veronica's cell. She answered with a crispness that told me she'd been up a while.

"You ready to eat breakfast?" I asked.

"I sure am. And don't forget, I have your laptop."

I wasn't about to forget that. After telling her I'd do the "shave and a haircut" knock in ten minutes and escort her into my room for breakfast, I disconnected and weighed the options of how to tell her that the clock had run out on our investigation. It was time for the one-way bus ride. Maybe I'd spring for an airplane fare, if I could get one on short notice. Or maybe Hector or one of his buddies would do the deed for me. But I didn't have time to watch her during my cohosting chores, and my return ticket to the Big Apple was dated Tuesday morning. Once the telethon started, it would be nonstop for twenty-four hours. The cleanup and final counting could be left to Johnny. He had the ever-capable Barry to help him, so that wouldn't be a problem.

No, my "problem" was coming by for breakfast.

We ate pretty much in silence, as if Veronica knew that the sand in the hourglass had almost all dribbled to the bottom. She'd brought the laptop and set it carefully on my desk before sitting down at the table, saying that she'd done more writing on the story last night. I smiled and nodded. The room service came and we settled in to eat. Finally, as we were both enjoying a postmeal, second cup of coffee, she said, "So the telethon starts tonight."

It was more of a statement than a question. "So it does."

She looked down. "Does that mean you'll be going back to New York, then?"

That one was a question, but it was obvious she already knew the answer.

"I was going to talk to you about that," I said. "I think we've taken this thing about as far as we can."

She looked up. "How can you say that? My grandmother's been communing with me. We're really close. I can feel it."

"Close to what? All we've really got are a bunch of theories and suspicious circumstances and no tangible proof of anything."

"That's not true. I told you I'm getting more visions."

I held up my hands. "I'm afraid it is true, my dear. And stow the visions in your magic carpetbag. This thing is getting more than a little dangerous."

"We've been being careful." Her voice cracked. "And we've got Grady."

"We can't keep expecting Grady to bodyguard us. He works for the hotel. Plus, we had a rather problematic encounter with a couple of rather tough guys last night."

"Tough guys? When?"

"At the fights. One of the reasons he and I missed the main event."

"What happened? Who were they?"

I smiled to defray her alarm a bit. "Two goombahs. Vito and Rocco. They tried to escort me behind the hotel for a little talk."

"Oh my God. Did you get hurt?"

"No, and they got arrested." I took a final sip of my coffee, which had chilled to tepidness. "Which is all the more reason to let the police handle things from here. We've opened a few doors for them. They're the guys with the investigative prowess and they get paid to take the risks. We don't."

"But the truth—"

"The truth will come out eventually. You have to believe."

"Believe? Do you know how long I've waited for the truth to come out about my grandmother's murder?" Her eyes welled up. "Do you?"

I was glad the phone in my room rang and gave me a reason not to answer her.

"Mr. Belzer?" an unfamiliar male voice asked.

"Speaking."

"This is Special Agent Falletti, sir. Federal Bureau of Investigation. I wonder if my partner and I could have a few minutes of your time."

"Now?" I checked the clock beside my bed. Quarter to nine on a Sunday morning. "It's a bit early in the day, isn't it?"

"I'm sorry, sir, but it's a very pressing matter."

I must have blanched a bit because Veronica read my face and mouthed, "Who is it?"

I recovered enough to raise an eyebrow and say, "Sure, I've always got time for the FBI. You want to come up?"

"Actually, sir, we'd prefer to meet in a public place."

That sounded ominous. I said I'd be down in the Marebello in five minutes. After I hung up I turned to Veronica. She had one of those incredulous expressions that people reserve for when they've heard really shocking news.

"Was that really the FBI?" she asked.

"They sounded like it. I won't know for sure until I check those little gold badges they give them in Washington."

"Is it about the case?"

"Could be. Now, look, it's imperative that you stay here in the room until you hear from me. Understood?"

"But—"

"No buts. We're dealing with some really dangerous people. Now that the FBI is involved, you know just how dangerous. You stay put."

She looked down. "Okay. I promise."

I was going to check to see if she was holding crossed fingers behind her back, but decided on another ploy. "You can keep my laptop and do some writing, so long as you get started packing."

"Packing? And then what?"

"And then, after I talk to the feds and check on Johnny, I'll see about having Hector drive you back to L.A."

Her lips turned downward in a pout.

"Veronica, like I said, I have to go back to New York. And it's time for you to go home, too. Didn't you say you have family in Waterton, Maine?"

"It's Waterville." She managed a trace of defiance.

"Wherever. It's time to get on with your life," I said. "Away from here."

Special Agent Andrew Falletti and his partner, Special Agent Stearn, were dressed like Will Smith and Tommy Lee Jones in *Men in Black,* except Stearn was a woman and their suits were blue. They stood just inside the entrance of the Marebello Room, patiently waiting like two well-dressed vultures. I guess it fit the bill for being public enough. The thought of going downstairs to meet two agents of J. Edgar's Agency in "a public place" was enough to raise the hairs on the back of my neck.

I walked past them, motioning for them to follow. The hostess seated us in a booth on the far wall, away from everybody else. Since I'd already eaten, I just ordered coffee. Falletti and Stearn followed suit. The waitress looked glum as she scribbled three coffees on her pad until I waved her close and said, "This is a special meeting, so if you keep everyone away from these tables, there'll be a big tip in it for you."

That brought a smile to her face.

I pointed to Falletti. "He'll do the tipping."

Falletti's mouth tugged into a hint of a smile. He had olive skin and a beard so heavy it probably looked like he needed a shave ten minutes after he set the razor down. Stearn was pretty, in an official sort of way. She almost reminded me of my female costar on the show, not so much in looks, but in the way she carried herself. Like a lady who is sure of herself and comfortable in her own skin.

The waitress returned with three mugs and a carafe. After she poured, she left. Falletti and I had ours black. Stearn loaded up on both sugar and cream.

"Is this public enough for you?" I asked.

Falletti's dark eyes shot around the room, then focused back on me. I guessed he was satisfied there was no one within earshot.

"What exactly was your connection to Edward Sikorski?" he asked.

"Connection? Not much. I only saw him once. Talked to him about some old cases from when he was on the LAPD."

"Which cases?"

He had a typical governmental knack for pissing me off. Like the guy from the IRS. A sense of proprietary arrogance, as if I were obligated to answer his questions without any explanation. Iconoclast that I am, I figured it was time to draw a line in the sand.

"Why are you so interested?"

This seemed to stun him. Knock him off his rhythm. His partner must have seen he was off his game and took over.

"Mr. Belzer, we'll ask the questions, if you don't mind."

I turned to her and smiled. "And what if I do mind?"

She looked more stunned than Falletti had.

Okay, I thought, you've slapped them back a couple of times. Now find out what the hell this is all about.

"The Brigid Burgeon case," I said.

They exchanged glances.

Falletti regained a bit of his composure. "For a book you're working on?"

Now it was my turn to be stunned. I had mentioned to Eddie on the phone that I was working on a book. But the only way the feds could know that was if they'd talked to him, or Veronica, neither of which was likely, or they had his phone lines tapped.

I smiled again. "Want to be in a chapter? I could talk a lot about J. Edgar and nice dresses."

"I'll bet you could," he said. "But I'd rather you just answer our questions."

"You want to repeat that last one? I don't remember it."

"I asked if you were writing a book."

"I'm always open to writing a good book. I happen to be a best-selling author, you know."

"And what did Sikorski tell you?"

"Not much. Just that Leo Russell was on the scene before he was. Ah, that was kind of strange because Eddie was working in a marked unit and Leo was in dicks. They're usually called to the scene after the fact."

Falletti nodded, his eyes shooting toward Stearn and then back to me. "Why are you so interested in the Burgeon case?"

I figured we could continue to play cat and mouse until the telethon started, but I had things to do. Like making sure Veronica got back to L.A. "It started about a week ago. An old buddy, who I hadn't seen in about thirty years, called me and wanted to talk." I gave them a quick thumbnail sketch of what happened to Paul and how Veronica and I had been drawn in to an expanding web where people were found dead with startling rapidity. I ended with, "Now, how about you telling me why you're so interested?"

The two feds exchanged glances.

"Come on," I said. "Haven't you ever heard of quid pro quo? That's Latin for something like, 'I scratched your back, now it's your turn.' "

"We work for the Bureau," Falletti said. "Consequently, we're limited as to what we may or may not discuss with civilians."

"And I am not a cop," I said. "I just play one on TV. Is that it?"

Falletti scratched his upper lip. It sounded like scissors on sandpaper.

"Are you in the practice of consorting with known figures in organized crime, Mr. Belzer?"

I laughed. "Hardly."

He sat there impassively for a few seconds. "Royce Ocean, the owner of this hotel. His real name's not Ocean."

I raised both eyebrows. "No, really?"

"It's Odaletti. You know him?"

I shook my head. "I've seen him from a distance."

"Does Mr. Leland know him?"

"You'll have to ask him."

"We intend to," Stearn said. I guess she craved some inclusion in our boy talk.

I looked at Falletti. "What if Johnny does know him? I mean, the guy's letting him do the telethon here."

"Which is what brought you to Vegas?"

"Right."

"And you running around asking questions that are making the wrong people nervous is part of your act?"

Well, what do you know? Falletti had a bit of the comedian in him. Or was it just a streak of rusty irony?

I made a sympathetic cluck. "Is that what I've been doing?"

"What happened last night?"

"Last night?" My eyes went up toward the ceiling as I did my best to convey extreme contemplation. "Let's see . . ."

"Vito Sodaro and Rocco Morelli. Two known figures in the Vegas OC map."

"Those guys were with the outfit?" I widened my eyes. "No shit."

"Mr. Belzer," Stearn said, "you'd do well to take this seriously. These people you're hanging with can be very dangerous."

"Ruthless, in fact," Falletti added.

I was beginning to feel that real uneasiness grab my stomach with both its icy hands. "Yeah, I saw *Casino,* too."

Falletti leaned forward. "Sir, this isn't a movie. Or a game."

I leaned forward, too. "You can call me 'Belz.' And I know it's not a game. Anything you can tell me that would help steer me away from unsavory OC types would be greatly appreciated and kept strictly confidential."

"As I said, we're limited in what we can and cannot say, but . . ." Falletti poured himself some more coffee, poured some for Stearn, and set the carafe back down. I guess I was odd man out for refills. But that was okay. The more I was hearing about the kind of people I'd made nervous, the less I wanted to visit the john by myself.

"But?" I continued for him.

"We work in the Nevada OC division. It's our job to monitor the activities of any individuals who are connected to organized crime, or who may be associated with it. Since this telethon thing began, there has been a slight influx of activity and individuals coming into the area."

"Such as?"

"Harvey Smithe," Falletti said.

"Him?"

Falletti nodded. "He's actually Dario Capacaza's illegitimate son from his liaison with a chorus girl. Matilda Kilvochek. Dario's legit son, Fabio, was killed five years ago. Dario had always done right by Harvey, making sure bills got paid and seeing to his education. But Harvey's intent on becoming a stand-up comedian, and now Dario's funding that dream, too."

"Except Harvey has all the talent of a wet blanket at a picnic," I said.

Falletti almost smiled again. "We know you administered a beating to Harvey a few days ago."

"I'd hardly call it a beating. I just caught him in a wristlock, is all."

"Still, activity like that could put you at risk for a retaliation."

"I'll keep that in mind the next time and make sure I follow through and break his arm. At least it'll make it worthwhile. Anybody else I should be on the lookout for?"

Falletti considered me carefully, then asked, "How well do you know Sal Fabell?"

"Sal? I don't know. We've met at a few parties, is all." I didn't mention that rumors of Sal's connections to the mob were as old as the lighted cowboy sign on Fremont.

"And you went to see him at the Mirage."

They'd obviously been watching as well as listening. I wondered what else they knew that would be kept under a secret shroud of "national security."

"To ask him to take part in the telethon," I said.

"And is he?"

"Tune in and see."

"Sal's real name is Salvatore Fabelli," Stearn said. "His father was a low-level mob guy back in Jersey. A bagman."

"Maybe it was rough times for immigrants back then," I said as matter-of-factly as I could.

"So what about Sal?" Falletti asked again. "He ever talk to you about organized crime?"

"I have nothing to say about Sal." That sounded a little too much like I was taking the fifth, so I added, "and that's because I don't know anything."

"How about Johnny Leland? He and Sal as tight as they used to be?"

I shook my head. Besides Sal, the last person I wanted to talk about with two feds was Johnny. It was time for some counterpunching. "You two ever heard of a guy called the Indian?"

Stearn looked like she'd been slapped. Even the imperturbable Falletti jerked fractionally at my last question.

"How do you know about the Indian?" he asked.

"I think he might have killed that friend of mine," I said. "Brigid Burgeon, too, as well as an older lady named Henrietta Perkins. And I'm sure we all know that Eddie Sikorski, in all probability, didn't conveniently fall down and drown in his own bathtub."

We sat in silence for about twenty seconds, Falletti and Stearn both giving me the hard stare, and me staring back and wishing that damn coffee in my cup was hot instead of tepid.

Finally, Falletti cleared his throat. "The Bureau is engaged in looking into these matters, Mr. Belzer, and they will be thoroughly investigated. In the meantime, I would strongly recommend that you refrain from stirring the pot with any unsubstantiated accusations."

"What about the things I mentioned?"

He blinked. "What about them?"

"We don't deal with half-baked conspiracy theories," Stearn said. "Just facts. Bring us something we can use, and we'll act on it. That I can guarantee."

"I'll keep that in mind," I said.

CHAPTER 19

You gotta love the feds. They waltz onto the scene to tell me to back off, because they're busy investigating and gathering evidence that, chances are, they'll never proceed on. And if they do, it'll be at their customary glacial speed. And then they'll tell me that all the stuff Veronica and I had uncovered during our interviews is just this side of worthless. I think "half-baked conspiracy theories" qualifies for just this side, right? But they had accomplished their purpose with me. I no longer had the fire in my belly to keep moving forward and asking questions designed to piss people off. It wasn't really like me, but I did have Veronica's safety, as well as my own, to think about. Plus, I'd promised Harlee I wouldn't get in trouble, and I'd already tiptoed along the line on that one.

The way things had worked out was for the best, I thought, as I parted ways with the *federales* and headed back up to my room. It was definitely time to get Ms. Holmes out of town. I dialed Hector's cell.

"Hey, boss, what's up?"

"Would you be available for that drive to L.A. this afternoon?" I asked.

"Yeah, sure thing. When you want to leave?"

"I'm thinking relatively soon. You available?"

"Oh, damn. I got to take this baby in for maintenance," he said. "Take me at least an hour. Maybe two."

"Take your time. Two hours ought to be perfect. Call me back when you're done and we'll see how things look."

"Sounds good, Belz."

As soon as I disconnected my cell jangled again. It was Barry. "Belz, where you at?"

"Just finishing up at the Marebello."

"Great. Can you come down to the ballroom where we're doing the telethon? We're trying to get things set up with the TelePrompTers and screens."

It was closing in on eleven o'clock. We had eight hours to go, so things were pretty much on schedule. When I got to the ballroom I was happy to see Grady briefing one of his guards on who had access and who didn't. I walked up and laid a hand on the big guy's shoulder.

"Thanks again for last night," I said.

He looked around and grinned. "Hey, careful what you say now. People might be taking that the wrong way."

I grinned, too, as I walked past him. "Whatever happens in Vegas . . ."

A group of techs were putting up the LED screen they'd use to show how much money had been pledged throughout the telecast. Surrounding them were four more immense screens that would simulcast the performing artists for the auditorium audience while the show was rolling. More techs were struggling getting those erected, and off to their right Barry was waving frantically at me to come down by the stage area. As I started down the aisle I saw Johnny pulling some wires under the black canopy. I walked up to him and frowned.

"Trying for a real heart attack?" I asked. "Why don't you let the techs you hired do their job?"

His mouth puckered and he dropped the wires, swearing. "These fuckers are slower than fucking molasses. I don't do it, it might not get done."

"I'm sure it will. You just got out of the hospital last night, remember? Plus, you're violating union rules."

He dusted off his hands and panted slightly. "Yeah, yeah, you're right, but look at that." He pointed toward them working on the big LED screen. "Shit, at the rate those guys are going, I'd be better off with one of them old fucking Solari boards to keep track of the pledges."

"Johnny, come on." I pointed to one of the chairs. "Sit down and rest."

"Okay, okay, okay, but did you see this?" A smile spread over his face as he sat and pointed to the other group hooking up the TelePrompTers. "Barry's transferring the whole script to the 'PrompTers so each person will be able to read their lines. Unless you want cue cards for your routine?"

"Johnny, relax. I've used TelePrompTers once or twice."

He glanced down and nodded. "Yeah, of course you have. I know. I'm just like the old mother hen, pecking at everything around the barnyard." Cocking his head, he motioned me to move closer. "What's the story with Little Miss Sunshine?"

"Veronica?"

"Yeah. You get rid of her yet?"

"I'm in the process as we speak. In fact, I was just going up to see if she was done packing when Barry called me."

Johnny looked excited. "Well, hell, don't let me keep you from that. The sooner that chick's outta our hair and on her way back to wherever, the better I'll like it. Where's she from again?"

"L.A. Mind if I have Hector give her a ride? It's on my dime."

"*Your dime?* Shit, *I'll* buy her a first-class ticket outta here if it'll be quicker. Take Hector. Tell him to drive her to Portland if he wants. On me."

I told him that wouldn't be necessary, and we sat down and started going over the protocol with Barry. Johnny jumped into things and started barking directions at his young assistant.

Overseeing the setup might be just what the doctor ordered for him, I thought. He obviously had a tendency to micromanage, and denying him the chance might be more stressful than letting him watch. Either way he would be fretting. I figured I'd go up and brief Veronica on the FBI's involvement. I owed her that much. Besides, if I used the right spin, maybe I could convince her that ending our participation and letting the Gee handle it was the best thing. Even if I was downright certain that what I'd told them would merit about as much attention as they gave the lost ark in the first Indiana Jones movie.

Johnny had caught me staring into space. "You dreaming about the bright lights or what?"

I smiled. "Something like that."

"Well, we've got about seven hours till showtime. You want to get your mind back in the game?"

"Sure," I said as we settled back to work.

It was almost four hours later, and I still hadn't heard from Hector. As I was riding up in the elevator, I called him.

"Sorry, boss," he said. "Took longer than I thought at the garage. They had to put in a new water pump. I told them to hustle."

"As long as they put it in the right way," I said. "Where you at?"

"I'm on Koval now, coming to your back door."

"Great, wait for us in the usual spot," I told him. I slipped the phone into my pocket and studied my image in the elevator mirror. I was the bearer of bad news, but to paraphrase that line in *The Three Musketeers*, the bearer has done what had to be done. Or something like that. I just hoped she was packed and wouldn't cry.

When she let me in her room after the knock, I can't say I was too surprised to see the place still in a state of disorganized comfort. Her defiant expression had already told me she hadn't packed at all.

"I've decided to stay and pursue things on my own," she said. "If you won't help me."

I looked at her antagonistic pout and sighed. "Let me break this to you gently. Earlier this morning I had a conversation with J. Edgar's boys. The FBI." I paused to let it sink in. "That means we've stepped on enough toes, overturned enough rocks, upset the apple cart so many times that those in authority are taking a serious look at things."

"Yeah, right. 'Those in authority,'" she mimicked. "You can't convince me that they're really interested. Your vibes are telling me you aren't even soundly convinced yourself."

She was right about that. And here I'd been pleased with my acting ability . . . but I guess it ain't easy to fool a psychic.

"Veronica, we're in a whole new ball game now. Remember I told you about the two tough guys I encountered last night?"

"Can't you hire a bodyguard?"

"The last time I tried that he set me up." I was about to go on when my cell phone rang. I fished it out of my pocket and looked at the screen. This one was a Las Vegas area code and exchange. I flipped it open and answered with a cautious hello.

"Richard Belzer, please." The voice sounded old. Real old, and weak, as if struggling to enunciate each word.

"You got him," I said.

"You interested in what really happened to Brigid Burgeon and Constance Penroy?"

His question stunned me. But I was leery. It could be the bait before the trap. "Who's this?"

"Name's Fred Gascon, but that's not important." He paused, exhaled and inhaled several times. "I need to see you on the sly. Soon. Ain't got a lot of time."

I took his last remark to mean he was in a race with the Grim Reaper, and he was losing.

"What can you tell me about Brigid and Constance?" I asked. No way was I going in blind to meet with a strange voice on the telephone. Veronica immediately perked up, her lips forming a small O.

"They used to call me . . ." His voice stopped. More sonorous breathing. "Freddie the Fox."

"Freddie the Fox?" I repeated.

"Yeah, that's me," he said. "You know Paul Venchus?"

"Yeah."

"Me, too." He punctuated that with a hacking cough that didn't sound very good. The kind that spells emphysema. Or worse.

"You all right?" I asked.

His laugh was almost as bad as his cough. "Far from it. But from the sound of it, I'd guess Venchus is dead."

"Good guess."

"How about another good one? Looked like natural causes, right? Messy. And we both know it wasn't." The cough started again. I tried to listen intently as his voice dropped to a hoarse whisper. "He sent me a letter . . ."

Breathe, dammit, I thought. Then talk.

"Gave me your cell number," he managed, then stopped again.

I wondered if there was anyone who didn't have it.

"Letter I just got today."

"So much for the speedy delivery service award."

"Cut the shit, Belzer. I gotta meet with ya. Now. What hotel you staying at?"

He was panting like he'd just run the hundred-yard dash. I waited and wondered. Was this legit, or was it a setup? They'd tried the smooth-talking shyster, the crooked politician, and tough-guy route, and failed each time. Maybe this was one more subterfuge.

"The Monticello. Why, you coming to meet me here?"

Veronica was practically tugging at my sleeve for me to lean down so she could listen. I shot her a chastising glance and shook my head.

"Do I sound like I could come to fucking meet you?"

"Freddie, how do I know you're on the level?"

"Yeah, Venchus told me you'd be cautious. Can't blame a man for that. I'm pretty cautious myself. My mama didn't raise no fool."

"Neither did mine."

I waited while he wheezed and hacked a bit more, then gave me an address after saying, "Write it down and bring it. I want you to give it back to me here. Ready?"

I scribbled it as he spoke. "You'll be there?"

"Yeah. And don't bring no cops or nothing. Get it?"

"Got it, but I have an assistant—"

"Veronica? She's all right. I want to meet her. Tell her to bring Paul's laptop. The one with the flower on the lid."

So he knew her name. And about the laptop. Still, that didn't erase all my suspicions. Rocco and Vito could have done enough digging to find that out. Plus, somebody had called the room of Ms. Veronica Holmes before. "Freddie, I'm still not convinced. How about we agree on a neutral spot somewhere in Vegas?"

"The horse's ass. You think I'm up to hitting the Strip? Do I fucking sound like I am?"

"Yeah, but like you said before, it pays to be cautious, right?"

"Venchus said to ask you something if you got cold feet."

"My feet are very warm at the moment." And I intended for them to stay that way.

He went into another coughing jag. When he stopped, his voice had dropped to a whispery trace of before. "He said to ask you if you were still writing jokes on napkins."

That wasn't something Rocco or Vito, or even the Indian, could have known. It was a memory of long ago and far away.

"That satisfy ya?" he asked.

"It does."

"Good. No cops, no cabs," he wheezed. "Nothing traceable. Rent a car, or something."

I told Freddie we'd be on the way.

Veronica stood there with a triumphant smirk on her face. "See? This was our big break, wasn't it? Just like I predicted. I knew this was going to happen. I *knew* it."

"Well, since your psychic info line is up and running once more, see if you can predict if we'll get back in time for me to put on my lucky underwear for the telethon." I grinned at her. "Just kidding. Let's save your mental cognitions for something really important."

We found Hector sitting near the back exit, just where I told him to be. He looked perplexed when we got in, and asked if there was any luggage.

"Not right now," I said. I handed him Freddie the Fox's address and he looked more confused.

"I thought we were driving to L.A."

"When we get back," I said. Veronica's eyes narrowed as she threw me a rebellious glance. But for once she kept her mouth shut. If this kept up,

I'd have to call Guinness and request a world record. But the day was still young.

After I told Hector to make sure he wasn't being followed, he grinned again and pushed his pompadour under his black chauffeur's cap. "Just like in one of your movies, huh, boss?"

"Except in the movies I carry a gun. *Vamos.*"

He did a swing-around through the parking garage and went out an exit I didn't even know existed. When we got onto Koval, the street that runs more or less parallel to Las Vegas Boulevard, Hector turned left instead of the right I was expecting. He must have seen my surprise and took his hands off the wheel to shrug.

"I figure taking Sands instead of Tropicana would throw anybody tailing us for a loop," he said. "I'll go west and catch the Twelve farther north, so we can go south."

Going west farther north to go south. It sounded like a Boy Scout's nightmare. But anybody tailing us would be most noticeable.

The circuitous routing took us a bit more than the twenty minutes I'd figured on, but it was worth it. As we exited the 215 Hector pulled in a parking lot across from the exit ramp and we watched for any suspicious cars. Unless they had access to a helicopter, I was reasonably certain no one had tailed us. I commended Hector on his diligence and told him to take similar precautions when he drove Veronica back tonight.

"If I go back," she said.

I knew it had been too early to start thinking about Guinness.

The house in question was typical Nevada. Tiled roof, adobe sides, painted a pale yellow, and a curving walkway to the front door. This one had been modified for a wheelchair ramp. I told Hector to cruise the block and I'd call him when we were ready. As we stepped out, my cell phone rang. Thinking it might be Johnny, I checked the screen and saw the "Unknown" script again. I hit the button to turn it off and shoved the phone back into my pocket. When I got back to New York I was going to have to find a way to trace that damn number, even if it was one of those disposables like Jock had said.

After ringing the doorbell and waiting in the heat, the door opened and a pretty blond woman of about thirty-five in colorful scrubs answered. Her name tag said JULIE in black letters against a gold background. I started to introduce myself when the same cranky old voice I'd heard on the phone a half hour before called out, "He's okay. Let him in." The nurse smiled and stepped back, opening the door wider. We went inside.

"He's refusing to take his medication until you arrived," she said. "You'll have to leave when I say if the pain gets too bad, okay?"

"Whatever you want," I said.

Nurse Julie smiled. "The morphine makes him groggy sometimes. But I'm sure he'll be delighted to talk to you. He doesn't have many visitors. Just his daughter."

She escorted us into the bedroom. Freddie the Fox didn't look so spry. He was propped up on the incline of a hospital bed with IV lines coming out of his arms and a catheter tube coming from under his white-and-black-checked gown and looping over the iron rung. A bag of clear liquid hung suspended over his head on a portable rack and the bag was connected to the IV line.

"Belzer," Freddie said. "You look just like you do on TV."

"I'll take that as a compliment." I held my hand out toward Veronica and started to introduce her when Freddie cut me off.

"Mary's girl." A smile creased his haggard face. "Connie's granddaughter. You look like your mother."

Veronica moved to the edge of the bed. "You know my mother?"

Freddie lay on the incline beaming for a few seconds. "Just from the pictures Connie showed me." He shook his head as a tear wound its way down the craggy territory of his cheek. "She was something."

"You knew her? My grandmother?"

He nodded, then winced. My guess was the pain that the morphine drip assuaged was starting to prickle. "She was a knockout, just like you."

She smiled and sat on the edge of the bed as he patted it.

He reached for the blue button on the IV line to give himself a jolt, but stopped. "Don't know how much longer I can do without. Been holding off till you got here. Once I start with the hits, I usually fall asleep pretty fast." He grinned as he winced again. "Who'da thought I'd end up a fucking junkie, huh?"

"Go ahead if it helps," I said. "We can come back later if you're too tired."

He shook his head, which caused him to grit his teeth. "Later's too late. Might leave without you." Veronica stroked his colorless hair.

"What can you tell us, then?" I asked.

"Whatever you want to know. I figure I got this last chance to make things right. Do what I shoulda done twenty-five years ago."

"How did you and Paul connect?"

"Pure serendipity." His lips parted in an ever-so-slight grin. "He saw me laying flowers on Connie's grave. Came up to me. Caught me at a bad time. I'd just gotten some bad news . . ." He paused and grimaced more heavily than before, then reached up and pressed the blue button. After a couple seconds the pain seemed to ease. Or at least he relaxed a little. "Listen, Belzer, maybe this ain't such a good idea. I ain't no rat. Never have been."

"I understand." I cocked my head toward Veronica. "But don't you think she has a right to know?"

After a few more ragged breaths, he said, "Yeah, maybe she does."

His head lolled back and he lifted his arm to point. "Shut that door so Julie don't hear."

I closed it and walked closer to the bed. "Freddie, what happened that night Brigid died?"

"Old Man Kaye made a deal with the devil to get rid of his number one son's little peccadillo." He hit the blue button again and rolled his eyes. "Brigid had one in the oven. Woulda ruined Markie Boy's political future if it'd come out. He was stupid in love with her, too. Head over heels."

"So Kaye arranged to have her killed?"

"Yeah."

"Who did it?"

"The Indian and a dirty cop named Leo Russell." He paused and rested. I hoped Nurse Julie wouldn't suddenly break down the door and throw us out. "Leo badged his way in. Brought the Indian with him. They held her down and used an enema loaded with barbiturates and watched her die. Russell was LAPD, but in Capa's pocket."

"Capa? Dario Capacaza?"

His lips twisted slightly into something resembling a grin. "Good boy. Done your homework. Guess playing a cop all them years on TV made a real live detective outta ya."

"I have my moments," I said. "Who's the Indian? Where did he come from?"

The shadow of his smile again. "From the reservation."

It was my turn to grin. Any man who could crack jokes on death's door deserved at least that.

"He was Kaye Senior's man. Agency hotshot. Stone-cold killer."

"Agency? As in governmental? Like the CIA?"

He nodded. "Him and Old Man Kaye knew each other from that. The Indian used to brag about his hits for the Gee, but the bastard got off on killing women. Always took a lock of their hair first."

"Leo's dead," I said. "Is this Indian guy still around?"

Freddie nodded. "As far as I know. He'd probably be pushing fifty-five or sixty by now. Still, that ain't that old anymore, is it?"

I shook my head. "What's he look like?"

"Long black hair. Wore it in a braid down his back. Big guy. Chest like a refrigerator, but don't let that fool you. Moves like a cat." He blinked and shuddered. "One of them big jungle cats."

"So why did Kaye Senior need Capacaza if he already had the Indian?"

"Needed Capa to have Russell get him in and out. Plus, Russell handled the investigation."

Which explained how he beat young Eddie Sikorski to the scene of the crime.

"What about my grandmother?" Veronica asked. "Did he kill her, too?"

Freddie's eyes glistened as he nodded. Another tear wound its way downward. "Me and her, we was . . . close. Real close."

"I know," Veronica said, smiling. "I read about you in her diary."

His lips pulled back, although in pleasure or pain I didn't know. "She thought the world of your mom and you."

He was starting to fade. His pupils were like saucers now, expanding against an edge of iris. "How did she figure out what happened to Brigid?" I asked.

His lower lip tugged back. "Me. I told her. We was close."

So while Freddie was courting Constance, she was pumping him for information. Questionable journalism ethics, but if she wanted that story bad enough . . . reporters have done worse. Freddie seemed to sense what I was thinking.

"It wasn't like that with her and me. We met by accident. She was a real knockout. Bought me a drink. Listened to me brag."

Maybe too many drinks, I thought. And the morphine was starting to whisk him away to oblivion. "And how did you know so much?"

He sighed. "Know why Capa's left me alone all these years?"

I shook my head.

"He knows I'm no rat, for one thing." Freddie paused. Blinked twice, like his eyes were looking at something beyond the horizon. "Plus, he knew better. Know why they called me the 'Fox'?"

"Because you're smart?"

He jerked slightly. "Fucking right I am. I was his tech man, back in the day. Taped everything. Videotaped it."

"Videotaped what, exactly?"

"His meetings with Old Man Kaye. About Brigid. When Kaye came back to him to have his son Larry's asshole buddy taken out in Reno. When Capa wanted to have his boy pass the gaming commission. Whenever we dealt with somebody important, I was taping it."

"Sounds like Capa has a thing about being able to blackmail people in high places."

"Yeah." His eyelids were drooping now. I figured he'd pass out any second. But he surprised me by shaking his head and looking almost alert. "But why Capa didn't dare ice me . . . I let it be known if anything ever happened to me, maybe a certain party in another state would send the duplicate tapes I made to the Gee. Capa couldn't have touched me if he'd wanted to."

My heart was racing with anticipation. "You still have the tapes?"

He shook his head. "Where you been, Mr. Movie Star? Nobody uses tape anymore. The whole world's gone digital."

"Digital?"

"DVDs," he said. "I converted everything to disks."

Veronica and I exchanged glances. She looked more worried than I felt. I ventured a few more steps on the tightrope. "Those disks would clear up a lot of questions."

Freddie's head sank a bit, his eyelids drooping again. A knock at the door and Nurse Julie's voice snapped him awake.

"Mr. Gascon? Are you okay in there?"

"Yeah, yeah, fine. Go away."

"I'm afraid you're overexerting yourself," she said. It was the kind of tone that told me she'd be busting through the door in no time.

"Five minutes," Freddie said. "Just give us that."

I heard Nurse Julie sigh, then say, "Okay."

Freddie motioned for me to check outside the door to make sure she'd left. I did and she had. She'd moved to the far side of the living room. Polite lady. Very well mannered and obviously didn't believe in eavesdropping. A secretive man's dream.

I closed the door and Freddie motioned me closer. He gripped Veronica's hand with his emaciated fingers.

"Sweetie, you gotta believe me," he said. "I was in love with Connie. Totally. I didn't know nothing about Capa having her killed. I would've found a way to warn her or something."

Veronica squeezed his hand. "I know that."

"She found out too much. Started asking that cop questions. He went to Capa and . . ."

"Who did it?" I asked.

"The Indian. His specialty is making things look natural." His mouth tugged downward and he began to sob. "She never knew what hit her. Capa never knew I was seeing her on the side. Never knew I was the one she was getting the info from. He thought it was Felix Stubenvelt. Had him killed. I felt like shit, but what could I do? He woulda slit my throat, too, if he knew it was me. So I let Capa go on believing he'd plugged his leak."

"Between the rock and the hard place."

"Look, I know I let Connie down, but she was already gone and I had my daughter to think about."

"Rough," I said.

"But when Venchus came along that day, it was like fate, you know? Another chance to set things right."

"We'll tell everybody," Veronica said. "Will you tell them with us?"

"I can't. No time left now. Plus, I gave my word to Capa I'd never rat to the cops."

"As you know, I am not a cop. I just play one on TV."

His head rocked back and forth in a nod. "I seen your show." He almost drifted off, but fought the slumber off once more. "My daughter comes out here once a week. Checks our PO box at the main office. That's how I got Venchus's letter with your cell."

Maybe Paul had been more protective of it than I'd given him credit for.

"When you get back to the hotel," he said, "you'll have a special envelope waiting. My daughter dropped it off on her way outta here." His eyes looked ready to close. "DVD inside. Should be interesting to you."

"Who was Felix Stubenvelt?" I asked. The name sounded vaguely familiar.

But Freddie didn't answer. He leaned his head back against the pillow and dozed. I watched as his breathing became slow and shallow.

We heard a knock at the door and Nurse Julie peered in. "I really must insist that you let him get his rest."

"Don't worry," I said. "We were just leaving. Just do me a favor and be careful. Don't open the door for anyone you don't know, okay?"

She frowned. "Is there something we need to be worried about?"

I smiled, debating how much, if anything, to tell her. Despite Freddie's feeling of digital insulation, I was concerned. But at this point, all I had were shadows and phantoms. And a vague description of the Indian.

CHAPTER 20

"There's no way I'm going back to L.A. now," Veronica said once we were safely ensconced in the back of Hector's limo and speeding toward the Strip again. Her mouth had set itself into a defiant little pout.

I pondered the ultimatum and the situation. We were close to breaking this one. The safest thing to do would be to get hold of Falletti and turn the disk over to him. The feds could take it and run with it. They'd love it, and Veronica and I would be out of the equation. No more goombahs staking out the men's room to tell me to back off. Overactive bladder sufferers everywhere could breathe a sigh of relief.

"All right," I said. "On one condition."

She canted her head slightly and asked with her eyes, saying nothing.

Had I really succeeded in finding a way to make her keep her mouth shut?

"We watch the disk when we get back," I said, "then Hector drives you home to L.A. tonight and I turn the disk over to the authorities."

"But what about our story?"

"You'll have more than enough to write it all up. I'll help you, if need be. But I can't be worrying about you all the while I'm doing the telethon." The mention of it caused me to glance at my watch. It was closing in on

5:45. Johnny would probably be frantic. We had a little over an hour before showtime. I tried to call him to tell him I was on the way, but got his voicemail.

"How close are we to the hotel?" I asked.

Hector shrugged. "Depending on how bad traffic is, I'd say twenty minutes. You want me to hustle?"

Twenty minutes would make it tight. "See if you can shave a few off," I said, "but don't take any chances."

He took off his chauffeur's cap and smoothed back his pompadour. *"Sí, señor."*

True to his word, Hector got us there in fifteen. Well, maybe fifteen and a half. As he dropped us off in front, I told him the plan remained the same. He was to circle around the block and wait for us at the back door. When I brought Veronica down, he was to leave for L.A. Surprisingly, she offered nothing in the way of protest. We went in through the front doors and I did a quick scan for any oversize, fifty-five-year-old Indians with refrigerator-size chests. I saw no one resembling that description, but the casino area was wall-to-wall people. Brad and Angelina could have been playing blackjack and no one would notice. Plus, I didn't even know who I was looking for. Just a vague description of a big, barrel-chested guy with black hair. Maybe turning gray now . . . unless he dyed it or had it enhanced like good old Uncle Lar. Something had been gnawing at me since Freddie had described the Indian and I suddenly realized what it was. The day we'd taken the monorail to go see Henri. The guy who'd followed us on the tram . . . he'd worn a baseball cap over long blond hair that looked about as real as a hundred-dollar bill with Elvis on it. Plus, his upper body had looked like it would have trouble fitting into a phone booth. If they still had phone booths. Could that have been the Indian? Had he been stalking us all this time? So close that he could have moved in for one of his "accidents" at any time? I dialed Grady's cell and got his voicemail, too. Great, I thought. We might be under the watchful eye of a CIA-trained assassin and not even know it, and Grady's phone is busy. Or turned off.

But the best place to hide was sometimes in plain sight. I took

Veronica's elbow and steered her through the crowd toward the front desk. We stopped at the VIP check-in lounge.

"I'm Richard Belzer. There was supposed to be a very important envelope dropped off for me in the last couple hours."

The girl behind the desk said she'd check and went back toward a sectioned-off area. She was gone for what seemed like an eternity. When she came back she was compressing her lips like she had unpleasant news.

"Mr. Belzer, I'm so sorry. Sharon said she gave it to Mr. Leland. She knew you two were working together on the telethon, and he came by looking for you."

I told her that it was okay and dialed Johnny's cell. He didn't know he was holding the key to a couple of quarter-of-a-century-old mysteries. It rang twice and went to voicemail. Frustrated beyond belief, I disconnected and tried Barry's number, and surprise, surprise, he answered.

"Belz, where are you?"

"I'm in the VIP lounge. Have you seen Johnny?"

"He was going around looking for you. Said he couldn't get through on your phone. He's a nervous wreck and so am I. I've got Sal on ice in a private room so he thinks he can surprise Johnny like he wanted. I've got to find Johnny and make sure this comes off all right."

"When's the last time you saw him?"

"He went off with Elliott Collins and that awful Harvey creature."

"He's back from rehab?"

"Unfortunately. But now I'm wondering where Johnny's at."

"I'm looking as we speak," I said. Then I heard the little chime that told me I had another call coming in. I told Barry I'd call him back and answered the call on hold.

Johnny's voice was a low whisper and he spoke so fast I could barely understand him. "Belz, where you at?"

"Near the front desk looking for you. Say, did you—"

He cut me off. "Listen, you got that girl with you, Veronica?"

"Yes, I do."

"Then both of you get the hell out of here right now. Have Hector drive you somewhere far. Don't stop for her luggage, or anything. Just go. Now. Fast. Got it?"

"Look, Johnny, I need to talk to you first. Did you pick up an envelope with my name on it at the VIP lounge?" I waited but no response came. Like I was talking to dead air. "Johnny? You there?" A check of the LCD screen showed me he wasn't.

"Where is he?" Veronica asked. "Does he have the disk?"

Johnny had sounded on the verge of panic. He wasn't the type to whisper a warning to me, telling me to vacate the premises for parts unknown—pronto—without offering an explanation, unless it was a bona fide emergency. And there was no way I was going to let him face something like that himself.

"Come on," I said, grabbing Veronica's arm and moving as fast as I could with her in tow toward the corridor that led to the back entrance. With my free hand I scrolled down and hit the button to try Grady's cell again.

"Where are we going?" she asked.

"You're getting out of here," I said. "Now, and without argument. I'm going to find Johnny and follow suit."

I figured there was no sense in telling her I was going to stay until I was sure Johnny was all right. Then I heard Grady's voice on the phone.

"What's up, Belz?"

"Where you at, champ?"

"Down by poolside looking for you. Johnny was having a conniption fit looking for you, so I told him I'd check around."

"Well, I'm back. And he's the one we're looking for now. I think he might be in trouble. He's supposed to be with Harvey Smithe and his agent."

"Yeah, they brought Harvey back about an hour ago."

"Listen, Grady, I'm taking Veronica out the back entrance and putting her in a limo for L.A. Can you meet me down there and we'll look for Johnny together?"

"Yeah. It'll take me a few."

"I'll wait," I said.

Veronica and I descended the escalator with her protesting all the way.

"I don't have to leave. I want to see that DVD." Her voice sounded plaintive. "Please. I think I have a right to see it, don't you?"

"Of course, and you will." I felt like the unctuous bank manager assuring the young couple their house would never be foreclosed on as he handed them the pen to sign the contract. But this was no time to debate. Johnny's voice had sounded urgent. Scared.

We proceeded down another escalator, bypassing the ones that would take us up on the monorail platform.

"Wait," she said. "I'm getting a bad feeling about this. A vision of something terrible about to happen."

"And I'm trying to prevent that vision from coming true," I said.

It was only a few short steps to the rear doors where I hoped Hector would be waiting. As we pushed through them, I saw the long, white limousine and felt a surge of relief. At least I could get her out of here safely. We came up on the driver's side and I tapped on the tinted window. It lowered and I was surprised to see a black guy wearing the chauffeur's cap. He looked up at me and smiled.

"Ready when you are, Mr. Belzer." He had a voice that sounded like Jack Benny's old buddy Rochester.

"Where's Hector?"

He smiled again. One of his front teeth had a gold cap on it with a Star of David design. Funny, he didn't look Jewish, but I remembered that Sammy Davis had converted for a while. "He had a family emergency. Axed me to cover. Name's Nate."

"He tell you where we were going?"

Nate shrugged. "Anywheres you want, I guess."

Was he trying to be cool or had Hector really talked to him? It was Hec's limo, that was for sure. I heard someone call, "Richard." Turning, I saw Elliott and Harvey walking toward us at a brisk pace.

"Have you seen Johnny?" Elliott asked. Harvey had a smug-looking smirk plastered across his face. I wanted to put Veronica into the limo and ride around the block until I could figure this one out. I yanked the door handle and opened it a crack.

I felt that familiar tingling on the back of my neck as I started to open the rear door. I'd have to find Johnny and assess this situation before I let her take off, but how? A ride down the Strip, I thought, and then I'd call another limo service. But I got the surprise of my life as I opened the door all the way. Johnny was inside, nursing a bloody lip. Next to him were goombah number one, Rocco, and a big, swarthy guy I didn't recognize. And Uncle Lar, resplendent in his artful grayish toupee, sat along the edge of the seat closest to the door.

Elliott and Harvey flanked us now, like two fence posts blocking that avenue or egress.

"Ah," Elliott said, "I see you have seen Johnny after all."

Harvey snorted a laugh.

I straightened up, ready to take Veronica and run in the other direction, when I felt a rather huge presence behind me, shoving something hard into my back.

"Move or scream and I'll blow apart your spine, Belzer."

The voice I recognized as Vito's, goombah number two.

CHAPTER 21

"Don't be rude, Vito," the heavyset, swarthy guy next to Johnny said. "Help the lady inside."

Vito kept the gun in my back and grabbed Veronica's arm, whispering, "Inside, bitch. Now, or your boyfriend here gets it."

I half expected her to spit back some sarcastic comment like, "He's not my boyfriend," but for the first time Veronica looked absolutely terrified. She leaned down and slipped inside the limo as meekly as a lamb. A lamb to the slaughter?

"Now you, hero," Vito said and shoved me inside, slamming the door after me. Johnny looked at me with glistening eyes, the trail of dried blood like a slash from his swollen lower lip.

"Sorry, Belz," he muttered.

"Shut your fucking mouth," the heavyset guy said. He pointed to the seat farthest from the door next to Uncle Lar. I helped Veronica over to it and sat beside her. The big man smiled. He looked to be in his mid-to-late sixties. His eyebrows were still dark and thick and almost met over the top of his nose. "See? Now ain't that more cozy?"

I searched for a wisecrack, albeit a modest one, considering the situation. My mouth felt dry, but I managed to say, "It'd be a lot cozier if we all transferred this to the bar."

The big guy laughed and pointed a finger the size of an Oscar Mayer hot dog toward me. "I heard about you, Belzer. Mr. Funny Man." He jerked a thumb toward Johnny. "And his friend. You been causing me more fucking trouble lately than a sore dick."

"And not nearly as much fun," I said. My throat still felt dry.

He guffawed this time, slapping Johnny's shoulder. "I didn't know he was this good. Shit. This guy's got a gift. And balls." His smile vanished, leaving an expression as cold as the inside of a freezer. "Too bad they're so fucking big."

"Capa, look—," Johnny started to say, but the big guy backhanded him, sending a new stream of blood down the side of Johnny's chin.

"Shut the fuck up. You ain't got the right to call me 'Capa.' You think I forgot how you tried to warn this fuck on the phone a few minutes ago? Betraying me? You think I forgot?" He glared at Johnny. "You musta forgot. Forgot how I handled things with Stubenvelt for you and Sal. You forget, motherfucker? You forget?"

His voice had elevated to a yell. This guy was a classic manic-depressive. Or maybe he was just a manic.

"Sorry," Johnny said. He looked totally deflated. I felt a raw pain in my gut just watching. I suddenly wondered if Johnny still had the disk on him. It could be our ticket out of this jam, or it could be our death sentence. I had to figure out a way to find out where it was.

"Mr. Capacaza," I said. "What's it going to take to resolve this?"

Capacaza's eyebrows lifted as he turned back toward me. "You know who I am, huh? Mr. Fucking TV Star. And you showed respect. Good. I like that."

"Johnny has a telethon to run," I said. "It's going to start soon. Why don't you let him go clean up and we can go to the Marebello Room and discuss whatever it is that's bothering you?"

He stared at me for a few seconds, then snorted a laugh. "Still playing the wiseass from your fucking TV show, huh? You think I'm as dumb and stupid as Tony Soprano, or something?"

"Not at all."

"Good, 'cause I'm not. And as for the fucking telethon, I got that covered." His lips pursed slightly as he reached over and slapped Lawrence Kaye's knee. "You ain't saying much, Senator."

Kaye licked his lips and shook his head. "Dario, this is not what I expected at all. I need to get back to a meeting."

He started to make a move to go out the door when Capacaza shoved him back into the seat.

"You stay the fuck put, you fuck. You come crawling to me because some washed-up reporter's making you nervous asking questions, and now you're pissing your pants after I'm tidying things up?" He snorted. "I been cleaning up your family's shit for so long, and here I am doing it again. But this time you're gonna help, like the man you ain't."

Kaye's mouth twisted into a grimace as our eyes met for a few seconds. He quickly looked away.

Capacaza's head swiveled back toward me. "I advise you to be very cooperative with my associates, Mr. Belzer." He pronounced my name as if it were a pejorative. I pondered the wisdom of giving him a palm strike to the nose, just on principle, but figured it wouldn't be the wisest move at the moment. Rocco was ensconced in the seat nearest the door with a stupid grin plastered on his ugly puss. I wanted to reserve a palm strike for him, too.

"Take them out to the place and turn them over to the Indian," Capacaza said. I felt Veronica stiffen beside me.

"Mr. Belzer," she whispered. "I'm scared."

Capacaza must have heard her and paused, barking out a derisive laugh. "You should be, sweetie." He moved forward and edged toward the door. Rocco leaned to one side so he could keep me covered with his gun the whole time. As Capacaza got out, Vito's huge form filled the door opening. He got in and sat next to Rocco, who used his foot to push Johnny over toward us.

"Maybe you two need a refresher course in what happens if you fuck with me," Capacaza said, pointing to Johnny and Lawrence Kaye. He looked at Veronica and me. "Have the Indian find out what they know." He grinned and did a little hand salute striking his index finger under the tip of his chin, like he was lighting a match. Obviously an Italian sign for good luck. I needed it.

"I'm going to go watch my boy perform on the telethon," Capacaza said. "He's gonna knock 'em dead."

"This seems like a lot of trouble to go to for the likes of him." I pointed to Kaye, who'd been sitting there shaking and sniveling.

Capacaza reached over and gave Uncle Lar a pat on the cheek. "Mr. State Senator here's been pretty good to me, so I can't complain. Plus, when his nephew is sitting in Carson City, he'll be even better." Capacaza smiled. "Ever wonder what it'd be like owning the fucking governor of Nevada? Almost as good as owning the president."

He slammed the door shut. The limo started rolling. My cell phone went off, but as I reached for it, Rocco leveled the gun at Veronica's head.

"I wouldn't answer it unless you want to see your girlfriend's brains splattered all over the inside of this car." He snapped the fingers of his free hand. "Hand it over, nice and slow."

I removed the phone from my pocket and stole a glance at the screen. Grady's number. I'd told him to meet me down here. He was probably looking for me.

"Give it here now," Rocco snarled.

I did.

He glanced at it and blew out a puff of air. "Must be your shine friend. But we brought our own superfly. Hey, Nate."

The screen lowered and Nate glanced back at us, the chauffeur's cap perched at a jaunty angle on his head. "What's up?"

"You know where to go, right?" Rocco asked.

Nate nodded.

"Then let us know when we get there."

The screen went back up, closing us in again.

"I think you're gonna enjoy meeting the Indian," Rocco said. His lips peeled back from his teeth. I guessed I wouldn't.

We exited the front way and turned right, heading northwest. But we turned left at Sands and proceeded west toward the I-15. From there, who knew where we would end up? It was starting to get dark, and I held a slim hope that once we did arrive I might get a chance to take one of the guns away from the two thugs. That's assuming I could get the drop on one of them without the other two shooting me first. I was certain Nate was armed, also. But even if I did manage to get one of the guns, would I be able to use it against two armed gangsters? I'd never shot a man up close and personal except on film. I'd handled weapons before, but my close-quarter handgun skills weren't up to date. Still, I had Johnny and Veronica to think about. Besides myself. I really wanted to be able to get home and hug Harlee again. For those reasons, I'd make the shots if I got one of their guns. No ifs, ands, or buts.

I noticed we'd gotten on the expressway and were heading south. Almost like that first time we'd gone out to see poor old Mrs. Perkins. It seemed like a lifetime ago now. In the distance the sun was starting to descend behind the mountains.

Johnny grabbed my hand and whispered, "I'm sorry, Belz. So sorry."

"It's not your fault." I noticed he was crying. "How's your lip?"

He brushed off the question with a shake of his head. "Why couldn't you just leave it alone like I asked? Why couldn't you?"

"What did he mean when he mentioned Stubenvelt?" I asked. "Who is that?"

"Felix Stubenvelt. He was Sallie's and my manager in the old days." His gaze went toward the floor. "Capacaza took us all out to the desert and had his guys beat him to death right in front of us. Made us watch. Told us that was what happened to stool pigeons and said we'd better not ever cross him."

"Us? You and who? Sal?"

He nodded.

"What did he mean by 'stool pigeon'?"

"He said poor Felix had been feeding information to some reporter about family business. It had something to do with Brigid Burgeon and the movie Sal had been making with her." Johnny wiped his eye. "That's why I was so worried about you nosing around. I know what he's capable of."

"So they killed him right in front of you?" I wondered why he hadn't notified the cops, but the expression on his face made me realize he'd probably thought about it and discounted the idea even knowing he should have. Being confronted with sheer evil can do that to you.

Johnny coughed. "Capacaza told us Elliott Collins was now our new manager, and we were going to like it. We tried to keep things going, but it all fell apart between Sallie and me. We split up. I couldn't get poor Felix out of my mind. I doubt he could, either. Maybe we just reminded each other of that awful night too much."

"And they've kept you on the string all this time?"

He nodded. "More or less. Whenever they needed something."

I thought about how Freddie the Fox must have felt knowing Stubenvelt had taken the death beating for him. No wonder he wanted to cleanse his soul before his appointment with the Grim Reaper. Even after twenty-five years. Which brought me to the disk again. "Johnny, what did you do with that envelope you picked up for me at the hotel?"

"Huh?" He looked confused. "What envelope?"

Shit, I thought. Maybe Capacaza had intercepted it instead. Our last ace and it was out of our grasp. But maybe these guys didn't know that.

"Listen," I said, "you'd better tell your boss that if we're harmed there's evidence that'll nail him to a lethal injection gurney. If he wants it back, we'd better turn this jalopy around right now."

Rocco and Vito exchanged glances and laughed simultaneously. "You think this is one of your fucking TV shows, asshole?" Vito said. "Save it for the Indian. He likes getting details out of people like you. Especially the broads."

I heard Veronica gasp.

"And I'm gonna enjoy watching," Rocco added.

I decided if I had a chance to go down fighting, I'd crush that little prick's Adam's apple first.

Outside it was too dark now to see much, although I knew we were still on the freeway. Finally we veered off, taking an exit. I looked in vain out the back window, between the heads of the two goombahs, hoping to see a pair of headlights following us in the slim chance that somehow the cavalry would come. No headlights exited behind us.

We slowed and made a right turn, then sped along a local highway for a few minutes.

My phone rang again. Rocco held it up and looked at the screen.

"Unknown?" he said.

"I've been getting a lot of those calls lately," I said.

"Relax," Vito said. "It's probably the Indian trying to figure out how far away we are. He's got that laptop thing."

Laptop thing? Had the calls I'd been getting been him tracing me the whole time?

"What are you talking about?" I asked.

Rocco laughed as he held up the phone. "Your fucking phone, asshole. It's like a homing beacon to a guy with the right hookup."

"And the Indian's got the state-of-the-art government shit," Vito said. "All he needs is your number."

I thought about it. The cell phone's signal pings off various towers, so he must have had some kind of telemetry to trace the signal once he called it. I'd inadvertently led him to each of the victims he'd subsequently killed. I massaged the top of my nose and felt the tightness in my gut increase. Why hadn't I seen this coming?

The limo slowed down and we turned right, traveled about half a block, and rolled to a complete stop. The screen lowered.

"We're here," Nate said, his voice sounding like a rusty pump. "Got to unlock it." Through the windshield I saw a ten-foot-high cyclone fence with three barbed-wire strands over the top of it. A dilapidated sign across the front said Private Property—No Trespassing.

"Yeah, you stay up here and guard the gate." Rocco pointed to Kaye. "You go up and drive us in, Senator."

"Me?" Kaye said. He swallowed nervously. "I can't do that."

"Do it, asshole," Vito said, gripping the door handle and opening the door.

Rocco pointed his gun at us. "And nobody else get any wiseass ideas."

As Kaye opened the door I caught sight of another sign behind the first one. Faded black letters on a peeling white background spelled it out:

Welcome to Western World—Cowboy Entertainment at Its Best.

Kaye's mouth twitched like a nervous rabbit as he tried to look me in the eye, but couldn't. He licked his lips and crawled out of the limo. Vito reached over and pulled the door shut after him. Nate stayed behind the wheel, staring first at Veronica, then Johnny, then me.

"Don't forget that spic is in the trunk," he said.

"Leave him in there," Vito said. "One less person to watch for now."

That must mean Hector, I thought. At least it sounded like he was still alive. But for how long? How long for any of us?

Nate got out and was illuminated by the headlights as he went to a pair of cyclone fence sections on hinges and secured by a heavy chain and padlock. He fished a key out of his pocket, unlocked the hefty padlock, and shoved one of the gate sections open. Kaye got in, shifted the limo into drive, and we lurched forward, sideswiping the other side of the gate.

"Watch it, dumb fuck," Rocco said. "Slow down."

Vito grinned. "That fucker can't drive any better than he drinks."

We drove past what had once been the admission booths and down a dark dirt road toward some ramshackle buildings. Most of them were one-story, if you could call them that, although a taller one stood in the middle. Probably the classic Hollywood representation of the western hotel over the Long Branch Saloon. Except plywood had replaced the swinging doors of this emporium. Every opening I could see had been covered. Other buildings featured dilapidated signs listing the structures as General Store, Town Bank, Post Office, and, of course, Sheriff's Office. Kaye rolled to a stop next to a big sports utility vehicle wedged in an opening between two buildings. A dark-colored Hummer. As its headlights flicked on, something jogged my memory and I was willing to bet that it was shiny and black, just like the one I'd seen at Mrs. Perkins's trailer park.

"Cut the lights and get out," Vito said to Kaye. Then, to the rest of us, "You get out, too, after Rocco does."

Rocco shot us another feral smile and scurried out the door. He positioned himself outside, the big semiauto hanging loosely at his side.

Maybe I could make a grab for it as I go out, I thought.

But as soon as I began to move Vito told me to hold it and grabbed Johnny's arm. "You go first," he said. "Then you, Belzer, then the broad.

Try anything, anything at all, and I'll put a bullet in her gut. Ever seen somebody die from being gut-shot? Takes a long while."

Veronica took in a series of short, truncated breaths. I realized she was sobbing. I put my arm around her shoulders and told her not to worry. I couldn't bring myself to say it would be all right.

Vito shoved Johnny out, then snapped his fingers at me. "Remember what I said." He motioned toward the open car door with the gun. "Move."

I went through the opening and felt the soft, sandy earth beneath my feet as I stood next to Johnny. It was dark, but the Hummer's lights provided enough illumination so that I could see the tracks of wetness on Johnny's cheeks.

"This is real bad, Belz," he whispered. "I'm sorry. So sorry."

I resisted the temptation to say, "Tell me something I don't know," and squeezed his arm instead. I looked around and saw the entire town was several hundred feet long with the old wooden buildings lining both sides. At the very end of the street a fence made out of logs formed a corral. It appeared to extend into infinity. I hoped we'd be just as invisible if we had a chance to run. Maybe, with a bit of luck and some old escape and evasion skills, we stood a chance at survival. But even if I was lucky, the chances of my escaping were slim. When I factored Johnny and Veronica into the equation, slim equaled none. But how could I leave either of them behind?

The door of the Hummer popped open and a big, barrel-chested guy got out, backlit by the headlights. His body rocked with a rolling gait as he strode over to us, carrying something that looked like a large notebook in his hand. I also saw the outline of a holster with the butt of a pistol sticking out of it. As he got closer I saw the broad, flat planes of his face, the high cheekbones, the long hair drawn back, mostly black but flecked with streaks of gray. Freddie the Fox had made a good guess about that. I wondered if he was still around, enjoying what little time he had left in his morphine buzz, or if the Indian had trailed us to the hospice house and tied up another loose end.

The Indian moved to the outer fringes of the headlights, then took out a remote and flicked it. The lights on the Hummer shut off, but there was just enough moonlight filtering down so I could see his smile. I could also see the notebook he was carrying was a laptop computer. With a hand-painted flower on the lid.

"Well, well, well, who have we here?"

"Belzer, the broad, and Johnny Leland," Rocco said. "The boss said he wants Leland back."

I didn't have to wonder what that meant for Veronica and me.

The Indian pointed to Lawrence Kaye. "Good to see you again, Senator."

Kaye nodded and averted his eyes. I wondered if he'd done the same when Capacaza's thugs had beaten his male lover to death in Reno.

"You've got pretty hair," the Indian said, moving forward and grabbing a handful of Veronica's curls. "I think I'm gonna have to cut off a little bit to keep."

I silently hoped she wouldn't remember what Freddie the Fox had told us about this guy's proclivities. But apparently she did.

"Does that mean you're going to kill me?" Her voice cracked, but contained enough defiance to demonstrate a good deal of pluck.

"Oh, right now you and I are gonna have a nice little conversation about this." The Indian held up the laptop. "Look familiar?"

To her credit, Veronica held his stare. "No, should it?"

He chuckled. "It should. I took it away from your boyfriend Venchus before I killed him."

She looked away and shuddered visibly.

"Look," I said, "why don't you leave her out of this?"

His face curled into a wry smile.

"A genuine television hero." His grin turned from wry to malevolent. "I've been having a fun time following you around. You saved me a lot of tracking."

"So I've heard. Now how about leaving her out of the equation?" I figured I had as good a chance trying to make a grab for his gun. It was a revolver, so there wouldn't be a safety to worry about. Just grab it and pull the trigger.

His grin didn't fade. Instead, he snapped his fingers at Rocco and said, "You bring anything with you to tie up Batman and Robin?"

"I can find something, I guess," Rocco said. "Plus, we got another one in the trunk. A stinking Mexican."

The Indian snorted. "Hey, watch it. He ain't so far removed from my people. Here." He threw two white plastic strips at Rocco. I watched as they dropped to the ground. "Use these ties. They're wire-reinforced. Behind their backs. Both of them."

"But the boss said—"

"I don't give a fuck what he said. I'm running the show here. You got a problem with that?"

Rocco stared back at the bigger man, trying to affect a tough look but failing miserably. Vito stepped forward and picked up the two strips, handing one to Rocco.

"I'll do it," Vito said, reaching for Johnny's arms. "You keep 'em covered."

Rocco spat, looking less like a gunsel and more like a nervous punk on the school grounds who had just avoided an ass-kicking by the top badass.

"Hey, you don't need to do this," Johnny said. "I won't run."

"You ain't gonna get the chance to run," Vito said, pulling his arms behind him. Johnny winced.

"That's right, funny man," Rocco added. They were like a sinister version of Laurel and Hardy, all right. And I hoped I'd have a chance to use the old stage hook on their faces.

"Your turn, Belzer." Vito grabbed the second plastic strip from Rocco and moved toward me.

I weighed the options of trying a technique on him to remain free. With Rocco a few feet away pointing a gun at me, and the Indian behind me, the wisdom of such a move seemed distinctly imprudent. I put my palms together to give myself as much wiggle room as I could. Maybe I would be able to work my hands free once the goons were distracted. I felt Vito tighten the ligature until the plastic bit into my wrists.

The Indian stuck the laptop under one arm and grabbed Veronica's with his other hand. He began pulling her toward the Hummer. "Come on, sweetie. You're gonna show me all those little passwords so I can open these documents."

"I'm not going with you! Help!"

He backhanded her across the face and her head jerked with the blow. I tried to lurch forward but Vito tripped me. Without my arms free to break the fall, my face skidded into the sandy dirt, my glasses almost falling off.

The Indian had Veronica by the hair now, with his other big hand clamped around her slim neck. She was drooling blood from a torn lip. He brought his face close to hers. "This can go the hard way or the easy way, sweetie." After tightening his grip enough to make her cry out in pain, he said, "And you ain't gonna like the hard way."

"Leave her alone." I thought how ridiculous and unpersuasive I looked lying on my stomach, barely able to lift my face out of the dirt. A second later I felt a kick hit my side. I rolled over and saw Rocco standing over me, pointing the gun at my head.

"Say the word and I'll do him right here," the rat punk said.

"Save it for later." The Indian pulled Veronica toward the Hummer and said, "Come on."

Her legs started with baby steps, then she fell to her knees. The big man lifted her to her feet and dragged her along. I didn't want to think about what he was going to do to her. Pausing at the door of the Hummer, he pressed his remote and the tailgate automatically swung upward.

He pushed her around the rear of the vehicle. "We're gonna turn this thing on, and you're gonna give me those passwords, understand?"

From my vantage point on the ground I could see their legs in back of the big SUV.

At least he hasn't taken her completely out of sight to do who knows what, I thought. I had to get loose, but the first task was getting on my feet. I rolled over on my back, the pain in my side starting to diminish ever so slightly. I managed to get to a sitting position and then tried to get my legs under me.

"Stay down," Rocco said. "Easier to watch you. You get down next to him." With that, he shoved Johnny, who collapsed next to me.

"Hey, watch it," I said. "He just got out of the hospital."

"So?" Rocco shot back. "You think I give a fuck?"

"Your boss said not to hurt him, remember?" I said.

Vito pushed Rocco back and then stepped away himself. "Just keep an eye on them for now."

I twisted my head toward Uncle Lar, who'd been skulking in a far corner. "Is this what you're buying, Kaye? Proud of yourself?"

He didn't answer.

"People are going to find out about this one," I called out. "Believe me, they'll find out."

His chin lowered to his chest, like he was saying a prayer in church. Or at a funeral.

"Keep your mouth shut," Vito said. "I don't wanna hear no more outta you."

"Yeah? Well, maybe your boss will want to hear that. We've got a disk of him and Old Man Kaye arranging a murder." I watched as Uncle Lar's head shot up. "And if anything happens to us, the disk is going right to the feds."

"Sure," Vito said. "And I got a bridge to sell ya."

"Wait," Kaye said. "What if he's telling the truth?"

"He ain't got no disk."

"Don't be too sure," I said. "You'd better call your boss now. Tell Capa he looks good on the disk, too."

Vito's fat cheeks framed his gaping mouth. I figured I'd thrown in whatever I had left to bait the hook. "Tell him Freddie the Fox gave it to me."

Kaye grabbed Vito's arm. "We can't let that disk go to the feds. My family would be ruined."

"Get your hands offa me, ya faggot," Vito said, pulling his arm away.

"Call him," Kaye said. "Please. Tell him what Belzer said."

"If you don't," I offered, "Capa's going to be mightily pissed." I kept working my hands together, trying to loosen the plastic strip. It wouldn't budge. All it did was cut into my flesh. Still, it was our only chance. I figured we had until the Indian brought Veronica back from the Hummer. Once that happened, the odds would be three to one again. I caught

Johnny's eye and something unspoken but communicative moved between us.

"He's telling the truth about the disk," he said. "I got it in the safe back at the hotel."

"Both of you fucks shut up," Rocco said. He moved over and pointed his gun at my head. "Wanna keep shooting your mouth off now? Wanna try to snatch the piece outta my hand again?" He stooped over and I brought my legs around and kicked him in the gut. He stumbled backward, bending over, and the gun in his hand discharged into the dirt next to me. I made one more try to break the plastic cuff on my wrists, arching my back and putting all my strength into it, but failed. I flopped like a fish in a boat.

"Belz, you okay?" Johnny yelled.

My ears were ringing a bit, but aside from a mouth full of dust, I was unscathed.

Rocco regained his footing and rushed over, pointing his gun at my head.

"I'm gonna blow your brains out, motherfucker!" He looked like a madman in the pale moonlight. The kick had sent him over the edge, but at least I'd gotten one in.

Before he could do anything else, the Hummer's rear lid slammed down and the Indian stepped around the vehicle, pulling Veronica with him. She was trying to wipe the blood off her chin with the back of her hand. Everybody froze in place around me as he strode over with her in tow.

"What's going on here, *Shamanse*?" the Indian asked. There was mirth in his tone, like he was enjoying the show. "Don't kill him yet. I still have to interrogate him first. Or did you forget?"

"This prick kicked me," Rocco said, still pointing the gun at me.

"Maybe you shoulda tied his feet, too," the Indian said. "But be careful not to get too close. He might do it again."

I'd relish the chance, I thought. Only this time I'd aim for his fucking jaw.

The Indian walked a few more steps with Veronica, then shoved her down next to us. She looked traumatized, her mouth crusted with a bloody stain.

The kid had put up a fight not to give him the passwords, but it hadn't made any difference. I twisted my hands some more and felt a tiny bit of give in the band. Maybe a few minutes more might do it.

"Put the girl and him over there," the Indian said. "But first, lemme get something." He popped a folding knife out of his jeans pocket and flipped the blade in place. It locked with an ominous-sounding click. Grabbing a handful of Veronica's hair, he pulled her to a sitting position and cut off a section. "I told you I needed a lock of your hair."

That meant we didn't have much time. I kept twisting my hands, trying to figure out a move.

He pocketed her hair and came over to me, stepping around in back and grabbing my collar. I felt myself being dragged as if I weighed less than a sack of potatoes. I saw the knife in his other hand and didn't figure he was going to take a hunk of my hair, too. The plastic band still held fast, but I still had a few legs-only martial arts techniques I'd learned. I'd go down fighting.

Some off-key, raspy singing distracted us momentarily. "Amazing Grace," sung in a drunken, repetitive refrain, over and over with humming to take the place of the words.

"Nate, what you doing, man?" Vito asked as the black guy stumbled toward us in the dim light, the chauffeur's cap pulled down over his forehead.

"Ammmmaaaaazzing grace, how sweet da sound . . ."

"You're supposed to be watching the gate," Vito said.

Nate stumbled toward Johnny and Veronica and pulled two baseball hats out of his coat pockets. "How sweet da sound . . ."

"What the fuck you doing, man?" Rocco said. "You fucking drunk or something?"

"Taking care of bidness," Nate said.

His voice sounded wonderfully familiar. He slapped a hat on Johnny's head, then Veronica's, then bent over even more and whispered something to them.

"What's that fucking *P'cate-wa elene* doing?" the Indian asked. All traces of amusement had vanished from his voice, as he held the knife blade inches from my face. "Get him outta here."

"Oh, I be going," Nate muttered, staggering toward the Indian and me. "I be going." With that he lunged forward, knocking his shoulder into the Indian and shoving him backward. Nate, or should I say, Grady, slapped something on my head and yelled, "Down, Belz!"

He collapsed on top of me and I saw flashes of light in the distance, accompanied by the cracking pop of rifle rounds. Vito and Rocco went down like they'd been poleaxed. The Indian had recovered from Grady's shove and was rushing toward us when three perfectly spaced holes ripped the fabric of his shirt along his huge chest. He slowed down, his legs trapped in slow motion under his massive upper body. The light was just good enough for me to see his lips curl into a snarl before he fell face-first into the dirt about three feet away.

The scene was suddenly besieged with men in black outfits, wearing bulky goggles and military-style helmets. They held weapons, too. Submachine guns mostly, but a few had handguns. They immediately began checking the fallen thugs, yelling, "Clear," and "Scene secure. Hostages all right."

Grady rolled off me and grinned. "Like Clint Eastwood said in that one movie, 'Don't go thinking we're engaged or nothing.' You okay?"

"I'd be a lot better if you hadn't crushed me," I said. "But all things considered, I've never felt so good being crushed in my life."

He helped me sit up, then get to my feet. Seconds later I felt the plastic binding cut from around my wrists. They were cutting Johnny's bonds, too. Veronica now rushed over to me as soon as she'd gotten to her feet and gave me a hug.

"Oh my God," she said. "I was so scared."

I patted her back. She was going to need some stitches in that lip. "It's okay. It's over now, kid. You're all right. We all are." I looked at Grady. "Nice of Nate to lend you Hector's hat. I take it he saw the light and cooperated?"

Grady took it off and admired it. "Shoore enough, Mr. Benny."

I smiled in appreciation at his nod to the master. "So how in the hell did you mobilize the cavalry so fast? Who are these guys?"

He grinned. "This was a joint federal, local, and"—he patted himself on the chest—"ex–law enforcement operation. You lucked out that the LVMPD SWAT team was doing its night shoot sniper qualifications at the Desert Sun Range a few miles from here." He lifted the hat he'd shoved on my head. "These were the target guides, specially painted with phosphorescent markings so they could be seen with night-vision goggles."

"And here I thought you'd brought me a new yarmulke," I said.

He laughed. "Luckily, we didn't need one for the senator. His toupee kind of glowed in the dark already."

"Don't you know who I am?" Lawrence Kaye was yelling as one of the SWAT cops was fitting a pair of handcuffs on him. "I'm a state senator. I'll have your badge for this."

"Pipe down, Kaye," I said. "And be glad you got those cuffs on. If you didn't I'd be tempted to go over there and kick your ass."

His mouth drooped open and his lips trembled.

"Proceed with your story," I said to Grady. "How did you find us here?"

"The feds had some kind of thing where they could trace your cell phone after we called you," he said. "Damnedest thing I ever seen. Never had nothing like that when I was wearing a badge."

"I'm just glad they put our tax dollars to good use," I said.

"I was coming to meet you," Grady said, "but when I got down I saw Hector's limo pulling away and Hector ain't driving. Harvey and Elliott walking toward me, so I asked them if they'd seen you, and they say no. It didn't smell right and after I tried to call you and got your voicemail, I figured they were lying, so I called Detective Kirby. He'd been waiting in my office with two FBI agents."

I held up my hand and smiled. "You did great, Grady. Saved my life yet again. But what time is it?"

He glanced at his watch. "Eight thirty-seven."

I went over to Johnny, who'd been standing there rubbing his wrists, his head bowed.

"Hey, buddy," I said. "We've still got twenty-two hours and twenty-three minutes left to go."

He looked up. "You saying what I think you're saying?"

"Officers," I said with my most direct elocution, "would one of you be kind enough to let our chauffeur out of the trunk so he can drive us back to the Monticello? We have a telethon to complete, and you have some more bad guys to arrest."

CHAPTER 22

After we determined Hector was shaken up but okay, Kirby called for an ambulance to take him and Veronica to a local hospital, and he and Falletti commandeered one of Vegas Metro's helicopters for one of the fastest rides I'd been on since the Cyclone at Coney Island. The rest of the SWAT guys had a massive crime scene to protect.

I'd called Barry before we'd taken off to tell him we were all right and were coming back. He listened and kept repeating, "Oh my God, oh my God," over and over.

"Barry, will you pull yourself together?" I said. "Tell me about the telethon."

"The telethon? It's going great." He sounded befuddled.

"Great? How can that be? Johnny and I are still here."

"It's Sal," Barry said. "As soon as he heard Johnny was AWOL, he stepped in and began emceeing. He's fabulous. So funny. He'll start to read the TelePrompTer, then make some funny joke about it."

"Ask him if he's keeping it clean," Johnny said. He'd been leaning close to my cell so he could hear.

"He's pretending he's half in the bag," Barry said, "but he's drinking apple juice. Can you believe it?"

"Yeah." Johnny smiled. "I can."

"As long as it's not prune juice," I said. "We may be a while."

Barry laughed, then made my night when he added, "Oh, Belz, I picked up an envelope for you at the front desk earlier. I meant to tell you."

A little light went off in my head. "Open it and please tell me there's a disk inside."

"It's a disk, all right. What do you want me to do with it?"

Rather than use my standard tried-and-true funnyman answer to that question, I used sincerity instead. "Guard it with your life and don't give it to anyone but me."

We touched down on the helipad on the roof of the hotel about fifteen minutes later, and Grady, Kirby, Falletti, Johnny, and I duckwalked until we were sure we'd cleared the blades. In reality, we were probably all under the danger height, but there was something to be said for being careful, especially after you almost bought the farm in a desert shootout. We went to a special elevator that took us down to the second floor where they'd already located Dario, bastard Harv, Elliott, and a couple new goombahs who must have replaced Vito and Rocco. Both of those assholes, I wasn't sorry to say, would be shoveling the devil's shit back into the blast furnaces of hell.

"There they are," Falletti said. "Let me get a contingent of officers and we'll go arrest the bastard."

"Those two greaseballs are probably armed," Kirby said. "We'd best wait until we can get them isolated from the crowd."

"You want them isolated?" I looked at Johnny, who smiled and nodded. "Leave that to us. Just have your troops ready."

Kirby and Falletti exchanged glances. "What are you planning, Belz?" Kirby asked.

"Just have the boys in blue waiting in the wings." I turned to Grady. "Where's the control room for the telecast at?"

"This floor. Down the hall." He cocked his head toward the door.

"Show me," I said.

Grady led us down a corridor and used his keys to open a solid-metal door. He held it open and I went inside, followed by Johnny and the two cops. Barry, wearing a headset, looked at us with saucer eyes and gave a squeal of delight.

"Johnny," he said, running over to give him a hug. "Oh my God, what happened to your face?"

"Long story." Johnny glanced at me. "A real long story."

"And one for another time," I said. I scrutinized the various monitors, each displaying a different angle of the telecast. Sal was on the center one now, delivering a monologue. The other monitors showed the crowd, the performing stage, the LED screen, and just about everything else. I didn't want to disturb the director so I tapped Barry on the arm. "Which is the live feed now?"

He pointed to the center monitor.

"And that goes automatically to the big screens?"

"Right. So the people in the auditorium can see the act in case they're too far away." He shrugged. "Standard setup."

"Can you disconnect the big screens from the live-feed telecast when I tell you?"

"Of course, but why?"

"I need you to play something on those screens that will bring down the house, but I don't want it broadcast live."

He tucked his chin down. "Okayyyyy."

"Relax, it's not X-rated, but it might have some bad language. You got that disk for me?"

"Sure." He started to reach into his pocket but I grabbed his wrist.

"You and Special Agent Falletti here review it on a separate monitor." I gave him a brief description of what to look for and what part to play as they hooked me up with a radio set to Barry's frequency and ear mike. "I'll give you the play-by-play, but I'll have to shut this off when I'm using the microphone or I'll get feedback."

"So how will I know when you're ready?" Barry asked.

"Keep your eye on Grady and me. When you see us do the high five, start the playback on the big screens in the ballroom."

"And keep the broadcast separate," he said. "Got it."

Grady had been standing off to the side, watching me. I hadn't thought about it until now, but this would most likely cost him his job. "You up for this, champ? I can understand if you'd rather sit this one out. Johnny and I can handle it."

He shook his head and smiled. "I think we both know I ain't the kind who finishes sitting on my stool and not answering the bell."

I nodded. "Thanks, Grady."

We took an elevator down to an area behind the stage and got a quick makeup powdering before walking around to the front, where Sal was doing a send-up of "I've Grown Accustomed to Her Face." It was borderline risqué because he was leaving the last word of the line out and just doing one of his famous leering grins, leaving little to the imagination as to what part of her anatomy he was referring to.

We stepped inside the backdrop and lingered behind the curtain. The bright ring of lights shone in front of us. Johnny froze.

"I don't know, Belz. What if he doesn't want to talk to me?"

"He's here filling in for you, isn't he?" I put my hand on his shoulder and felt him shivering. "Johnny, it's okay. It's time." And I gave him a shove.

Sal's head swiveled backward, then he faced the audience again, raising his eyebrows, and said, "Here's another face I was accustomed to about twenty-plus years ago." He held out his hand toward Johnny and the audience erupted in cheers and applause. "I'm glad you're finally here," Sal said. "I need a break to go to the john. This stuff's going right through me." He held up his near-empty apple juice.

Never one to let the moment pass without a wisecrack, I thought.

Johnny stood there, with the most wonderful smile I'd ever seen, the tears wet on his face. It was the second time tonight I'd seen him cry, and definitely the better one. They hugged so spontaneously that I don't think they were even cognizant of the standing ovation they were getting. I stayed just beyond the folds of the curtain. I keyed the mike. "Barry, after their reunion, get ready to switch the broadcast signal on my thumbs-up. Got it?"

"Roger, Belz," he said in my earphone. I watched the two of them a few seconds more, then whispered to Grady to stay where he was until I motioned for him to join me. With that, I shut off the radio and flashed my biggest smile as I walked onstage to join Johnny and Sal.

Sal's fingers yielded the microphone as easily as slipping a bottle away from a slumbering toddler.

I stepped away from them and said, "Together again, at last, ladies and gentlemen. Sal Fabell and Johnny Leland, two of the greatest acts in show business."

The applause continued and Johnny and Sal, their arms around each other's shoulders, turned and acknowledged the crowd. I motioned for Grady to join me up front. When he got there I held my arm high, my thumb raised straight up, and started my count. I gave Barry about thirty seconds to switch the signal to a prerecorded segment, and spoke into the microphone.

"Ladies and gentlemen, I'm Richard Belzer, Johnny and Sal's cohost tonight. Isn't it great to see these two legendary stars together again?"

The applause and cheering were deafening. I waited until it had almost died out and said a few more words, ending with, "And I also have to announce a program change. Comedian Harvey Smithe will not be appearing as scheduled. We're arranging a replacement as we speak. I'm sure this won't inconvenience or disappoint anyone. After all, how could it?"

The crowd roared with laughter, but at that point I could have told a joke about the Asian bird flu and it would have gotten some laughs. I handed the mike back to Sal, who immediately started hamming it up. I walked to the side, away from the lights. Sure enough, I saw a group of four men moving down the center aisle toward the stage. I stepped quickly toward Grady and lifted my arm. "Gimme five, bro."

Our hands smacked together and we continued through the backstage opening. I switched on the radio and whispered, "Falletti, this might be a good time to tell Kirby to move in."

"Ten-four."

Grady and I went to the rear curtain area and were met by Elliott Collins, Capacaza, and the two replacement goombahs.

"Gentlemen," I said, "so nice of you to join us." Capacaza's mouth was already gaping in surprise. "Yeah, it's me, in the flesh. Too bad you didn't send the A team."

His lower lip jutted out and he made a frustrated snort. "Never mind that. What do you mean saying that Harvey ain't gonna be on the show?"

"I figured one big idiot from your family was enough." I pointed to the big screens. The crowd had pretty much fallen silent, and the coarse dialogue between much younger versions of Capacaza and a man I recognized as Mark Kaye Sr. filled the ballroom in larger-than-life images.

"I want that bitch dead," Kaye was saying. "Do we understand each other?"

"Perfectly," Capacaza's younger self said with a smile. "And I got a guy who can help us out. He's LAPD, and he's mine. But first, you fucking mick bastard, you listen to what *I* have to say."

I tsked-tsked and waved my finger in front of Capacaza's face. "Dario, you can't use the F word on prime time. Didn't you ever hear George Carlin's old routine?"

"You Jew bastard," he said, reaching for me.

"You got a real limited vocabulary." I popped his prominent nose with a palm strike and before the goombahs could react, Grady laid one of them out with a quick one-two and Kirby had the other one down with a hit from his Taser. I stared at Elliott like I was going to break his legs. He must have known I could do it, too, because he backed up and cringed.

"Go ahead and take a shot at the son of a bitch, Belz," Grady said. "The motherfucker deserves it."

I considered this, but the abject fear in Elliott's eyes made me hold back. In another second one of the cops was drawing his arms behind his back and cuffing him.

"Nah," I said to Grady. "He's got enough problems. He's probably going to have Harvey as a cellmate."

After two more days the desert dust had pretty much settled, for better and for worse. The better included an announcement that Mark Kaye III had dropped out of the governor's race, citing "family concerns." Another one in the better column was the press release that good old Uncle Lar had "entered a clinic for rehabilitation citing an alcohol problem." But off the record Falletti told me that the senator was "singing like a canary

in a cage," and had agreed to testify for the Gee in some sweeping indict-
ments.

"So long as they keep him caged," I said.

And finally, Dario Capacaza had collapsed after being taken into cus-
tody and suffered a major stroke. They'd rushed his comatose form to the
hospital, but the devil must have called in his marker because Capa never
regained consciousness. I put that one in the better column as well, cynic
that I am.

Sal invited Johnny, Veronica, Grady, and me to sit at the front tables
for his show the following night, and we all sat around afterward talking
till the wee hours. Waking up the next morning and feeling the effects of
all the red wine I'd had was the worse.

And that was about it. Even the swelling on Veronica's lips had started
to go down and she was still turning heads when we exited the tram taking
us to the gates in McCarran International Airport as we prepared to leave
Las Vegas. The occasional pinging of the airport slot machines served as a
reminder of what we'd been through. And how far we'd come.

"Do not ask for whom the bell tolls," I said. "It was almost for us."

She shook her head and smiled. "I knew you'd save us."

"Yeah, well, that's one of your psychic predictions that I'm glad did
come true."

Veronica gave me a hug as they made the announcement for first-class
boarding for her flight to Portland, Maine.

"Looks like I'll have time to play a few slots before my flight takes off,"
I said.

"Oh, Richard. This has been . . . unbelievable. How can I ever thank
you?"

"Just write a good story and put it under both your and Paul's names,"
I said. "And identify me as 'Celebrity X.' "

"You're joking, right?"

I looked down at her. The swollen lip aside, the makeover had turned
the caterpillar into the butterfly, all right. And everybody thought *Pygma-
lion* was passé. It just goes to show that the great ones, like George Bernard Shaw, never go out of style.

"Me? Joke?" I smiled. "Well, I *am* a pretty good comedian, right?"

"And a wonderful man. If it wasn't for you, I'd be—" She gave me a kiss on the cheek and I felt the wetness of her tears. They were making the last call for first-class boarding, and as we broke our embrace the mascara had left dark tracks on her face. After a quick glance at the loading gate, she tried to talk but began the hiccuping sound that so often accompanies feminine crying. Finally she was able to eke out, "I'll miss you."

"Don't worry," I said. "I'm just as close as your favorite rerun."

Emotion tugged the ends of her mouth down and I gave her a pat on the shoulder as a gentle send-off.

She turned, picked up her carry-on, and gave the ticket to the attendant. Just as she stepped into the jetway, she stopped and waved, the tears flowing full force now.

I waved back. "Take care, kid. Call me and let me know how you're doing. Ah," I milked the pause for all it was worth, "you do have my cell number, don't you?"

ACKNOWLEDGMENTS

Mike Black has proved invaluable in the creation of this new novel and what I said before bears repeating . . .

I am not a cop but I play one on television. . . .

For over a decade and a half I have had the good fortune to play the same character, Detective Sergeant John Munch, on *Homicide: Life on the Street;* and *Law & Order: SVU,* not to mention (although I will) as many as ten guest appearances on other prime-time shows.

Even with that extensive fictional experience, there's nothing like the real thing. That's where Mike Black comes in. A twenty-eight-year veteran police officer in the south suburbs of Chicago who has worked in various capacities, including patrol supervisor, tactical squad investigator, raid team member, and SWAT team leader, he also holds a black belt in tae kwon do and, perhaps best of all, has five cats.

The combination of his real-life experiences and being a gifted writer of four novels and two nonfiction books was invaluable in crafting *I Am Not a Psychic!*. Quite simply, the book could not have been created without his insight, diligence, talent, and graciousness of spirit. I will be forever grateful to Mike for our collaboration and look forward to a continuing creative relationship.